EBURY PRESS
THE NAGA WARRIORS 2

Akshat Gupta is a national bestselling author, a TEDx speaker, and an accomplished screenwriter and dialogue writer. The Hidden Hindu series, authored by him, has sold over one lakh copies, with each book becoming a national bestseller. Akshat is well-known in the publishing industry, as well as in the Indian film industry, with several films and web-series signed under his name.

From the bestselling author of **The Hidden Hindu** trilogy

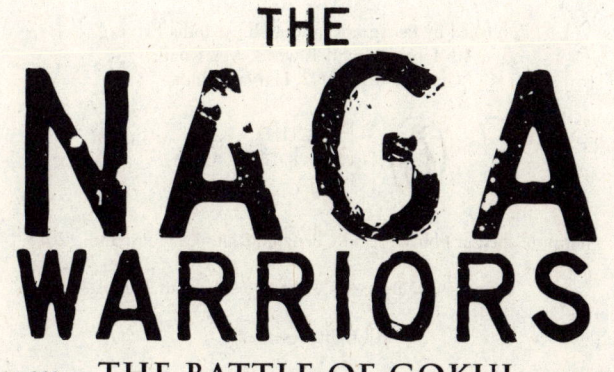

THE NAGA WARRIORS

⫸⫷ THE BATTLE OF GOKUL ⫸⫷

Vol. 2

AKSHAT GUPTA

EBURY
PRESS

An imprint of Penguin Random House

EBURY PRESS

Ebury Press is an imprint of the Penguin Random House group of companies
whose addresses can be found at global.penguinrandomhouse.com

Published by Penguin Random House India Pvt. Ltd
4th Floor, Capital Tower 1, MG Road,
Gurugram 122 002, Haryana, India

Penguin
Random House
India

First published in Ebury Press by Penguin Random House India 2025

ISBN 9780143465942

Typeset in Bembo Std by Manipal Technologies Limited, Manipal
Printed at Replika Press Pvt. Ltd, India

www.penguin.co.in

MIX
Paper | Supporting
responsible forestry
FSC™ C016779

Contents

1

Echoes of War

Thomas, the hiker, was still plagued by a persistent question, 'How did the nameless Naga know so much about something that happened hundreds of years ago?' He wanted to know if the nameless Naga was ageless and was named Adhiraj when he fought alongside Ajaa and Shambhu ji against Sardar Khan. But the nameless Naga was gone, and gone with him were numerous unanswered questions about what happened next in the Battle of Gokul.

Thomas's mind strayed back to the heart-thumping tale of the heroes, as according to the nameless Naga, every element vividly depicted the bravery and sacrifice that characterized the Battle of Gokul by bringing the past to life. He began thinking what would have happened with Ajaa, who stood strongly along with seventeen other sadhus and *sadhvis*.

Shambhu ji, the helpless sadhu bound by his oath, could not admit to his own son that he was the king of Surajgarh and Ajaa's father, even though together they represented the unity of strength and faith. If Shambhu ji represented fire, then Ajaa was his flame, their hearts as pure as the Ganga emerging from the Himalayas.

The weight of the memories of the nameless Naga had left a lasting impression on Thomas. The incomplete yet unforgettable tale of the Naga warriors, lost in time, seemed alive in his eyes as he reflected on the past night's experience with the nameless Naga who was now nowhere to be seen.

Thomas knew that he would never forget the most captivating instance of Shambhu ji's return to battle, riding a bull. Thomas could almost hear the resonating shouts of 'Har Har Mahadev' ringing in his ears as Shambhu ji, riding the bull, led the grand procession, just as Lord Shiva himself had mounted Nandi, and the other old Naga sadhus followed him. The scene was a heavenly display of power and solidarity. The heavenly account of the Battle of Gokul captivated Thomas since it demonstrated the Naga warriors' unwavering spirit and unbreakable bond that nearly destroyed the entire army led by the Afghan commander Sardar Khan.

Thomas could still feel his heart heavy and eyes moist as he thought about Vanraaj, the wanderer with a powerful physique that hinted a life spent in the woods, and his beloved Dulari, the elephant, a symbol of Lord Ganesha, who led a herd, acting as an unexpected reinforcement that turned the wave of the battle in favour of the Naga warriors. Dulari's majestic build and elegant movements, combined with her almost intuitive understanding of Vanraaj's emotions, made her a sight to behold. Vanraaj and Dulari used their skills as a strategy to combat the Afghans with great valour as they fought with vigour and gave all they had when the Naga warriors needed it the most. Tragically, in the end, their bodies were sliced into pieces by the Afghans. Nevertheless, the numerous snakes Dulari carried on her back and that Vanraaj unleashed just before dying were the final blow on the shattering hope of victory for Sardar Khan and his army. The snakes that came to the battle to support the Nagas, who were Shiva devotees, represented Vasuki—the king of snakes that rests on Shiva's shoulders, coiling his neck and registering his presence against the Afghan *asuras*. It was a courageous fight and an honourable death for Vanraaj, Dulari, and the other elephants, while little Golu and Vanraaj's Neelkanth silently wept watching the death of everybody he knew as family. 'What would have happened to Golu after that?' thought Thomas.

Besides young Golu, Thomas could not stop thinking about Namah, Bhola and Shivay—the three young Naga sadhus whom Mathadhish had named Cheetah Dasta. The fastest and fiercest among all the Nagas, noted for their ability to dodge obstacles and run with the aim of finishing the mission. Despite knowing about their assured death, they ran without weapons towards Sardar Khan's troops during the final conquest, mesmerizing the men with their fearless charge. Despite being struck by arrows, they did not waver. Their constant dedication, true spirit and high speed were evident in their ability to locate and target soldiers hypnotized by Mathadhish, turning them all against each other, all by the chant of the three strongest words: Har Har Mahadeva.

The sadhvis' bone-chilling laughter, with their features painted dark, their tongues out, mocking, and hair unfettered and jutting, was like Shyama and Adyama, representing the ferocious face of Goddess Kali. The laughter of these sadhvis was so strong that many Afghan warriors, including their commander-in-chief Sardar Khan, started to lose their morale just by virtue of their presence. The sadhvis shouted resolutely, 'You were in thousands and we were just 111 in number. Look at what's left of you while we still stand tall with our spirits intact.' With their fists clenched, the eighteen surviving Naga sadhus wiped away their sweat and blood—a sight to behold when courage met overwhelming odds.

The last stand of the Naga warriors was represented by eighteen sadhus and sadhvis, the pillars of strength and devotion, including Sadhvi Adyama and Shyama, Mathadhish, Adhiraj, Ajaa, Shambhu ji, Krishna and others. The surviving sadhus, through their devotion and strength, created a strong force of indestructible warriors, their combined energy symbolizing unwavering determination.

Thomas, while still wanting to know about the last Nagas standing, couldn't help but think about Dhruv, the committed teacher who imparted the values of harmony and enlightenment to his students. He was heartbroken to see little children killed and brutalized, their blood staining the earth he had sworn to protect. Despite his strong belief in non-violence, everything changed for him when he witnessed the brutality of the merciless and cruel Sardar Khan and his army, slaughtering innocent believers of Shiva and Vishnu. With a renewed sense of commitment, Dhruv rose up and transformed himself from a calm instructor to a warrior prepared to protect.

Dhruv travelled to Gokul to fight the merciless invaders, but Ajaa had other plans for him. Ajaa saw potential and determination in Dhruv, entrusting him with an important mission to find the Nagas in the Himalayas. He was tasked to find them due to his excellent tracking skills and to fulfil the promise he made to Ajaa. Ajaa urged Dhruv not to surrender, even to Yamraj, the God of Death, before conveying his message to the head of all the Matha and Nagas up there. The message to the devotees of Shiva residing in the mountains was that the land of Lord Krishna needed them down on the battlefield. With the promise to deliver Ajaa's message, Dhruv started off on his trek to the Himalayas, but Thomas wanted to know what happened to Dhruv after he left.

Disheartened and hopeless, King Vedant, hiding his cowardly self, refused to participate in the battle supporting the Naga warriors. However, Vishnu devotee Krishna, the commander-in-chief of Vedant's army, valiantly stood up to his own monarch to fight for the Nagas against the Afghan army, becoming one of the eighteen last warriors standing against the forces.

The sun casted a golden hue over the crisp mountain as Thomas began his descent, the air filling his lungs. Gripping on the old book, the map and the *shankh** next to him, he

---

* Conch, a tropical marine mollusc with a robust spiral shell which may bear long projections and have a flared lip.

reflected on the nameless Naga's account of the battle of Gokul. Every passing minute deepened the mystery. The more he pondered it, the more questions he had. Each step down the path needed the utmost attention, but there was something that suddenly caught Thomas's eye. He noticed two sets of footprints, clear and prominent, leading up towards the mountains, slowly fainting and disappearing in the mist. Thomas knew that the footsteps were of the nameless Naga and his subordinate who sat on the mouth of the cave the previous night. Thomas paused, caught in a dilemma—whether to continue down the path he had already started, staying true to his journey, or following the footprints moving uphill. He stood at the fork in the path, his heart pounding in anticipation, torn between following the map guiding him back to civilization or the footsteps leading up the hill, which might lead him to the nameless Naga who held the answers Thomas sought.

Thomas was curious to learn more about the narrative, but fortune was shining upon Madhav, the Naga who had been sitting at the mouth of the cave last night. 'I have heard all that you have told the foreigner,' said Madhav, walking behind the nameless Naga, eager to hear what became of Ajaa, Shambhu ji, Mathadhish, Krishna and each and every last sadhu and sadhvi.

The nameless Naga carried on narrating further as he proceeded to walk with the unwavering human spirit . . .

2

Ajaa and Khan

'What happened next? Has the tale of courage and sacrifice been lost in the chronicles of history?' asked Madhav, the Naga following the nameless Naga. The nameless Naga shifted his gaze from the hilltop he was aiming at towards his subordinate and after taking a deep breath, he recounted:

The seventeen last remaining Naga warriors and Krishna stood determined against Sardar Khan's overwhelming army. Each of the Nagas, ready to face their fate, joined the battle cry 'Har Har Mahadev'. The wind carried the scent of fresh blood and fallen heroes. Ajaa, Shambhu ji, Krishna, Adhiraj, Sadhvi and a handful of Nagas still breathing stood in silence, awaiting a full-blown attack from Jugal Kishore's regiment. However, the silence was broken by the pounding hooves of a single horse running towards the last eighteen defenders of Gokul standing in formation. To their surprise, an Afghan soldier, riding the horse and holding a white flag, approached them.

Dismounting swiftly, he approached the Nagas in fear with a sealed scroll.

'A message from Jugal Kishore,' he said, offering it to all of them, not knowing whom to address as they all looked alike, soaked in blood.

Ajaa's fingers grasped the parchment, unsealing it to read the brief and clear-cut words. It read:

> To the leader of the Nagas, the battle ends now. No more blood will be shed. I offer a truce, with no conditions imposed on you all.
> Accept it and we shall be on our way back to our designated places.
>
> —Jugal Kishore

The message was sharp, a truce, an end to the bloodshed. No flattery, no lengthy prose, just a blunt declaration. Krishna exhaled, relief was evident in his eyes. 'They have declared their defeat by offering this truce,' he murmured, glancing at the Naga sadhus and sadhvis. For a moment, a shadow of happiness passed through his eyes. The unconquerable odds they had faced seemed momentarily forgotten. But Ajaa, holding the parchment, looked up with sharp eyes, his thoughts consumed by something else.

'This isn't victory. It's a pause. Remember those who stood beside us, the ones we lost. We cannot let their sacrifice be in vain,' Ajaa said firmly.

Shambhu ji nodded, 'Jugal may offer a truce, but our battle is with Sardar Khan.'

'If he is spared now, he will return in the future; better prepared,' said Sadhvi Adyama.

Ajaa's gaze turned to the messenger. 'Sardar Khan has to be punished for the deaths of so many lives on both sides. Tell Jugal Kishore to send Sardar Khan on this battlefield. His death only can be the condition of truce.' Every face that the messenger could see was in sync with Ajaa, and there was no disagreement or discussion among them on the statement that Ajaa had just made.

The messenger was shocked to his core by the audacity of eighteen injured men and women who were ready to fight against Jugal Kishore with an army of thousands on Sardar Khan's side, who was still commanding more than a hundred Afghans himself. Krishna was also surprised by the collective decisions of the Naga warriors, made without any hesitation or fear of death.

The messenger nodded and walked back to his horse.

As he mounted his horse and retreated, the Nagas stood tall, their determination unwavering, their spirits unbroken. They would see this battle to its rightful end, no matter the cost.

Jugal Kishore anxiously waited for the messenger to return from the Naga base. As soon as he entered, all eyes turned to him, expectant. Sardar Khan was also seated in the camp.

Clearing his throat, the messenger began, 'The message of the Nagas is clear: they demand Sardar Khan's head. They want him on the battlefield and declare that the

battle can end only with either their death or the death of
Sardar Khan.'

A murmur ran through the tent at these words, and all
eyes turned to Sardar Khan, awaiting his response. Jugal
Kishore couldn't hold back a chuckle, his laughter breaking
the tension. 'You wanted this battle, didn't you? And now,
it seems, it's down to your own head. If you wish to face
those death distributors, then go ahead.'

Sardar's jaw clenched, his pride wounded. 'You mock
me. But I will ruin them with the strength I have with your
fleet now. They won't be standing for much longer!'

'But,' Jugal Kishore interjected, his voice firm, 'you will
do so with the men that remain by your side. Do not expect
any reinforcements from me. I cannot afford to participate
in this madness invited by you. If I do so, I too will face the
wrath of Ahmed Shah Abdali for marching and indulging in
a battle not sanctioned by him.'

Sardar Khan's gaze met Jugal Kishore's, a fierce
determination burning in his eyes. There was palpable
tension in the tent.

'You have two options,' said Jugal Kishore, 'One—you
go out there and finish what you started and then Abdali
punishes you for the loss of his men, cannons, horses and
camels. Two—you run away and hide till Abdali finds you
and punishes you for the loss of his men, cannons, horses
and camels. Ohh! Is that sounding the same only to my ears
or to yours too?'

Sardar Khan helplessly clenched his fist looking at Jugal
Kishore's smiling face, imagining it torn apart from his body.

'But ya! I have a third option too. Go surrender to these Nagas. Maybe they will grant you an easier death than Abdali because I know for a fact that Abdali's punishment will be way more painful before you die,' said Jugal again, smirking.

Sardar, without waiting for any further words, turned on his heel and began issuing orders to his remaining soldiers, preparing to kill the eighteen.

The battlefield was a region of silence, disrupted only by the impending collision of opposing forces. Sardar Khan, at the forefront of his hundred men, looked like a titan. Standing at an almost otherworldly height of nine feet, his presence was spine-chilling. Every inch of him exuded raw power, his muscles rippling beneath his armour. His eyes, narrowed slits, held the promise of approaching doom for his foes.

Opposite him stood the bleeding sadhus with the bold sadhvis. As they charged forward with the rallying cry of 'Har Har Mahadev', the sudden appearance of brave Krishna, with the grace of a seasoned warrior, moved fluidly amongst the enemy, his blade a blur. He kept his promise, counting aloud with each enemy he took down. He was determined to kill at least thirty enemies alone before falling as he had promised his former king Vedant.

Adyama had both the skill and the speed that pumped up the other sadhvis too. With her *khadga**, she ran towards

---

* Khadga is a sword, long or short, and is used along with a *kheṭaka* or shield made of wood or hide

Sardar Khan's men as the landslide crashed to the ground. Screaming in a terrifying manner, with her tongue out, wide-open eyes and her hand raised with khadga, she charged towards the Afghan soldiers to kill them. When the Naga woman attacked, she was no less than any Naga man.

On the other side, Shambhu ji and Mathadhish, along with a few legless Naga sadhus, were holding their ground and every one of them was handling more than three enemies. Shambhu ji's tiredness was evident to all those who were fighting alongside him. It was a matter of minutes till the Afghanis did not notice and declared Shambhu ji a weak link that could easily be eliminated to break the formation.

Amidst this chaos, Ajaa was a force to be reckoned with, standing ready to take on Sardar Khan. Though he stood at a solid six feet, compared to the towering figure of Sardar, he looked smaller. Sardar Khan, watching Ajaa, was sure that he could kill him and gave a thunderous order for his men to stand back. This was personal. This was a duel of honour. The ground seemed to shake as the two behemoths approached each other, the gap between them closing swiftly.

Ajaa seemed no match in front of Sardar Khan's height and weight, but what Ajaa might have lacked in size, he made up for in pure strength and speed. His muscular frame, coated in ash, moved with the precision of a panther. His dreadlocks, symbols of his ascetic life, whipped through the air, adding to his fearsome appearance. His one eye was on Sardar Khan and another on his guru, Shambhu ji, whom he did not yet know was also his father.

The sight was breathtaking. The inhumanly large Sardar Khan, a symbol of brute strength and power, versus the agile, ash-covered Naga warrior, Ajaa. Their eyes locked, filled with the promise of a fierce battle to come. The moment had arrived, and Neelkanth's eyes were on them, flying high above them, waiting for the first strike. It felt as if Ajaa was warming up since the start of the Battle of Gokul for this moment.

Ajaa stood tall and firm, a figure of tremendous grandeur and heavenly presence as the personification of Lord Shiva, the most powerful deity known for his cosmic and supreme fighting capability. His posture was erect and regal, representing the balance between fierceness and tranquillity that defined the greatest warriors. Just as Shiva battled formidable asuras with unmatched bravery and grace, Ajaa was now certain to confront the enormous Sardar Khan. Ajaa's appearance was awe-inspiring, radiating a different kind of power—a spiritual and disciplined strength refined through inner mastery. His body was covered with patterns and symbols that resembled the sacred ash that Shiva wore himself. Calm yet determined, Ajaa was ready to release the hurricane of well-trained moves and attacks. However, it wasn't just the physical resemblance to Shiva, it was also in the spirit he exuded. The air surrounding him sparked with an otherworldly force, with his eyes intense and focused, reflecting the depth of every Naga warrior who had seen countless battles and emerged victorious.

Sardar's gigantic sword, a monstrosity of sharpened metal, whistled through the air with every swing. Each of his powerful blows bore the weight of his towering frame, making the very ground tremble, but Ajaa, with his smaller yet sturdy sword, countered each attack with a precision and swiftness that seemed almost supernatural. Their swords collided with loud clangs, sending sparks flying. Every strike and counterstrike became a mesmerizing dance of death.

Sardar, using the sheer weight of his giant sword, aimed a heavy blow at Ajaa, who sidestepped just in time, causing the weapon to hit the ground. Using this momentary imbalance, Ajaa lunged, managing to slice Sardar's arm. The wound was not deep, but it angered the giant Khan even more. Sardar, roaring in fury, quickly recovered and launched a storm of attacks. Ajaa blocked, dodged and countered, drawing blood from Sardar's leg.

Yet, for every cut and bruise Ajaa inflicted, Sardar responded in kind. A sudden, swift motion saw Ajaa's shoulder sustaining a wound, bearing a stream. Blood dripped onto the battleground, joining the essence of the countless warriors who had fallen before.

In the peripheral vision of this brutal dance, Shambhu ji's final stand unfolded. He had fought with the fervour of ten men, taking down adversary after adversary. But their overwhelming numbers began to take their toll. With sweat and blood blurring his vision, Shambhu ji, exhausted, barely noticed the soldier who managed to slice his sword arm. The weapon dropped from his grasp, the sound echoing ominously in his ears. Unarmed and weakened, he was soon surrounded from all sides. As the Afghan swarm closed in, his fierce gaze remained unyielding, even in the face of the inevitable death.

On the other corner of the battlefield, the sight was both haunting and divine. These were the sadhvis, their faces reminiscent of the fierce Goddess Kali. Their eyes, blazing with an otherworldly fire, held tales of battles from the past. Their dark dreadlocks flowed freely, dancing to the rhythm of their charge, much like the wild tresses of Kali during her destructive dance. With their tongues out, they emulated the very essence of the Goddess Kali, embodying her wrath and protective zeal. Their presence was a declaration, not just of their prowess but of the divine feminine power they represented.

Sadhvi Shyama, a woman of spiritual strength and firm resolve, stood next to a broken and wounded Naga sadhu laying on the blood-soaked earth. Who was breathing in short gasps as he struggled to exhale against the shooting pain torturing him. The Naga's silent eyes seemed to plead with Sadhvi Shyama to release his spirit, ready to transcend the suffering of mortal life. With all the remaining strength gathered, his lips opened and he whispered a barely audible 'Thank you', in gratitude. With a heavy heart, Sadhvi raised her khadga, the holy sword filled with the power to grant liberation. The surrounding air seemed still. Sadhvi whispered a prayer, raising the blessings of the divine to guide the Naga's soul to its rightful place beyond the physical pain and turmoil. Sadhvi, with her calm and serene eyes, held a promise of peace. The Naga warrior's gaze softened with a fleeting smile of relief as he surrendered to welcome death. The khadga met its mark with a swift precise motion and the Sadhu's unbearable suffering ceased instantly.

Sadhvi Adyama, after taking down more than fifteen soldiers, was also surrounded on all sides. She continued piercing her khadga into the chests of Afghan soldiers, standing with one foot on a dying Afghan, terrifying everyone around her. With her red eyes wide open like Maa Kali and a broad smile decorating her face, she picked a fallen sword in her other hand and killed five more before being attacked from behind by the coward asuras, causing her to collapse to the ground.

Adhiraj and Krishna took advantage of the chaos and multiplied their kills while Shambhu ji, still fighting and refusing to give up, was attacked from all sides by the Afghanis until they brought Shambhu ji on his knees.

Shambhu ji was bleeding to his end. Krishna and Adhiraj, fighting on different fronts, wanted to rush to his rescue, but were helpless and surrounded by soldiers. Krishna had multiple cuts and slashes across his body, but his mind was fixated on the number of kills he had angrily promised King Vedant. Shambhu ji was slowly closing his eyes for the last time after which he would never be able to see Ajaa ever again. He was putting his last few ounces of strength left in him to keep his eyes open, desperately searching for Ajaa on the bloodied chaos of the battlefield.

Meanwhile, Ajaa, his best prodigy and only son, was locked in a fierce one-on-one combat with Sardar Khan. Every clash, every grunt, every move seemed like the dance of death. As Sardar's large and heavy sword clashed against Ajaa's slowly cracking sword, the two found themselves grappling with sheer physical power, their faces inches apart, sweat and blood dripping from their eyebrows to eyelashes.

Another unapologetic and powerful blow by Sardar Khan on Ajaa's defending blade and it broke in two making Ajaa fall on the ground. Ajaa, with his body bruised and bleeding from countless wounds, remembered his Shiva and called upon a reservoir of strength that seemed almost divine. With a roar that echoed across the battlefield, he threw aside his broken blade. And with renewed vigour and the power of the gods seemingly coursing through him, Ajaa wielded the *trishul* with deadly precision.

Sardar Khan, with his sword, charged with fury, his fists and remaining weapons flaying with brutal force. However, Ajaa, guided by the power beyond human understanding, met each strike with the precision of a god. Though slowed down by exhaustion and blood loss, he moved with firm determination. Ajaa was about to fall, to never stand back while, with a blurry vision, Shambhu ji located him and kept watching him as if trying to fill his heart with the face of his son and his valour.

Both father and son were on their knees bleeding to death, tired and wavering. Ajaa now was hardly able to breathe, blood dripping from every part of his body, weakening him with every passing moment. Everybody present alive there could tell that it was the end for Ajaa. Some eyes were moist seeing Ajaa dying and some were glittering with happiness for Sardar Khan's victory; some felt defeated and some felt victorious, some were silently weeping and some were cheering loudly. Sardar Khan turned and looked at

Jugal Kishore before beheading Ajaa to take his head as a trophy, but in the defining moment, Sardar Khan strike a little carelessly, not expecting the exhausted Ajaa to be left with any more moves or motivation. Ajaa speared Sardar Khan with a final powerful swing right in the middle of his eyes. His trident ended his reign of terror once and for all. Blood was gushing out from Sardar Khan's eyes as he screamed in agony, his cries so loud that they shattered the morale of all the other Afghans fighting for him. The points of the trident not only blinded him but pierced his brain too. Jugal Kishore, with his men, calmly watched all of it from the top of a plateau. Another set of eyes watching it all was of Neelkanth who was still above Ajaa and Sardar Khan.

Amid this chaos, Ajaa, gravely wounded and gasping for breath, started to drag himself toward Shambhu ji, who was still on his knees, unable to move, yet his eyes were stuck on Ajaa. Words were beyond them now; their eyes did the talking. Their smiles, despite the agony, spoke of pride, of the fulfillment of their duties, of a brotherhood unbroken. Ajaa had moved a few inches closer to Shambhu ji when an Afghan soldier pierced Ajaa's back with a javelin, driving it through his heart and into the hard crust of the earth. With one hand still towards Shambhu ji, the lionhearted soul let out his final breath, leaving behind a legacy for the pages of the past. Old and overwhelmed, helpless and hopeless, injured yet in his senses, Shambhu ji laid on the ground with his dead, frozen eyes looking at Ajaa, expecting the unexpected that Ajaa, his prodigy, his pride, his prince, would stand and walk to him to give fire to his dead body.

Madhav, silently listening, felt the nameless Naga's voice choking in pain as he was still unaware that the one he was following in the impossible terrains of the Himalayas was Adhiraj himself who fought in the Battle of Gokul alongside the Naga warriors and witnessed the great Ajaa dying while he as Adhiraj kept killing the handful of unorganized Afghan soldiers.

The sadhvis laid dead and brutally injured beyond recognition. Mathadhish's body had fallen with his hands and legs cut off. Other Naga sadhus were all scattered lifeless and I realized then that there were only four men still standing—Krishna, searching for more Afghanis to kill, Sardar Khan screaming in pain, searching for his death, Shambhu ji, searching for salvation, and me, searching for life in any Naga sadhu or sadhvi on the battleground that was finally silent.

'We have lost enough men for this small town that could have easily been bypassed by that dying dumb Sardar Khan. He was a fool to think that he could defeat the Gods of Gokul. It is cursed for us. Bury the bodies of the dead and then it's better to return,' said Jugal Kishore and decided to turn back.

'Sir! But Sardar Khan? He is still alive, wandering among the dead,' said a commander under Jugal Kishore.

'Bury him alive with his men! He is now a dead man walking,' ordered Jugal Kishore.

The battleground was full of men, but all dead. It was noisy again, but this time, with the crowing of crows and vultures. Adding to the hauntings was Sardar Khan, worse than the dead screaming in pain for somebody to kill him. Amidst all of this were Krishna, the Vishnu devotee, Golu, the son of the brave elephant Dulari, and Shambhu ji, the father who saw his son dying and me—I was thinking where to start collecting our fallen warriors and their borrowed weapons that were to return to our gods and goddesses in temples.

It was a landslide moment for Madhav to learn that the one he was walking behind was a hundred-year-old man with no signs of ageing. 'Who are you?' asked the shocked Madhav, stopping to walk so that he could absorb what he was told.

'You will know who I am at the right time. For now, it is not about me. It is about the heroes of Gokul,' replied the nameless Naga and started climbing again. Madhav followed him.

Jugal Kishore's troops started digging trenches to bury the dead Afghan soldiers and we along with Golu started collecting wood to burn ours.

In the abandoned war ground, where the remains of a brutal fight were found scattered, Krishna, Golu and I collected wood from the nearby forest, hardly a few miles away, to honor our fallen Naga sadhus and sadhvis. Amidst all this, while crows and vultures were having their feast on the scattered body parts of men, suddenly a blue-throated bird, wings a deep black, and beak sharp and determined, landed softly upon Vanraaj's lifeless body. It was his Neelkanth, the same Neelkanth that once used to travel with Vanraaj and Dulari. The bird's presence signified a silent farewell to Vanraaj from the natural world. Vanraaj, known for his boundless compassion that had always shared a deep connection with nature's creatures, seemed to draw the bird to him even after his death. Seeing this Neelkanth, I realized that the bird was with us all along—from Vanraaj's arrival in Gokul to his final and glorious end as a fierce warrior.

After offering respect, Neelkanth left Vanraaj and Dulari and flew and sat on orphan Golu's back. Gokul, once a place of heroic clatters, was now a grave inactive place for heroes whose memories tangled with the silent and emotional tribute of the bird. 'Ajaa died and so did Sardar Khan. The battle ended. Gokul was saved. What was left of it then?' asked Madhav thinking it was over while walking behind the nameless Naga in the vast ice-covered terrains of the Himalayas.

'I too thought that Gokul was saved till time taught me that there is always an after-effect. The battle ended but the war was about to begin.' The saga of Naga warriors was far from over. The wheels of fate continue to turn, and the book of the future harbours the chapters even more gruesome and ghastly.

'After-effect! War! What do you mean?' asked Madhav curiously.

The nameless Naga answered, 'Unaware of the death of Ajaa and all the other Naga warriors, Dhruv was headed to the gigantic mountains of the Himalayas to find the ocean of Nagas in the snow. They were unaware of the fierce battle of Gokul. As he entered the unfamiliar mountains, he heard the sound of crawling from a distance behind him. He immediately turned to check if he was in danger as the sound was clear enough for him to judge that it was not a small snake or reptile, but some creature the size of a crocodile or full-grown python. He looked around for quite some time but couldn't notice any living being around him.'

Thomas, in present, while searching for his way back to the land with the help of the map he had picked from the cave of the nameless Naga, was feeling the same as Dhruv had felt centuries ago. And like Dhruv, he too could not find anything crawling and following him. But both were sure of their instincts and knew for sure that they were not alone.

3

Fire of the Pyre

In a constant state of nervousness of being chased by some crawling creature, while searching his way back to the land with the help of the map, Thomas opened the book he had picked up from the cave along with the map and shankh, and began turning its pages. To his surprise, the book was in English, as if it was intentionally prepared for him. It had facts about the mysterious divine powers of Nagas that the world is still unaware of. Thomas decided to read it on his journey back to the plains.

From above the plateau, standing at the edge of it, Jugal Kishore was looking at his men, alive in hundreds, digging trenches to bury the rapidly rotting army of dead bodies. Amidst hundreds of men collecting corpses of Afghans, Krishna and I were checking if anyone outside was still breathing. Poor Golu, in tears and unable to express his grief in words, picked up his mother's trunk and brought it to me with an innocent, impossible hope in his eyes that

I would bring his mother back. He then walked back to Dulari and took out all the javelins and arrows from Dulari's and Vanraaj's bodies and pampered them both one by one before cautiously sitting near his dead family, making sure that his weight did not hurt their wounds. Unfortunately, he did not understand the definition of death. I could feel Golu's pain in my heart and walked to him. As I sat near him, Golu laid his heavy heart and bulky head on my lap, while the Neelkanth settled on my shoulder. I knew that very moment that I was going to be with Golu as Vanraaj was with Dulari.

A tired Krishna walked near the dead body of Ajaa, still pierced with a javelin. Not knowing who and what Ajaa was, he treated the dead body as respectfully as any other and took out the javelin that was still standing erect on Ajaa's corpse. As he pulled it out, he heard a voice in pain. For a moment, he felt the voice was from Ajaa, but soon realized that it was another Naga sadhu. He looked around and saw Shambhu ji bathed in blood, still on his knees. Krishna left Ajaa and rushed to the aid of Shambhu ji, who lost his consciousness and balance as Krishna put his hand under Shambhu ji's head before it hit the ground. He sat and carefully turned the body of the old Naga, ensuring none of his wounds caused much pain, unaware that the worst wound lay not in his body but in his soul—the wound of the loss of his son. Krishna took Shambhu ji's head on his lap and tried to offer him water, but Shambhu ji could not drink a drop. Shambhu ji was half-dead. The remaining half, still alive, was hallucinating that Ajaa was walking towards him with a smile to hug him and call him by the name he craved for but never heard in his entire life—Baba. That meant 'father' in his kingdom. Ajaa's wounds were still aching in Shambhu ji's heart as he gazed at his dead son. His eyes were still fixed in the direction where Ajaa had fallen. But from Krishna's perspective, so many Naga sadhus lay dead in that direction that he could not comprehend why or for whom Shambhu ji was reaching out. His eyes were still frozen on the blood gone cold in Ajaa's veins, but Krishna could not understand where Shambhu ji was still trying to crawl and reach. In an effort to understand Shambhu ji's last wish, he carefully studied Shambhu ji's face—only to be met with the shock of his life. Krishna recognized the dying old man. 'That is undoubtedly King Dhyanendra!' he assured himself in disbelief. Shambhu ji, without looking at the face of the helper, half-dead and half in trance, was still stretching his hand towards his dead son, Ajaa.

'King Dhyanendra!' said Krishna. This was a name Shambhu ji heard after decades, the name his father gave him before the Nagas named him Shambhu. The name caught the attention of the old man and he looked at the face of the voice, trying to recognize Krishna. 'Me! Krishna! The commander-in-chief of Haripur,' said Krishna, trying to help him remember. Shambhu ji, failing to recognize anything as blood from his body was draining faster than the moments left in his life, though unaffected by anything, was still trying to stretch his hand towards the dead Ajaa. Before Krishna could ask Shambhu ji anything, and before Shambhu ji could request to be taken to Ajaa, life drained out from him completely. Shambhu ji died. With his hand stretched, Shambhu ji's soul left his body. He was too weak to speak, but his last wish was to touch his brave, fallen son and student, Ajaa. Krishna could not understand and Shambhu ji could not speak—'Ajaa was my son.'

The dutiful pair of father and son—the king and the prince—left behind two unfulfilled wishes: The urge to hold his son for Shambhu ji and the desire to know his father for Ajaa.

With eyes downcast and lost in deep thought, the nameless Naga gazed at the horizon and spoke to Madhav, his follower, 'The silent companion of life is death that walks with it from the very moment we are born. It reminds us of the fragility of our existence and the fleeting nature of both glory and suffering. Yet, it is at the time of facing death that we truly understand life.'

I was looking at all of that from a distance while searching for life in the bodies of the dead warriors and so I walked to Krishna while Shambhu ji's head was still on his lap. 'This man that you see dead is . . .' I wanted to tell the real identity of the old man and his relation with Ajaa to Krishna, but Krishna intervened and said, 'I know! He was King Dhyanendra. Let us do the needful. Collect wood and mortars and do the rituals. I have to go to Surajgarh.'

I knew Shambhu ji's real identity as Mathadhish once told me, but I was surprised how he knew Shambhu ji's real

name and why the commander-in-chief of Haripur wished
to go to Surajgarh's kingdom.

'How did you know Shambhu ji's previous name and
why do you have to go to the kingdom of Surajgarh?'
I asked.

'Because that's King Dhyanendra's kingdom. I owe that
to him,' replied Krishna, as he respectfully laid Shambhu ji's
head on the ground and stood to drag the other dead bodies
closer to Shambhu ji's.

'I want to know how you knew him,' I asked curiously.

'While I was relatively young and was commanding the
army of Haripur under King Vedant's father, we attacked
Surajgarh to dethrone King Dhyanendra and make it a part
of Haripur. The battle continued for days, and we lost to
King Dhyanendra. I was caught alive and was taken to the
king to be beheaded. That is what the kings used to do with
the enemies. But he was different.

"I can let you live only if you promise to never attack
my boundaries again," King Dhyanendra said, offering me
my life.

I replied, "I can't promise you that. I am the commander-
in-chief, and I am bound by my oath to obey the king of
Haripur. If he decides to attack you again, I will lead my
troops back to your door."

I was on my knees and ready to die, but he did not
kill me.

He said, "I am impressed by you, Commander. Your
loyalty won over your death. If you would have pleaded
and accepted my terms, I would have surely ordered my
soldiers to kill you. You did not fail to do your duty even in

the face of death, nor did you lie to save yourself. You are a man of honour, true to your king and a pure soul. What's your name?"

"My name is Krishna," I replied, surprised by the generosity of King Dhyanendra.

"Go back, Krishna, and tell your king that I am no enemy. Tell him that all the kings should be united against anything that attacks the godland from outside. These different provinces and kingdoms are sibling lands. We are all the sons and daughters of the same motherland. We should be united as a fist against the external forces. Also tell him that if next time he attacks my people, then Haripur will be merged with the Surajgarh's kingdom and his legacy will be lost forever."

With these words, King Dhyanendra returned my honour and life and gave me my sword back. Haripur never attacked Surajgarh kingdom. He was a true king as he always stood for his neighbouring kingdoms in adversities and never asked anything in return for the aid he provided.'

The long and deep trenches were dug by Jugal Kishore's men for burial and tons of wood were collected by us for a large funeral. We were ready for the mass funeral while the soldiers were throwing the rotting bodies in the trenches on the orders of Jugal Kishore.

Krishna wanted to burn the body of Shambhu ji separately so that he could take the ashes back to his kingdom, but I denied his wish saying that he belonged with all the other Naga warriors.

'Ajaa and all the other brave Naga sadhus and sadhvis were burned together and I performed the funeral rituals for all of them,' said the nameless Naga, with both his voice and heart heavy. Madhav followed him and listening to all of it, kept a hand of condolence on his shoulder. The nameless Naga recollected himself and firmly said, 'The demon named Sardar Khan was buried alive with blood flowing from both his eyes, as was ordered by Jugal Kishore. At his end, Sardar Khan was seen walking inside the trenches above the dead bodies of his own soldiers, trying to blindly find a way to come out of the ditch. Jugal Kishore stood on the plateau, watching the unceremonial fate of Sardar Khan as the living men threw soil on Sardar Khan, burying him alive, deep with the dead. While Sardar Khan was going below the earth that we call *pataal lok* (the underworld), the fire of the pyre in the Naga's farewell was so high towards the sky that it seemed as if the Fire God himself wanted to escort all the Naga warriors to heaven with all due respect.

Jugal Kishore and his men departed from the outskirts of Gokul to report back to Ahmed Shah Abdali, while Vedant left from the other side to return inside the walls of Haripur. Gokul, though broken, stood with pride, and the proud Naga warriors died to save it.'

While the nameless Naga kept wandering with his junior narrating the never-heard history, Thomas was walking down the hill with the unknown mysteries and supernatural powers of the Nagas. But in order to understand the Nagas, one had to understand Shiva. So, the pages began with an explanation of the cosmic dancer, who embodies the eternal cycle of creation, preservation and destruction.

The pages read, 'He presides as the Lord of Death and rebirth in the cosmic dance of existence. He dissolves the physical form, turning it into sacred ashes that symbolize purification and transcendence. In his embrace, death becomes a gateway to *moksha*, the ultimate salvation. Through Shiva, the end is merely a beginning, a return to the infinite source of all existence where every dissolution is followed by a divine renewal.'

As the bodies of Ajaa and Shambhu ji, along with the fallen Nagas were consumed by the sacred flames, their ashes ascended as offerings to Shiva. In his embrace, they attained salvation, their spirits merging with the cosmic dance. Through Shiva, their end became a divine renewal, eternal evidence of the cycle of life and liberation.

The bodies of the offenders were buried, while the defenders were given the path to Shiva through fire. Krishna, Golu and Neelkanth, seated on Golu's back, attended the cremation not knowing that they were surrounded by the souls of Naga warriors bidding farewell, as I performed the last rites called *Antim Sanskar*.

While we faced the heat of the cremation, Dhruv could feel the chills in his bones as he began his ascent, each step weighed down by the responsibility of his mission. He regarded this duty as Ajaa's orders. As the chilling winds of the Himalayas kissed his face, he found solace in the thought that the legacy of the Nagas would forever be immortalized. He looked non-existent in front of the vast and numerous Himalayan peaks. Dhruv continued the long and difficult journey in the vast terrain of the Himalayas as the message he carried was invaluable. The Himalayas, one of the most majestic mountain ranges in the world, stretches over 2400 kilometres across five countries namely, India, Nepal, Bhutan, China, Pakistan. Its vastness encompasses some of the highest peaks of our planet, including Mount Everest, which soars to an awe-inspiring 29,029 feet. The range varied in width from 200 to 400 kilometres, presenting an imposing barrier that divides the Tibetan plateau to the north from the Indian subcontinent to the south. These towering peaks and vast stretches of rugged mountain rendered Dhruv so directionless that he was lost in the overwhelming majesty of the mountains. Days and nights blurred together as he wandered, unable to keep track of time, swallowed by the immensity of the landscape. But what did not blur was the crawling that could be heard but not seen still following him. The grandeur of the Himalayas with their snow-covered summits and deep valleys mirrored the profound challenges and introspective depths of Dhruv's quest as he sought the ocean of the Nagas, hidden within this breathtaking and unforgiving terrain.

While Dhruv was unable to keep track of time, it was nearly the end of the third day since the bodies were burnt and buried. Krishna was preparing for his trip to King Dhyanendra's Kingdom, Surajgarh. 'His kingdom needs to know that they are orphaned by the Afghans, that their father, their king died fighting like a lion,' said Krishna, preparing to leave while Golu, alongside me, was busy trying to take out the conch hanging on my waist.

'Golu! Don't!' I said while pretending to be angry.

'He is just a speechless kid, who has recently lost his mother. He sees a guardian in you. Handle him gently. Elephants are very smart beings and loyal family members,' Krishna taught me.

'I don't know what to do with him and myself,' I said, a little tensed and upset.

'Look around you. There is so much to do. There will be a day when the residents of Gokul will return. Prepare to welcome them and take pride that you and your clan of Nagas saved their village. You are a Shiva devotee. Be the first two spokes of his trident. Recreate what's destroyed and preserve what's saved by your brothers so that the villagers can get their homes back. I shall return to Gokul soon,' said Krishna, hugging me and patting Golu's head.

'Be a good boy and grow up quickly,' Krishna told Golu and turned back to depart. While leaving, he said, 'his name is Gajraaj from now on. Don't call him Golu any more.'

While Krishna was leaving Gokul, Vedant was entering Haripur. The sunset painted the sky with shades of orange and crimson, as the sprawling city of Haripur came into view. Vedant and his vast army entered the city gates with the banners of victory flying high. The streets echoed with their triumphant march and Vedant falsely pretended to be the hero of the battle. But the celebrations were not shared by all.

As the sounds of festivity filled the night there, somewhere else the news of Sardar Khan's death and Gokul's defeat was about to ruin an invader's inner peace.

Jugal entered the tent where Abdali was seated on a *takht**, a kind of raised platform. He was familiar with all the faces present in Abdali's tent other than one puzzling figure with a wicked mysticism. Her face had a long and sharp scar running down her cheek, crossing her lips till her chin, a permanent reminder of a jinxed past. She was dressed in a dark, intricately layered robe, part armour, part cloak, with the reptilian charm of an occultist with unnaturally bright eyes, exuding an unsettling power. The edges of her garments were lined with ancient Persian letters, glowing dimly with dark energy. Her hands, always hidden beneath long, flowing sleeves, were anticipated to weave powerful spells and invite malevolent forces. Around her waist was a belt decorated with precious stones, each with a suspicion of dark magic trapped in it. Neymat was her name, Jugal Kishore learned later.

Neymat stood nearby, her presence a silent testimony to the gravity of the situation. In the corner, a family of an Afghan soldier in uniform, his two wives, and their eight children were tied and trembling in fear. Their faces wet with tears, their bodies curved in a squat position. The atmosphere was thick with dread, the air itself seeming to hold its breath in anticipation of Abdali's reaction.

---

* (in Eastern countries) a sofa or long bench, or a bed.

Abdali was quiet and the silence that enveloped him was nearly dense. After looking at Jugal Kishore's unhappy face and sensing that he had disappointing news to share, Abdali's gaze then landed on the betrayer. At this point, the already terrified family of the traitor appeared to shrink even more.

Now, in frightened stillness, they were going to see the horrible sight. An oppressive quiet descended upon the room as Abdali's eyes burned with wrath. Sitting with a terrifying composure, Abdali summoned the traitor while hiding his rage. 'Come here,' Abdali said. Nervous, the betrayer stepped forward. 'Take my sword and cut your foot,' said Abdali, calmly. The courtiers were shocked and confusion surged through them, while Neymat was thrilled, her excitement clearly evident in her eyes, as Jugal noticed.

'M-my lord?' mumbled the traitor in disbelief.

'I asked you to cut your foot,' Abdali repeated calmly. The soldier shook as he gave him his sword. 'Use my sword to do it,' Abdali added. Pale in anticipation and trembling in terror, the accused lifted the sword to do as ordered in one shot.

'Naah Naah! Not at once! Use the sword as a saw and cut your bone slowly as wood is cut.' Neymat had mischief in her eyes. She was undoubtedly enjoying the events in the tent. The traitor saw his family. He knew that his death was assured, but if he refused to follow the orders, he would have to see his family die right in front of his eyes. He swallowed his saliva in fear, set the sharp sword on his leg, closed his eyes and started cutting his flesh and bone slowly.

The courtiers were horrified to see the blade piercing the flesh and blood gushing out of it as water. The soldier shouted in pain; his face contorted as blood shot forth. Cries of shock and contempt filled the room, but nobody moved. Abdali said, 'Cut it! You can do it.' The soldier let out one last scream before he severed his own leg from his body. Blood gushed forth and pooled on the ground. The courtiers could not stand to see it and looked the other way. Some even covered their eyes and voice, but Neymat had her eyes and mouth both wide open in amazement and amusement. With the hope that his punishment was served, he looked at Abdali for mercy.

'Roast it now,' ordered Abdali. The soldier was pulled to a fire while he writhed in agony.

An iron rod was brought over and handed to him by two other soldiers. The traitor picked up his severed foot and pierced it with the iron rod to grill it over the flames with horrific efficiency. The traitor groaned, his face dripping with sweat, and foot gushing blood, hardly awake. The aroma of roasting flesh filled the room, turning stomachs. The foot was burnt, and the traitor looked at Abdali again, expecting the end of the torture.

'Now serve it to everyone. You will distribute it among the courtiers,' said Abdali.

The courtiers looked at each other with dismay. The pale, trembling betrayer readied himself to execute Abdali's directives and stepped closer on one foot to a courtier. Their commitment and loyalty were put to the test at every turn. Though there was tension and a sense of dread in the air, nobody dared to disobey Abdali's directives and the courtier lifted his hand to pick the flesh of the foot in total disbelief.

'It was a joke! You don't have to eat it. You people have no sense of humour,' said Abdali sarcastically before turning to Jugal and questioning, 'Yes, my dear!'

A thick quiet fell over the tent as Jugal started to tell the story of what had happened at Gokul and how Sardar Khan had died. Gathering all courage once more, Jugal said in a quiet voice, 'Against my orders, Sardar Khan decided to attack Gokul on his way to Haripur, for his personal profits. The fighting at Gokul unlike any other battle I had seen before. The sound of booming cannons and thundering chants of Har Har Mahadev made the ground quiver, and the air was thick with smoke and the stink of death. The forces fought each other fiercely in an effort to gain total control. Sardar Khan commanded troops in this with bravery and unflinching determination.' Jugal spoke shyly and almost fearfully, yet with a fake admiration. All of Sardar Khan's soldiers rallied as he led charges against the enemy, inspiring them with his presence and influence felt everywhere. Sadly, he was hit by enemy fire and he fell during the conflict. Jugal continued despite the sight, feeling intense terror and distress. 'Now that's called a good sense of humour,' said Abdali, addressing all the men standing inside, hearing Jugal Kishore.

Nobody laughed as they knew it was a taunt that may fall heavy on anybody. Abdali kept looking at Jugal's face. Abdali's voice sliced through the air like a sword again. 'Is

Sardar Khan still alive?' His voice carried a palpable anxiety that made everyone in the room shrink back, their eyes wide with fright and their breathing shallow.

'No, my king! We lost him.' Jugal tried to explain and reassure Abdali that they had done their best. Jugal tried to explain his case and ask for forgiveness. Abdali, burning with rage, said, 'Sardar Khan disobeyed my commands! How can he die? I would have punished him severely for his treachery. I should've killed him with my own hands!' Abdali's rage sent shivers down everyone's spine. His outburst went on, and the dread increased with each word. Then it stopped just as abruptly as it had started. Abdali paused for a moment and turned towards Jugal asking him, 'Is that village still standing?'

'Yes, my lord!' replied Jugal Kishore in fear and disgrace.

'What is the name of the village you said?' asked Abdali. Neymat replied, 'Gokul! It is said to be the village of one of their worshipped Gods called Kanahiya. Ruining it will spread the word in far lands too. We must set an example of this.' It was a brutal and scary suggestion from a beautiful and soothing voice.

'Where are my commanders?' Abdali again questioned Jugal calmly.

Jugal answered, 'I will have to check, my lord,' with a dry mouth and a blank thought. 'I was travelling for the last couple of days.' Jugal Kishore hesitated to respond out of concern for Abdali's wrath.

'Neymat!' Abdali called.

After comprehending the signal, Neymat quickly responded, 'Shenshah! On the eastern side of Vanga (now Bengal), is General Sarfaraz moving towards the central, accompanied by 7000 troops, 300 horses, 200 camels and ten cannons. He can reach Gokul at the earliest. In the western region of Bharat, Commander Zoravar and Malik Akhtar are commanding an army of 8000 men, 600 horses, ten cannons. Commander Azharuddin is in the central region with 5000 men, 300 horses and ten cannons. He is the closest to our camp and here we have around 10,000 soldiers, fifty cannons, 1000 horses and 1000 camels, including what Jugal Kishore ji has brought back alive. Overall, an army of 30,000 soldiers, 1900 horses, 1500 camels and seventy cannons.' Neymat was taunting Jugal Kishore, demonstrating her promptness by having all the figures and their placements at her fingertips.

'Jugal, you are rusting now,' Abdali exclaimed with a tone that pierced Jugal's eyes. Jugal Kishore sensed that his status and dignity were rapidly disappearing from Ahmed Shah Abdali's eyes.

With a command that resounded with might, he ordered, 'Send my message to all the commanders to approach Gokul. Tell them all to surround Gokul from all sides and wait for me. Azharuddin and his troops will join us on the way. Order them to kill all Pandits, impregnate all women, convert all children to Islam and burn everything on their way. The bravery of the Nagas, their indomitable spirit, and the epic battle that unfolded cannot be documented and will not go down in history for generations to come. I will set an example of Gokul for the times to come so that nobody ever even imagines standing against my forces ever again.'

Jugal, standing next to Neymat, wore a worried expression. He expressed his confusion and fear for Abdali's army, saying, 'If we do this, all the Hindus and Sikhs might come together and unify against us, which would result in a dangerous situation for our army, my lord.'

In response to the concern, Abdali stated, 'Unify? No, they can't. They won't. They pose no threat to us.'

'How can we be so sure?' asked Jugal, concerned about Abdali's confidence.

With his eyes going back to Jugal Kishore, Abdali questioned him, 'What is that word you people use for sight . . . far and close?'

Jugal took a moment to recollect, but before he could answer, Neymat responded, 'Drishti, huzoor. Sarp Drishti and Garud Drishti.'

'Ya! That one . . . the snake sight. That is not going to be a threat to us,' Abdali said, nodding, 'Due to their Sarpa Drishti, they are weak because they only consider short-term gains and they will remain so. Our biggest strength is not in our army or our fighting skills or our mission. Our biggest strength is their Sarp Drishti,' said Abdali with insistence.

Abdali's gaze now shifted coldly to the traitor's family. He asked Neymat, 'What do you think should be done with them all?'

Neymat replied with full authority, 'Traitors will always produce traitors. They are undeserving of another opportunity.'

With a merciless finality, he smiled as if proud of Neymat and ordered his men to murder all the eight children of the traitor who was still alive and present in the tent.

'It will be useless to kill them all, my lord! Give them to me and I shall sacrifice them for a cause that will strengthen you,' Neymat said, looking at the children with greed. Abdali signalled his soldiers to deliver the children to her sacred space. The repercussions were immediate and serious, leaving a lasting impression on everyone in attendance as well as in the tent. Abdali gave his last order before heading out of the tent. 'Take the traitor's two wives and give them to our soldiers for as many offspring as possible with them. Their newborn will obey me and remain faithful to my cause.' With determined expressions, the soldiers moved to comply. When Abdali left, the tent was marked by his rage. Everyone there was horrified by the image of the blood, screams and roasted human leg, which served as a haunting reminder of the price of betrayal. The depth of Abdali's cruelty screamed out loud in the hearts of Jugal Kishore and the others. Jugal clearly understood that this time he had a bigger and smarter rival. And to sustain, the strategy this time could not to offend the mysterious Persian, but to be in her good books.

At a calm moment, in the snow, Madhav enquired, 'Garun Drishti . . . Sarp Drishti! What did Ahmed Shah Abdali mean?'

The nameless Naga started explaining about ancient wisdom. 'In times of conflict, men's destiny is decided by their choices, which are shaped by the views of Garuda

Drishti and Sarpa Drishti, that means shortsightedness and farsightedness. Drishti signifies vision, Sarpa denotes snake, and Sarpa Drishti refers to a short-distance, snake-like vision that denotes concentrating on minor, short-term benefits without taking the long-term effects into account. However, Garud means eagle and Garud Drishti refers to the vision of an eagle, which is farsighted and represents the ability to plan long-term benefits strategically and ready to face short-term losses for the bigger purpose. Understanding this distinction is essential to comprehending the decisions, and strengths and weaknesses of leaders.'

'But what relevance does this have to our war?' the Naga following the nameless one enquired.

'Vedant had a Sarp Drishti. He could only think of the lives and land of his kingdom and people missing out on the bigger purpose of saving his own kind that may lead to saving the country and the land of Bharat. The temptation of shortsightedness must be resisted as we embrace the knowledge of foresight. Because of this, we shall not only prevail in combat, but also create a future based on morality and fairness, explained the nameless Naga. His words captivated Madhav, who thought about how important foresight is in wartime. 'You see,' the nameless Naga remarked, 'Abdali relied on the kings having Sarpa Drishti, the limited vision that caused them to be too focused on their immediate needs to see the long-term effects of their actions. It is because of such kings then and politicians now that we are still fighting a war for our land, culture, beliefs, women and temples today.'

'What do you mean by "Still fighting"?' asked Madhav, trying to understand the present scenario.

'The only things that the Hindu civilians think of today are food, clothes and shelter for the family. Their food must be lavish with variety, clothes be branded, and shelter be huge with extra bedrooms in a posh locality. They still do not understand that if they do not save their culture and religion, their food will be snatched away from their mouth, their clothes will be torn in mobs and their shelter will be occupied by force.'

Madhav was taken aback by the harshness of the horrifying imagination.

'It is a harsh statement, I know, not soothing to your ears but unfortunately true,' concluded the nameless protector of dharma.

He took a sigh and added, 'About 2000 years ago, Adi Shankaracharya was a great visionary who created us —Naga soldiers—and taught us to defend and preserve dharma. He embodied Garuda Drishti in a way that his forward-thinking and foresight ensured the dharma's survival and flowering for future generations. The inefficient short-sightedness of kings of those times gave Abdali the confidence of his brutal strategy and victory.'

The subordinate added, 'The lands belonged to the kings, who thought Sarpa Drishti would not be bound in time to cause any real threat. But if even a tiny group had the Garuda Drishti, they might foresee the dangers of war and band together to protect their country and people.' I *see now, after paying close attention to nameless Naga and seeing how important the right vision is for leadership and decision-making.*

The nameless Naga, realizing that his fellow Naga clearly understood the meaning and difference of the two sights that every person should understand, switched his focus from Abdali and Neymat to Krishna and said, 'Meanwhile, Krishna burdened with the sad news of King Dhyanendra, continued his journey from Gokul towards the Kingdom of Surajgarh. The road was long and tiring but Krishna was steadfast in his mission to honor the memory of King Dhyanendra.'

Madhav curiously interrupted, 'Abdali was preparing to ruin Gokul! Ajaa and Shambhu ji died. Krishna left from Gokul. It was just you and Golu . . . I mean Gajraaj in Gokul. Who will save Gokul?'

'Dhruv and the Nagas of the Himalayas will,' said the nameless Naga with pride.

'What about Dhruv? How far was he from finding the Nagas in the Himalayas?' Madhav asked, eager and concerned.

4

Queen of Hearts

While Abdali was preparing to summon all his four commanders, each as ruthless and cruel as Sardar Khan, Dhruv was climbing a steep path still feeling a crawling sound following him when he unexpectedly encountered a beggar, shivering by the side of the track. The man had dark skin and grey hair. His lips had numerous cracks and so did his feet. Wrapped in tattered robes, he appeared weak and hunched over. His tattered clothing wrapped loosely around his shrunken frame. His matted grey hair fell across his weathered face and eyes that held a lifetime of experience. His hands trembled as he tried to stand with the help of a makeshift stick.

'Spare some food for a hungry man?' the beggar asked softly.

Moved by the beggar's difficulty, Dhruv offered him some of his provisions. 'Here, take this,' he said, handing over some food and water. He also removed his stole and draped it over the man's shoulders. 'You look cold. This will help,' Dhruv said. The beggar was deeply moved by Dhruv's gesture and thanked him gratefully.

'Who are you and what are you doing here?' asked Dhruv, concerned.

'My name is Varya. I am lost in this never-ending world of mountains. And who might you be?' asked the beggar in a shivering tone.

Dhruv responded, 'I am Dhruv from the village of Gokul. I seek Naga sadhus who live in these mountains. Have you seen any around?'

Varya nodded thoughtfully. 'I know the way to some extent. The path is dangerous, but with determination, you will reach your destination. You fed me and gave me your stole to get rid of the cold. I will help you as much as I know and have climbed.'

As the two continued their journey, Dhruv enquired about Varya's origin. 'I belong to nowhere and have been on a lifelong quest for spiritual enlightenment. I have been wandering through forests and mountains, seeking the path of salvation and the divine presence of Shiva. My journey has been filled with meditative solitude, profound reflections, and a deep connection to the natural world,' said Varya.

Together, they climbed for days and survived the nights. During the journey, Dhruv noticed that Varya had a strange ability to sense danger and guide him away from perilous paths. But surprisingly, he could not feel or hear the creature following them. At one point, they encountered a treacherous river crossing. Varya decided to walk ahead, finding the safest path to ensure Dhruv reached the other side unhurt. 'Careful here,' Varya warned, as they navigated a narrow ledge. 'The rocks are loose,' added Varya. Dhruv and Varya moved forward steadily. Despite the challenges, he remained focused on his goal. They became friends, cared for each other and shared food. Dhruv told Varya all about his life and the reason for his journey to the Himalayas. Varya heard about Ajaa and his devotion to save his Gods. Losing the count of days and nights, the two men approached the next milestone. It was dark by then, and the only sound heard was the haunting sound of chilly winds all around them. Under the light of the moon, Varya stopped and pointed ahead, saying, 'Beyond this point lies the unknown terrain that I have not explored.'

Varya looked at Dhruv with a tired smile and said, 'I cannot go beyond this area. It's a long journey ahead, and I am not fit and strong enough to continue. The deficiency of oxygen and the increasing cold are more than I can bear with my fragile body and advancing age. I suggest you too should return from here.'

Dhruv nodded, understanding the gravity of Varya's condition but knew that he had to go on. He held Varya's hand gratefully and thanked him for he couldn't have come this far without his help. Sensing Dhruv's resolve, Varya placed a trembling hand on his shoulder. 'Go with courage,' he said to him softly. 'Your journey is far from over, but you have the strength to see it through,' Varya added.

Dhruv glanced at the stole he had offered Varya when they first met. Noticing this, Varya offered it back but with a smile, Dhruv refused, saying, 'You need it more than I do. Keep it. It will help you on your way back to where we met.'

Varya had gratitude for Dhruv's kindness. 'You are a kind man, Dhruv. Not only food and this robe, but you have also given me the most expensive gift in this mortal world.' Dhruv seemed confused.

'Time! The most expensive gift anyone can give. I am a beggar, and I have nothing to offer in return but it seems I have given you a part of me that will be with you always,' said Varya, smiling.

'Part of you! I don't understand. What do you mean?' asked Dhruv, confused.

'Time will answer your question. Now go ahead,' replied Varya, hugging Dhruv.

With a final nod of gratitude and respect, Dhruv turned towards the mountains, the weight of Varya's words and his journey ahead pressing upon him. He was now standing at the base of enormous mountains, with snow and swirling clouds covering their peaks. The cold seeped through his garments, freezing him to the bone, and the thin air made breathing difficult. The track ahead twisted through thick woodlands and rocky terrain, making it narrow and steep. As Dhruv ascended higher, the trees grew fewer, and the surrounding terrain transformed into an isolated stretch of ice and snow. Everything around him was changing but the only thing constant was the crawling sound. But he could never find anything whenever he turned back to look for the source of the sound. Even though his lungs burnt and his legs hurt, the idea of discovering his purpose kept him going. He could make out the towering mountains, their sharp peaks piercing the sky. His destination, however, was still far away, and hidden by mystery and the possibility of discovery. Dhruv paused and took a moment to reconsider his previous route. Although the journey was challenging, he had a strong sense of resolve. He recalled Ajaa's words, which gave him the courage and strength to move forward. 'Dhruv, may my Shiva be with you as you proceed.' Though he still had a long journey ahead, he was ready to face any obstacles in his path and continued climbing.

While Dhruv's search seemed unending, Krishna reached a position from where he could see the far outlines, a distinct viewpoint, and a wider angle of Surajgarh, the kingdom of the late King Dhyanendra. Krishna was able to observe the castle walls from a distance, which formed a strong layer that protected the kingdom.

The massive gates were shut, and guards were stationed along the border, keeping a vigilant watch. The kingdom's specifics were hidden behind the walls, but one could still sense its majesty and significance. A surge of will and determination swelled Krishna's heart. He was almost at the finish line of his difficult and long journey. Though the journey had been hazardous and drawn out, he was filled with hope and sadness upon seeing the kingdom. He carried the heavy responsibility of delivering the devastating news of the king's passing, knowing it would bring great pain to the citizens of Surajgarh. The stronghold stood as a testament to King Dhyanendra's might and legacy, and Krishna was determined to carry out his mission in a way that honoured the king's history. Krishna inhaled deeply and moved forward; his sight fixed on the distant grip.

As he approached the kingdom, he was filled with astonishment. The fortress's imposing walls, visible in the distance, reflected the kingdom's splendour. The fortress's gates were magnificent, and the tall guards he initially mistook for strong-built men were actually striking women with powerful physiques that spoke volumes about their strength.

'My name is Krishna, and I was the commander-in-chief of Haripur. I demand to meet your king,' asserted Krishna, standing at the entrance of the fort.

'We do not have a king. We serve the queen,' said the elegantly dressed woman guard at the gate, proudly. Another gatekeeper, a commanding woman, stepped forward to intercept him and enquire about his purpose. Both these females were taller than Krishna, their imposing physiques making it clear that no one could pass without their consent.

Krishna respectfully responded, 'I have urgent news regarding King Dhyanendra. Please notify your queen of my arrival.'

The senior commanding officer narrowed her eyes and assessed Krishna before signalling a junior guard, who quickly disappeared through the gates to inform the queen. After half an hour of silence, the guard returned, and Krishna was allowed in. Eager to convey the message and learn more about the great protector of the kingdom, Krishna followed her through the enormous gates. The sun was about to set when he stepped inside Surajgarh.

Krishna was astonished by what he was witnessing and observing. His eyes widened as he entered the gates and saw the women of the royal fleet with swords riding horseback, their erect postures and keen eyes filled with furious determination. Their royal uniform conveyed authority and grace, proudly upholding the safety and security of men working in all professions.

The kingdom's men worked tirelessly in the fields and other laborious workstations. They were motivated by a sense of duty and affection for their masters. They were aware of the security and dependability of their future under the leadership of a queen and her well-deserving army of women. The mission was to ensure the safety and well-being of all people living within the kingdom's borders, regardless of their background or current circumstances. He could see the women managing the division of resources, labour and land cultivation the same way that a queen ant organizes her colony's complicated actions and is always concerned about the welfare of her people.

The kingdom welcomed the refugees with open arms, offering both its hospitality and its gates to those fleeing trouble from other kingdoms, allowing them to start a new life with dignity while acknowledging the hardships they endured. This stance also reflected the kingdom's broad belief in the value of life. This inclusivity extended beyond their subjects to embrace people of all backgrounds and religions, not just Hindus.

Hindus and Sikhs felt secure within the boundaries, and they shared a common goal and objective of safety and harmony. This revelation represented the living embodiment of the unwavering resilience and strength of these cultures, situated at the centre of this matriarchal realm, such as Swayamvar, which allowed women to choose their own partners, laying the groundwork for the evolving nature of power through mutual respect and affection. It highlighted the democratic principles that permeate every aspect of life.

As a result, rather than exerting control over her subjects, the queen promoted an inclusive and cooperative approach. This sense of security allowed refugees to interact openly with locals, sharing their inspiring stories of resilience and hope. It highlighted the kingdom's remarkable commitment to unity and supported the recognition and appreciation of diversity in backgrounds, cultures and religions. The nameless Naga went on to describe the queen's kingdom as being like the Bharat of old times, which had always represented hope and unity.

Just as Bharat maintains harmonious relationships today with diverse nations such as Russia as well as the United States of America, as well as Iran and Israel, so did the queen cultivate alliances with various kingdoms, even those that sometimes stood against each other.

In addition to being a symbol of morality and empowerment, she encouraged her people to fight back in the face of opposition. She successfully defended her kingdom against external threats and pressures, fought invading armies and bravely protected her people from harm. She inspired her subjects and helped them build better futures for both their families and the kingdom. The queen was revered as Annapurna Devi, the Goddess of Food, who provided nutrition to the hungry. She embodied the essence of Goddess Lakshmi, bestowing wealth and prosperity on the people of her kingdom. She was an idol of knowledge, like Goddess Saraswati for enlightenment. In times of war, she stood tall and fierce like Goddess Durga, commanding her armies with unrivalled strength and valour. For decades, her people saw in the queen not only a ruler but also a mother, as her unwavering commitment to their well-being fostered hope and unity throughout King Dhyanendra's kingdom. The queen's legacy would endure for years in the heart of this unique matriarchal society, where women ruled freely and justice reigned supreme.

As he moved closer to the palace gates, he heard happy and free folks singing in satisfaction.

In the realm of the rivers and wines,
Reigns a queen with a heart that shines.
Elegance in her strides,
Courage in her eyes,
Our queen stands a beacon
In the lows and highs.

Her name is held in tales to be told,
Proving a ruler of wisdom and bold.

With compassion as her guide and love as her shield,
She nurtures her people with her loyalty revealed.
From distant lands, people come seeking aid,
In her mercy queen never once delayed.
Welcoming with an open-heart all in need,
Offering comfort and hope with every deed.

Encroaching threats and darkness loom,
Queen stands as hope, dismissing gloom.
Feeding the hungry, healing the ill.
Lifting the fallen with firm will.

In her kingdom, peace and joy rules,
As the queen's love flows like a soft embrace.
With trials and triumphs, she leads with grace,
She is a revered figure in our hearts—her palace.

It was getting dark by the time Krishna entered the royal courtyard of the palace. He was astounded by its magnificence and beauty, having journeyed from the outskirts of death, destruction, bloodshed and warfare. The courtyard had a distinct presence, infused with tradition and grandeur. Krishna was captivated by the striking towers surrounding the courtyard, which were made of marble and gold and gave off a golden gleam when the lamp's rays reflected on to them. The marble sculptures and gold ornaments on the walls gave the halls an otherworldly beauty. Krishna was astounded by the palace's majestic splendour. He absorbed its calm and composed ambiance and felt enveloped in a deep sense of relaxation as the serene melody of the fountains flowed in harmony with the peaceful aura of the courtyard. The colourful flower beds that encircled the fountain provided a soothing scent to the surrounding area. The entire courtyard was decorated with golden silk drapes and the chandeliers illuminated the palace in a light comparable to that of stars in the sky. The women had distinct brightness on their faces and were dressed in silk.

Not only did the majesty of the courtyard and the confidence of the women within leave Krishna speechless, but there was also a unique dynamic that set the kingdom apart from others. The women held positions of power and authority, exuding strength and command, while the men served as attendants, their movements marked by grace and deference. They stood beside female ministers with swirling decorative fans, while others stood at the corner ready, their eyes alert and attentive to the needs of the women they served. He observed men serving and pouring drinks and attending to the needs of the courtiers with dedication. The scene was a stunning reversal of traditional roles, showcasing the kingdom's progressive nature. This was a place where capability and valour defined position and seats, not gender.

As he approached the royal throne, he was drawn to an unusual figure from a distance. Krishna's interest grew as he turned to face the blurred figure that was gradually becoming clearer and eventually revealed to be the queen. Her poise and assurance were evident, as was her magnificent regal crest, which radiated light. Krishna came to realize that she was a queen of extraordinary strength and intelligence.

The magnificent hall reflected the power and majesty of the royal Queen. Krishna was greeted warmly by the queen and her courtiers. He was impressed by the queen's demeanour, a blend of strength and modesty that earned her the respect of everyone she met.

'Greetings! Your Majesty. My name is Krishna. I was the commander-in-chief of Haripur,' said Krishna, introducing himself.

'Yes! I am told who you are, Commander. I wish to know what brings you here from Haripur. I remember Haripar once attacked us. Do you want to try another battle with us?' the queen asked with grace in her voice, but suspicion and alertness intact.

'No, my queen! I don't serve the new king of Haripur any more. I am here because I recently had the honour of fighting alongside King Dhyanendra. I saw the valour, courage and power he fought with. I am a witness to a lot of things in the past few days, and I come bearing news that may bring both sorrow and pride to this court and you,' said Krishna humbly with his head bowed down.

'What's the news?' asked the queen. Her voice had both anxiety and concern.

With all of his resolve, Krishna responded, 'Your Majesty, I saw the heroic deeds of Naga warriors under King Dhyanendra, who led them with unparalleled bravery to turn the tide of battle in our favour despite overwhelming odds by confronting an opponent ten times larger than us.'

'What exactly happened, Commander?' another tense voice interrupted, enquiring about the reason for Krishna's visit. Krishna had a serious vision as his gaze drifted to the face of the voice. A beautiful young woman in her early twenties stood beside the queen with a distinct aura of power and authority around her. Her dark hair, elegantly styled and studded with sparkling pins, fell gracefully down her back. Her keen eyes never missed anything, and she observed the world around her with a burning intelligence while wearing a form-fitting and armour-like robe, meticulously embroidered with symbols representing the kingdom's strength. She maintained the elegance of a young leader while also displaying gentle tenderness and regal composure. A sword hung at her side with a gem-adorned handle as a tribute to her position as commander-in-chief of the queen's troops.

Before he could continue, the queen ordered, 'Answer the princess!'

This made Krishna realize she was Chandrika, the princess, King Dhyanendra and the queen's daughter. Krishna paused for a moment, awestruck, as he recalled a face from the recent past that resembled the princess. The face that flashed in Krishna's memory was of Ajaa. He turned to the queen, asking if she had a son. The queen's discomfort, as evidenced by her pale face, caused Krishna to think intuitively about the situation and immediately recall why Shambhu ji stretched his hands towards Ajaa as he took his final breath.

Krishna realized that Shambhu ji was implying that he was powerless and could no longer pamper his son.

This assisted Krishna in connecting the dots and discovering that he was standing in front of the queen and princess with the burden of not one but two grief-stricken reports—the loss of not only the king but also the prince.

Krishna approached the queen and princess again and said softly, 'King Dhyanendra and Prince Ajaa fought bravely, protecting everyone and our land. Together they stood as symbols of bravery and solidarity, surrounded by enemies. Ajaa killed Sardar Khan, the commander-in-chief of Ahmed Shah Abdali, and won the battle of Gokul before falling. King Dhyanendra witnessed his son, and your prince, die.'

'And, my king?' asked the queen leaving her throne, with her voice trembling in sorrow.

'He took his last breath on my lap,' answered Krishna with his voice low.

There was a brief silence in the great hall of courage and strength. The queen and princess choked up, overwhelmed with emotion, but still stood firm and strong. Their hearts were heavy with loss but their spirits unshakable.

Despite being shattered by the news, they knew they had to remain strong for their people, understanding that their duty to the kingdom outweighed their own pain and loss. Thus, despite the ongoing suffering, they resolved to guide and protect their people, embodying the saying, 'When the going gets tough, the tough get going.'

'Is there anything else that you are here for, Krishna?' the queen asked, regaining her composure as she shifted from a grieving wife and mother back to a queen.

Krishna stood before the queen and princess; his face filled with concern. 'Your Majesty, the people of Gokul are in need of your protection because our land is suffering and facing constant threats from invading armies. I have the zeal and intent to help them, but without partners, my efforts seem meaningless.'

Turning to her daughter, the princess, who was also the commander-in-chief of the queen's army, the queen said, 'We cannot let Gokul suffer. We won't abandon them. We'll take Gokul under our wing.'

The queen confidently announced, 'Our king and prince sacrificed their lives for the people of Gokul, and it is now the duty of this kingdom to ensure that none of the Naga lives have gone in vain. Gokul is under my protection now.'

She turned back to Krishna and said, 'I give you 300 women warriors and 100 horse riders from my regiment of Durga defence forces. Together, you set boundaries and protect people and land from invaders. The princess will command this mission and ensure Gokul's well-being.'

Princess Chandrika stepped forward with determination and said, 'I will lead the army and do everything in my powers to restore peace and prosperity to Gokul.'

While the nameless Naga was narrating about Krishna getting a small army led by the princess of Surajgarh to protect Gokul, Thomas, who was really absorbed in the book, discovered some amazing information about a supernatural power of a Naga clan. It was about the soul catchers, believed to be a mystical and fearsome Naga clan in ancient lands, admired for their terrifying powers. These Nagas possess the rare ability to capture and control souls— both of the living and the dead, good and bad. Once trapped, these souls, within their sacred tridents, become powerful weapons that the sadhus can unleash on the battlefield and use when they wish. Their striking appearance included bodies covered in sacred ash, dreadlocked hair resembling twisted serpents and eyes burning with a fire, adorned with skulls and bones. They carry tridents alive with the energy of countless captured souls, embodying their mastery over life and death.

These Naga sadhus not only fight with mere physical strength, but also with the power of the unseen mystical forces they command. They can summon storms of unforgiving spirits, paralyze enemies with fear and even control the minds of warriors, turning them into puppets, changing the course of war as a result.

These soul controllers are guided by ancient forces in their actions to serve a purpose beyond human understanding. Conclusively, these Naga sadhus possessed the power over souls that granted them control over both the living and the dead. As long as they walked the earth, they remained the guardians of dharma.

The text in the book explained the historical significance of Shiva's army and its connection to an enigmatic clan of Naga sadhus to Thomas. He developed an interest in the prehistoric tales about heavenly Nagas and their paranormal superpowers. While Thomas was about to turn to the next page of the book, the crawling sound of something moving around him caught his attention. Feeling unsafe, he decided not to stay there any longer and moved on.

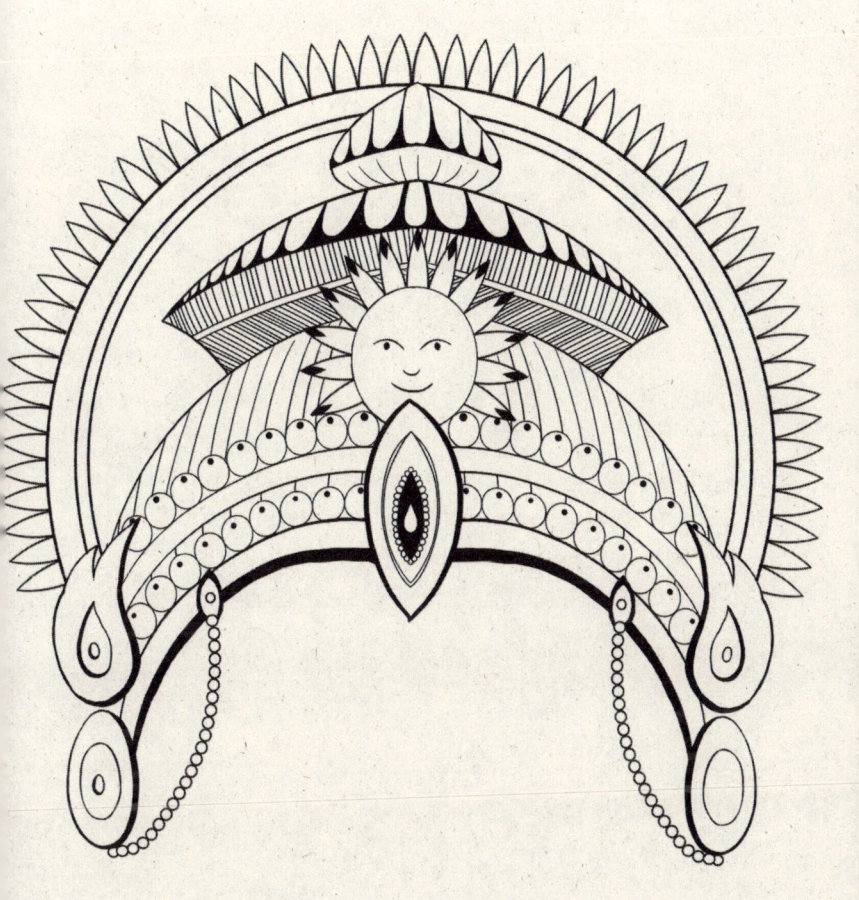

5

Arrow and Arrival

With the bitter cold piercing his skin down to his bones, Dhruv slogged through the snow-covered pathless heights. The journey ahead was dangerous, made even more so by the violent and snow-laden winds that blurred his vision. He could still feel something crawling around him. Something bigger than him in size. Not a snake as the crawl was not regular, but he never could find anything whenever his eyes searched for any form of life around. At nights, with scary whistles of the breeze, he often felt he was not alone and that he was being watched. It was often said that these mountains were not for the faint of heart, with their treacherous terrain and extraordinary snow beasts. Although Dhruv had heard these stories, he had never given them any credence. That is, until now, when he heard growls and sniffs that were inhuman. He was certain that some creatures surrounded him, and the danger was closing in. However, he couldn't tell which direction the sound was coming from, as the chilling waves felt directionless, and the snowfall was heavy. He then heard the thud of heavy paws on the thick layers of snow and quickly jumped to one side just a moment before a pair of dangerous and massive snow bears emerged from the swirling snow, their eyes blazing with greedy desire.

As they advanced, their massive shapes moved with incredible agility, sending shivers down Dhruv's spine. These massive snow bears were said to be fierce guardians of their frozen territory and the divine mountains. The snow bears' white fur blended seamlessly with the chilling environment, making them nearly invisible until it was too late for the prey. The bears attacked Dhruv furiously and he ran for his life. He could only see one of the two bears chasing him because the second creature took another route to attack from the front. In no time, Dhruv found himself blocked on two sides. Saddened by the certainty of his mission's failure, he sank to his knees, surrendering to the powerful forces of nature, ready to be torn apart. 'I am sorry, Ajaa. I could not live up to your expectations. I am sorry that I failed you. Shiva knows that I tried my best to reach the chief Mathadhish with your message.' Imagining Ajaa and Shambhu ji to be still fighting against Sardar Khan and his army, Dhruv thought about all the Nagas defending Gokul. This was the final image etched in his heart as the bears ran towards him from both sides. Ready to experience the unbearable pain of being torn into pieces, his flesh eaten and bones scattered, Dhruv closed his eyes. He could feel the bears closing in quickly, but then they stopped suddenly. Dhruv opened his eyes to see why he was still not attacked. He found the bears looking in one direction and falling back, howling in fear. Dhruv noticed a few arrows lodged in the snow around him, forming a boundary that the bears seemed afraid to cross. The arrows had a peculiar multicolour band tied to their tails. Right then, another arrow whizzed through the air, passing just beside Dhruv and landing near one bear's foot, as if warning it to retreat. The snow bears quickly turned and fled, while Dhruv turned to find the source of the arrows. A figure with his next arrow fully stretched in his bow walked towards Dhruv. He moved like a shadow through the cold terrain. Dhruv noticed it was a hunter-like tribal man, with piercing eyes that seemed to look straight into people's souls.

He looked tough, his forehead covered with cloth that tied his shortmatted hair. His rough skin was shielded by a cape of thick material made up of white fur, protecting him against the biting cold of the mountains. His arms and calves were covered in stiff leather garments. His intense and sharp eyes reflected his alertness as he skilfully handled a bow, with feather-tipped arrows and a dagger hanging on his waist. His presence was both impressive and fearsome and showed deep bonds or connection with the wild. The hunter walked close to Dhruv who was still on his knees.

'Who are you and what are you doing here?' asked the hunter in a friendly tone.

'My name is Dhruv, and I am in search of the Naga Matha to meet the chief Mathadhish,' Dhruv replied.

'I did not ask your name. I asked, who are you? I did not ask you where you are going. I asked you, what are you doing here?' said Kirat.

Dhruv was clueless. He had no idea what to answer.

'You saved my life. You are a godsend for me,' said Dhruv hesitantly, thanking the tribal.

'You have to be cautious in these mountains,' Kirat said. 'Every nook is full of danger.'

Dhruv responded, 'I am grateful to you. You are the reason I am alive. Who are you?'

'I am a resident of these territories,' said Kirat.

'What's your name? Where did you come from to save my life?'

'My name is Kirat. I live in the Valley of Rice.'

'Why did you save me?'

'I felt you there and knew you'd need protection and help,' said Kirat. 'Take this bow and some arrows. You may need it in your journey ahead.' Kirat assisted Dhruv in standing up and led him away from areas where other dangerous animals could attack him.

While the tribal was ensuring that Dhruv was not attacked again, messages to attack different provinces on the way to Gokul were sent to all the Abdali's four commanders stationed in different corners, who were soon to start for Gokul with their entire cavalry and resources.

Meanwhile, Jugal Kishore, aware that he was upsetting Ahmed Shah Abdali, felt a growing sense of fear. He knew that if he didn't act quickly and decisively, he could even be killed. Abdali's remark about him 'rusting' deeply affected him. With Neymat emerging as a potential replacement, the threat became more real than ever. Jugal's mind questioned and remembered the fate of the traitor soldier who was forced to cut off his own foot as a punishment. That haunting image reminded him to be smart, methodical and prepared because failure was not an option for him. His very survival depended on his ability to rise to the challenge and prove his worth in the face of increasing pressure.

He called one of his trusted men and ordered him to fix a meeting with Neymat so that he could get to know her better. Another spy was called and asked to keep a close eye on Neymat's actions. Jugal was curious to know what she was planning to do with the children of the traitor that Abdali punished.

'While all the four commanders were getting their orders to move to Gokul, I worked tirelessly, hammering nails and repairing the broken mud walls to rebuild the huts and houses in the village, which had been destroyed by Sardar Khan's invading army. Gajraaj, who was growing rapidly, was always around me, trying to help. But whenever I asked him to bring anything, he always picked up the wrong things,' said the nameless Naga, smiling while remembering the cute little elephant who grew rapidly, as if his senses had told him what he must be ready for in the days to come.

'Gajraaj was mischievous, distracting me by trying to snatch my shankh off my waist and pulling my arm, insisting that I blow the shankh over and over again. I tried to be patient, but irritation occasionally crossed my face. I would climb on Gajraaj's back to repair some higher sections of huts and houses while he stood still, obediently supporting me, his eyes twinkling with mischief. Those moments reflected a combination of hope and sorrow. On one side, we were rebuilding huts, houses and temples, bringing new life into the village. On the other, we were forced to confront the remnants of Sardar Khan's brutality when we discovered a hut filled with blood-soaked clothes and mutilated body parts. With a heavy heart filled with agony and sorrow, we set everything on fire, the flames overwhelming the dreadful memories and clearing the way for a new beginning.'

'Where are we going?' asked Madhav the Naga follower, as it seemed a never-ending journey.

'You will know in time,' replied the nameless Naga walking ahead.

As the nameless Naga and Madhav ascended the mountain, Thomas was descending with the help of the map, carrying the book about the Nagas safely.

Deeply engrossed in the book, he turned to another page that had writings about the hypnotic powers of the Naga Sadhus—Masters of Mind and Mysticism. Nagas, being channels of divine energy with the ability to transcend the physical form, were well regarded in ancient times. The most amazing ability they possessed was to hypnotize the opponent and make them hallucinate, which was nearly unbeatable on the battlefield. Thomas instantly recalled Mathadhish, the master of hypnotism, one of the oldest members of his matha, who had the power to change the course of battles and had done so successfully, fighting alongside Ajaa and Shambhu ji against Sardar Khan.

The hypnotic power of the Naga sadhus was not a mere skill learnt through practice. It was a blessing of the Adi yogi, Lord Shiva, who is the master of all mystical arts. The Nagas attained this skill through deep meditation and years of intense penance in reverence of Lord Shiva, who not only controlled their minds but also the minds of others. It's manipulating the energies of the universe that's nothing but the *prana* (soul) of all living beings. Hypnotism goes beyond merely looking into someone's eyes or waving a hand before their face. It is a spiritual process involving multiple stages.

In the initial stage, the Naga sadhus would gather in an isolated spot and begin the process of absorbing energy. They did so by sitting in a circle with fire in the centre, indicating the eternal flame of consciousness. They also covered their bodies in ashes, wearing only the sacred Rudraksha beads, representing detachment from the material world, and chanting ancient Vedic mantras, praying to Lord Shiva. While they chanted, they focused on their breath, drawing in the prana from the air around them and directing it into their forehead, the focal point of their mystical powers, which would vibrate with energy. The energy created at the point of Shiva's third eye was the key to their hypnotic abilities, eventually becoming the force they later unleashed upon their enemies.

After the creation of the energy, the sadhus would begin the process of synchronization, which was a crucial step that ensured Nagas were mentally and spiritually aligned.

By locking eyes with each other, they would form a mental bond that could channel thoughts, feelings and intentions without uttering a word. Working in unison allowed them to amplify their hypnotic power, and help them overcome their enemies' minds. The principle advantage of this power was that their minds were protected from any external influence. The sadhus, deeply synchronized and energized, would engage in a powerful ritual involving rhythmic chanting and a sacred drumbeat. With the intensity of the ritual increasing, they could enter a trance-like state, becoming vessels of divine energy. Their chanting, using a secret mantra known only to the Naga warriors, had the power to invoke Lord Shiva's hypnotic abilities, enabling them to transcend the physical world and use spiritual influence with precision. Consequently, the purpose for which these powers were acquired was to heal people mentally, making them forget traumas, extracting secrets from their minds and getting things done on orders. Nagas, with their glowing eyes, had the power to peek directly into their opponents' minds and investigate the void of one's own soul, where all fears and insecurities lay naked. They also used these powers at the time of war.

Nagas would lock their eyes on the targeted soldiers, causing them to feel dizzy and experience blurred vision. With each passing second, their minds would get heavily influenced with the echoes of chants heard by them, yet inaudible to those not targeted. Following this disorientation, the Nagas induced a powerful emotion of fear by creating and projecting images into the minds of the soldiers, often causing them to mistake these illusions for reality.

With the soldiers disoriented and consumed by fear, the final stage of the hypnosis could begin—'The Command'. Once the sadhus had fully gained control over their enemies' minds, they would implant a single thought that the soldiers could not resist. It could have been anything from dropping their weapons to turning against their own army or killing themselves. Completely under the influence of the sadhus, the soldiers would obey without question, overwhelmed by the hypnotic power and having no will of their own.

The power of hypnosis was not just a tool for war but also a means to protect the sacred lands of the Naga warriors, ensuring that no invader could ever conquer their home. The hypnotic power of the Naga sadhus, a force that safeguarded the sanctity of their people, was a shield that no army could ever try to breach in their territory.

As Thomas meticulously studied these details, the storm of mysticism in his head grew fiercer while he pieced together the ancient history and significance of these sacred texts.

Meanwhile, the nameless Naga continued narrating and walking.

Vedant, the King of Haripur, who entered the gates of his kingdom with his army with the banners of victory flying high, pretended to be the one who pushed back Abdali's army. He didn't know then that these fake stories of his victory against Sardar Khan were soon going to cost him.

This fake blabbering soon reached the ears of one of Abdali's commanders named Sarfaraz Khan, who also happened to be Sardar Khan's younger brother.

'King Vedant killed Sardar Khan and Abdali's army ran back, defeated by Haripur! So, this is what the people of Haripur know about their king? I wish to hear this lie from King Vedant himself about how bravely he fought and killed my brother!' exclaimed Sarfaraz, burning with a fire of personal vengeance for the death of his brother.

Sarfaraz Khan was not only of similar size and weight but also shared the same temperament as Sardar Khan. At that moment, he received Abdali's message, which, on reading, made Sarfaraz smile.

'What is it, Sir? You are smiling,' asked his subordinate captain.

'"Burn everything on the way", says this message,' said Sarfaraz excitedly.

'So?' the captain questioned again.

'So, King Vedant and his beloved Haripur are on our way to Gokul,' said Sarfaraz opportunistically.

'Prepare for attack. Our first target is Haripur. We start tomorrow morning. I want to meet King Vedant,' ordered Sarfaraz.

Abdali's formidable army surged towards Haripur at high speed, with ominous clouds of dust signalling their approach. That very day, Chandrika, the princess of Surajgarh, leading a relatively smaller troop of 300 female soldiers and 100 horse riders, known as the Durga Defence Forces, marched out of the gates of Surajgarh with Krishna to reach and set up their camps in Gokul. The queen stood above the passage walls of her fortress, silently looking at her daughter leading the Durga Defence Forces like a tigress.

The queen was kind but also wise. She knew that sooner or later the Afghans would come to her doors to destroy the ethnicity and contentment of her kingdom too.

'Order the blacksmiths to prepare 1,00,000 more arrows,' instructed the queen while standing on the high walls of her fort with her *garuda drishti*, anticipating the future and preparing for it.

'1,00,000 arrows! 1,00,000 is a huge number. Why do we want so many arrows? We don't have enough archers to shoot that many,' asked her new commander, who replaced the princess.

'We have given medicines at the time of disease to our neighbouring kingdoms and food at the time of their drought. We have given gold for their financial needs. Now is the time for war and they will need weapons. Send 25,000 arrows to my daughter in Gokul,' said the queen.

'Also send them messages immediately,' she added.

'And what should they read?' asked the commander.

'"Do not make the mistake that Vedant made when he had the choice",' the queen's voice was firm and clear.

The kingdom was at work. The blacksmiths were smelting iron, and the courtyard was flowing with ink on parchments for other kingdoms, while Princess Chandrika was on her way to Gokul where Gajraaj was growing up with me.

'I can't imagine how it would look, watching all of them fighting shoulder to shoulder for Gokul,' said Madhav, visualizing the scenario in his head.

'Yes. It was beyond imagination, impossible to describe the grandeur in words,' said the nameless Naga, looking forward and climbing.

'But there is so much to hear from you before they all reach the battleground of Gokul. I am thinking, where will you take me next?' asked the Naga follower with curiosity.

The nameless Naga started narrating further about Vedant. 'And then, I swung my sword and killed three men in one shot.' It was Vedant, flaunting how bravely he fought in front of the children of his dead predecessors. The kids were hearing all this as if a story was being narrated to them, and thinking it to be true.

'My king, informers tell us that a huge army of Afghans is heading this way and that they shall be reaching our walls in two to three days,' said one of the distressed courtiers.

King Vedant was speechless on hearing the information while the children waited for him to finish the brave tale of his lies.

'The courtiers are waiting for your orders and request your presence, my king!' said the courtier who came with the news.

Nobody knew that not one but many troops were moving towards Gokul from different directions, while directionless, Dhruv walked in the vast terrains of the snow mountains, with his bag in one hand and a bow in the other. The arrows were hung on his waist.

It took three days for Krishna and the princess to return to Gokul. Right outside the city, Krishna was engulfed by the recent memories of death and destruction, blood and bond, scream and strength that took him back to the valour of the Nagas and the inability of Vedant to make the right decision. When Krishna entered Gokul, it was in a relatively better shape than how he left it. Gajraaj was the first one to see Krishna, filled with excitement at his return, while I was surprised by what Krishna brought with him. An army of fearless females, it seemed to me. It took me no time to understand that the one leading the women warriors was Ajaa's sister. His reflection was prominently noticeable on her face.

Both Krishna and Princess Chandrika were greeted by Gajraaj and me. Gajraaj's heart leapt with joy at the sight of Krishna, and his enthusiasm overflowed as he greeted the two warmly. For the princess, it was her first encounter with us but for Krishna, it was a reunion. With the female warriors by their side, Krishna and the princess had journeyed back to Gokul, ready to lend their strength once more. Together, they would work tirelessly, fortifying the village's defences and restoring the homes of its residents, united in purpose, preparing for the looming threat.

'He is Adhiraj,' Krishna introduced me to the princess.

'They fought beyond what I could explain in words,' I said, mentioning Ajaa and Shambhu ji.

'Where did they fall?' the princess asked with a grave face.

Krishna and I walked to the battleground followed by the princess. The soil was still soaked with blood, and the condition of the ground was screaming out its current past loudly.

The princess sat on her knees and touched the ground as if searching for the touch of the father that she never knew and the brother she could never play with.

Consoling the princess, I said, 'They are still here. Ajaa and Shambhu ji! In the air you breathe, in the soil you touch, in Gokul that they stood for, killed and died for, they are still here.'

'Set up our camp here,' the princess ordered her soldiers in a strict tone. It demonstrated her courage and determination that she chose not only to stand but also to sleep on the battlefield itself. The Durga Defence Forces were at work. The camp was to be set on the very mouth of the beast called war.

'An army of more than 30,000, including a horse cavalry of nearly 2000 riders, and camel cavalry of 1500 and other soldiers handling 70 cannons against the Durga Defence Forces of just 300 soldiers and 100 horse riders, that too all women. It is impossible to win. How is Gokul still standing?' asked Madhav following the nameless narrator.

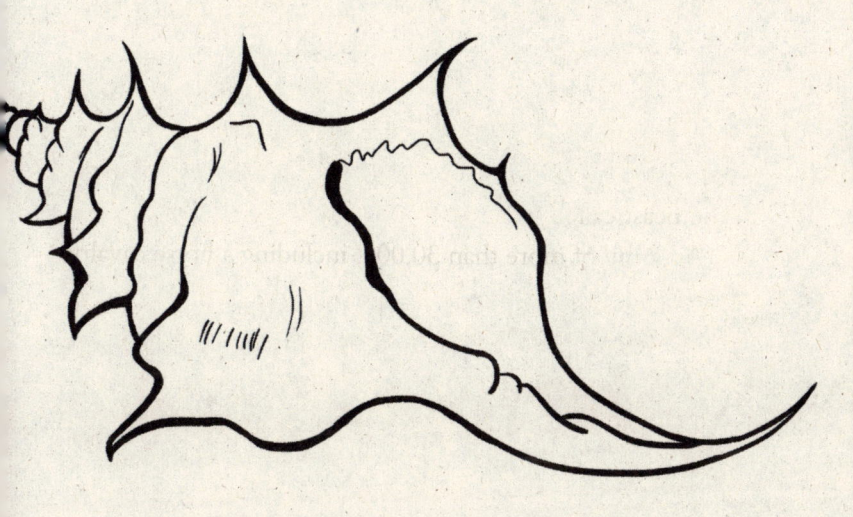

6

The Crawler

After three days of a clueless and tiring trek through the Himalayas, Dhruv clung to hope, searching endlessly for signs of the Naga Matha. Meanwhile, in Gokul, Krishna worked night and day, setting up barricades and restoring homes to prepare for the approaching danger. He was assisted by the small yet formidable army led by Princess Chandrika and composed of brave female warriors. Three days of hard work and the camp was set on the battleground of Gokul. Three days of non-stop smelting of iron and the number of arrows were increasing every hour in Surajgarh.

Three days of rigorous travel of messengers from Surajgarh and the kingdoms all around receiving the message from the queen. Many refused as they were not ready to unite under a woman. Some had their own differences with their neighbouring empires to fight alongside them as brothers and some decided to put their weapons down merely on knowing the size of Abdali's army. But some, indebted to the queen's favours and realizing what was at stake was more than their kingdoms and their lives, decided to send a part of their armies to face the moving forces of Ahmed Shah Abdali.

After three days of travel, the troops of Ahmed Shah Abdali, led by Sarfaraz Khan, arrived at the gates of King Vedant's kingdom, Haripur.

Very soon, the once serene city braced itself for the onslaught of destruction. The land darkened with the shadow of Sarfaraz's intentions, their banners fluttering ominously in the wind. The first assault struck Haripur like a thunderbolt. Cannons roared, shaking the very foundations of Vedant's lies of victories and valour against Sardar Khan. Houses crumbled under relentless bombardment, their inhabitants fleeing in terror amidst the chaos. Streets that once echoed with laughter and trade now resounded with cries of anguish and despair. Within a few hours, Haripur's resistance was crushed under the relentless advance of Sarfaraz's troops. The Afghans stormed through the gates, their swords gleaming in the fiery glow of burning buildings. The clash of steel and the cries of battle echoed through the city streets.

Vedant, watching helplessly from his palace, saw his kingdom engulfed in flames. His decision to remain neutral in the battle of Gokul now seemed like a fatal mistake as his people were paying the price right in front of his eyes. Once a ruler, he now felt the bitter sting of regret as he witnessed the heights of cruelty from the lofty walls of his palace.

Vedant, sensing the imminent danger, gathered what remained of his 200 loyal soldiers and entered the secret door just moments before Sarfaraz's men breached the palace gates. The secret door would lead them directly outside the kingdom's walls. These hidden passages within the palace were designed for such emergencies, though not for kings to flee. It was for the females, elderly and children. Accompanying Vedant were the women and children of his palace.

Getting down the tough terrain, Thomas took a break as it was getting dark quickly. He found space in the narrow passages of a huge crack in the mountains. He built a fire for warmth and opened the book again. The next few pages were about the giant Nagas.

In a remote land, hidden within dense jungles, misty valleys and mountains, there existed a community of giant Nagas. These Nagas were not merely warriors; they were titans, towering over others and embodying ancient powers. Their presence alone struck fear in the hearts of the bravest as they possessed immense strength and unmatched combat skills. It is said that the origin of these giant Nagas stemmed from the union of earth and prehistoric waters, making them the protectors of sacred mountains and lands. However, their presence endured in stories and songs, passed down through later generations. It is said that when the world faces its darkest hour, the giant Nagas will return to tip the balance in the battle between good and evil.

Describing the physical appearance of the giant Nagas, the book noted that they were massive creatures, standing between 15 and 20 feet tall. They had strong muscles, and their bodies were covered in shiny, thick scales ranging from dark green to deep blue, making them nearly invincible against weapons. Their sharp claws could easily tear through the flesh and bones of opponents. Despite their size, they moved gracefully. These giant Nagas had prominent cheekbones and mouths full of sharp teeth. Their eyes were particularly striking, glowing fiercely. Despite having a strong urge to dominate and conquer enemies with their brutal instincts, they were intelligent and skilled in the art of war, protecting their territory.

Giant Nagas used their immense size and strength to their advantage, hurling enemies across the battlefield. Just the sight of them could instil fear in anyone present. They were also chosen to fight enemy champions and leaders because of their unbeatable strength in one-on-one combat.

'Did giants really walk the earth in ancient times?' thought Thomas.

His question was answered somewhere in the mountain heights by the nameless Naga speaking to his follower, Madhav.

'Is there any evidence that giant humans, surpassing normal humans in size and strength, ever lived on Earth?' asked Madhav.

From Bharat to America, the proof of these living giants can be found in nearly all mythical, ancient texts and scriptures. Not only us Hindus, but the religions of Islam and Christianity also have made references to them. For instance, Yajuj and Majuj are mentioned in the Islamic faith and Nephilim Giants are mentioned in the Bible. Ravan's brother Kumbhakarna, who was a *rakshas*, is mentioned in the Ramayana and the Mahabharata. Bhim, one of the Pandavas, married a *rakshasi* called Hidimba. Hidimba was a giant female, and they had a son named Ghatotkacha, who later caused massive destruction to the Kaurava army, favouring the Pandavas during the war fought at Kurukshetra.

Madhav interrupted in excitement and asked, 'But does this mean that giants were real? Or is it only our imagination?'

The nameless Naga smiled as he answered. 'Some claim that giants never existed on Earth. It's merely a rumour that a select few people shared so as to protect their clans that these giants were defending and saving.'

There has been scientific proof that giants and humans co-existed in the Indian subcontinent and in other parts of the world. Scientists have now established that 15,000 years ago, humans and giants lived and raised children together.

A great deal of information has been found regarding the proof and evidence of giants till date. The discovery of large weapons by archaeologists, such as double axes in Greece, which are not the same as a regular axe. Noremitsu, a gigantic sword, was found in Japan. Huge axes had been found in Germany and in Morocco, along with many skeletons, including giant bones of all sizes and shapes. Not only that, but giant footprints, that are significantly larger than those of an average human, have also been discovered. These 1000-year-old footprints can also be seen on hills and mountains.

All these proofs and findings suggest that the presence of giant humans on Earth was real, making it impossible to disprove these historical accounts and legendary myths. There is an old archaeological site called Cahokia in Illinois that is well known for its stones and tombs. Brad Olsen, the author of *Beyond Esoteric*, led extensive and in-depth research at the site. There is a possibility that these giant remains were buried in these graves, which would have measured 12 to 18 feet in length. However, their large skeletons vanished from that location later.

A thousand years ago, 50,000 people called Kah Okiya lived where their homes had sophisticated irrigation systems and textiles. They were very knowledgeable about large-scale infrastructure and constructed around 200 tombs that resembled pyramids. It was testified that as soon as the giants passed away, these mounts were constructed out of respect for these giant humans. They were composed of huge stones, similar to Domans, and symbolized the giants' resting place.

According to alternative theories, these tribes' rulers were 12 to 18 feet tall, extremely strong, and skilled fighters. These massive beings taught people from other tribes farming, animal husbandry, crafting weapons, combat and other skills. Their association with the almighty or extraterrestrial beings was the reason for this. Additionally, the heights of statues constructed on Easter Island matched those of the actual gigantic figures, with one typically standing 13 feet tall. There are not just ancient proofs. In the year 1918, Harold and Addie Wadlow gave birth to a child who became the tallest person ever measured at 8 feet 11 inches. Though he passed away at the age of twenty-two, it's said that he continued to increase in height throughout his life.

According to researchers, there is still evidence of these giant humans' DNA in us. When that gene predominates, the infant is abnormally large and tall. Regina Meredith travelled to Sardinia in 2019 with her team to conduct research for her book, *The Giants of Sardinia: Visitors from the Stars*. She reported discovering some giant human bones which she forwarded to an Italian institution for further inspection. Reports confirmed that such bones belonged solely to humans, and the Rh group, which is the most prevalent in DNA, was exceptionally distinct. Regina stated that the genetic material was unique to the planet and that the DNA still persists in us.

Famous explorer Marco Polo wrote a few things about travelling around Asia in his book about his trade. When he went to China, he observed giant humans standing guard outside the royal palace, measuring 15 feet in height.

Marco Polo was taken aback upon seeing them. It is stated that these massive humans possessed a great deal of cosmic and linguistic knowledge. They worshipped Eronaci gods, as well as Sumerians, Babylonians, and other figures from the Mesopotamian civilization, all of whom were huge in size, almost twice as large as humans, and had red hair. They held great significance in both North America and Siberia. One can see their paintings in Egypt, which indicate the existence of giants in prehistoric times.

However, how can these discovered skeletons and bones not be real? Naturally, giants would have lived on this planet in the distant past. Science may try to reject this, but when more secrets are uncovered in the future, no one will be able to ignore the fact that giants once roamed the earth.

Anyway, there are more giant questions and incidents that need to be shared and heard, one of which I am narrating to you—the incident where Vedant had once believed he could negotiate with the Afghans, thinking his kingdom would be spared, but he was mistaken. Betrayed and cornered, he managed to escape through a hidden tunnel with a handful of loyal soldiers. The journey to safety was tense and full of guilt for Vedant as they navigated through smoke-filled passages under the crumbling streets, pursued by the relentless fury of Sardar Khan's brother, Sarfaraz. Eventually, Vedant and his band of survivors reached the outskirts of Haripur. They fled into the wilderness, leaving behind the smouldering ruins of their once magnificent city. Vedant's heart was heavy with loss and regret, knowing that his kingdom had paid the ultimate price for his selfish cowardice.

On the other hand, Dhruv continued his journey selflessly and bravely. The hunter's mysterious words about the dangers ahead echoed in his mind, but determination fuelled his steps. He felt a renewed sense of purpose, driven by the need to reach his destination and seek the help necessary to save Gokul. As he neared his destination, a palpable sense of anticipation hung in the air. He could see the ancient matha in the distance, a sanctuary he hoped would hold the answers and the aid he sought. But while Dhruv was navigating the treacherous path towards the Himalayas, his senses were on high alert. He heard faint, eerie sounds again, as he had been experiencing since the start of his mountain climbing. It felt to him almost like someone crawling on the ice. The noise was subtle, but when he looked around, it stopped, and he saw nothing. He dismissed it as the sound of shifting snow and pressed on.

But as he took his first step into the sacred grounds, a shadow fell over him. A terrifying figure resembling a giant emerged from the shadows. He was larger than any man Dhruv had ever seen. This towering entity, its body entwined by countless serpents, was a dreadful being of immense power with many arms. It marched towards Dhruv and let out a roaring challenge. The sky thundered, and the wind howled, swirling snowflakes in a wild dance. That massive figure, bigger than any human Dhruv had even seen or read about, descended upon him with an aggression that shivered through the mountains. Soon, the giant figure attacked Dhruv. He fought valiantly, but the colossal being's strength was overwhelming. The creature lunged at him with incredible speed for its size, its massive claws slicing through the air. Dhruv ducked and rolled to the side, narrowly avoiding a blow that would have surely crushed him. The ground shook with the force of the giant's aggression. The gigantic being, eyes blazing with fury, swung its massive paw at Dhruv, who barely managed to block the blow with his hands. The impact sent him sprawling backwards, and he felt the earth tremble beneath him. Dhruv's quickness was his only advantage. He rushed around the beast, striking quickly and retreating before it could counter-attack. But the creature's size and strength were overwhelming. It reared up on its hind legs and brought its full weight down to crush Dhruv.

The ground cracked and split where it landed, but Dhruv had already moved, his instincts and speed keeping him alive. Despite his skill and determination, Dhruv knew he could not keep this up for long. The creature was relentless, and each clash left him more battered and bruised. He needed a way to turn the tide of this unprovoked fight. Suddenly, a suspicious-looking figure, a man in a terrible state, covered in boils and looking contaminated as if he had been burnt and muddied, crawled up slowly and held the giant's feet. The snow settled on his face and back, freezing like it does on statues and rocks. He seemed half-buried in ice as only the upper half of his body was visible. He was so weak that he could not stand on his feet. The giant, busy beating up Dhruv and trying to kill him, attempted to brush off the hands gripping his feet, but the hold was tight, and he couldn't free himself from the fragile-looking man. This incident momentarily distracted the giant, drawing his attention to the new arrival, allowing Dhruv to slip away. Without wasting any time, the giant entity attacked that crawling creature like a predator. Its rage was fierce. Despite his weakened state, the man somehow tolerated and sustained all the giant's deadly blows.

The crawler was neither speaking a word nor attacking the offender. He wasn't even trying to defend himself, yet his grip remained firm, further agitating the giant. At times, the fragile man looked lifeless with no expressions of pain or fear of death. He just blinked every time the giant hurt him to free his legs. The giant then broke the hands holding his feet to get rid of the grip of the strange man crawling on the ground. His feet were freed now but his focus now shifted from Dhruv to his unexpected saviour. He lifted the man, held him by his legs and started bashing him against a rock. While the giant was busy beating the life out of the man, Dhruv got back on his feet and seized the chance to escape. He walked away as fast as he could. The snowstorm intensified, reducing visibility. Dhruv was sure that the man who had crawled to stop the giant was dead as nobody could survive the continuous thrashing on the rock. The giant continued bashing the sick, dying man, and the splatters of blood coated the rock, surrounding him in the white, glowing ice. Dhruv was sad that he could not thank his saviour, but he decided to use the snow breeze to vanish and save himself from the enraged giant. As Dhruv realized the giant had stopped screaming in anger, and turned to look at the man who had come from nowhere to give him a window to escape the giant. Dhruv saw the giant holding the man by his feet, hanging him upside down in the air. Dhruv was in pain, both physically and mentally, realizing that someone he did not know and would never meet again had given his life to save him. But what happened next was unbelievable for both Dhruv and the giant.

While the giant hung the man by his legs, blood dripping from his broken body, his head crushed and face dislocated, the man—who seemed almost lifeless even before the giant touched him—suddenly opened his eyes again. He looked straight into the giant's eyes as if taunting him and asking, 'Is that all you have?' The giant was panting and confused. Hanging upside down, the man shifted his gaze from the giant to Dhruv, who was barely visible in the distance through the snow breeze. The man then smiled, sending chills of horror through Dhruv and agitating the giant, who screamed again, as if responding to the undying man, saying, 'Why don't you die?' The giant, increasingly frustrated and still holding the man by the legs, swung him into a snowdrift, burying him temporarily. Emerging from the snow, the man crawled out with great effort. The giant stomped towards him, shaking the ground. It tried to crush him under its foot, but he rolled aside, narrowly escaping and camouflaging himself in the snow in less than a second. The giant frantically searched for the man, determined to kill him, but both he and Dhruv had vanished. Dhruv could no longer see the giant or the man either, as thick snowflakes obscured his vision. However, driven by his unfaltering focus on the mission, he continued to move forward through the blinding storm.

At sunset, I noticed the princess standing alone, gazing at the sky in the exact spot where Ajaa once stood, tormented by thoughts of not knowing his parents and bloodline. I felt a sense of déjà vu as I walked towards the princess, just as I once walked to Ajaa before the war.

'I once stood right here with your brother, and he shared the reason for his frustration. What's troubling you, Princess?' I asked.

Princess Chandrika, with a touch of sadness and curiosity, asked me, 'I have heard so many stories about my father King Dhyanendra and my brother Ajaa, but it is like I barely know them. You were so close to them. What were they truly like?'

Keeping the warmth in my tone, I told her, 'King Dhyanendra—Shambhu ji, as we fondly called him—was majestic, with an aura almost otherworldly, like Shiva himself had returned to walk among us. The way he carried himself, the way he spoke, people were in awe of him. Shambhu ji was a man unlike any other I have ever met.'

'At fifty-four, he was a Naga—a warrior sage with a face etched with the wrinkles of time and experience. Yet, despite the seriousness imprinted into his features, his eyes always sparkled with mischievous light, hinting at the playful spirit that resided within him,' I added.

'A mischievous light?' the princess asked.

My eyes lit up as I remembered Shambhu ji's playful nature. 'Yes, it was part of his charm that made him so unique. Shambhu ji had a warm spirit that lived in his heart, though it was hidden beneath a hard outer shell—much like a tough nut with a sweet kernel inside. He was a man of contrasts. His work, as he moved through life, was artless, unselfconscious, just like Hanuman, the mighty avatar of

Lord Shiva. There was no pretence about him as he was who he was. He would roam around the grounds of Gokul with a light, almost playful step, as if he was engaging in a silent game of hide-and-seek with the world around him. It was as if nothing could weigh him down and yet, everything he did was with purpose.'

The princess said, 'This sounds almost magical. Tell me more.'

'Exactly. It felt that way. And Shambhu ji's aura was concrete, filling the space with a presence that was both comforting and awe-inspiring.'

I paused, lost in thought for a moment. 'He was tall, with broad shoulders and a strong frame, but there was grace to his movements. His eyes were deep, calm, like still waters that hid depths. His beard was thick, streaked with a few strands of silver—signs of the battles he had fought and the wisdom he had gained. His mere sight was enough to instil both respect and devotion in anyone who crossed his path.'

Princess Chandrika smiled with sheer pride.

'Princess! Shambhu ji was an ideal of strength, wisdom and commitment to dharma but to us, he was more than a legend. He was a father, a guide, a mentor.'

The princess, with her eyes shining with admiration, said, 'What about Ajaa, my brother? What was he really like, Adhiraj?'

'Ajaa . . . he was something else. A force of nature, really. He had this presence that commanded attention, even before he spoke a word. His eyes . . . they were intense, filled with a fiery determination. He had a strong jawline, but there was a softness there as well. A balance between strength and kindness. His body was a testament to his strength, with tight and corded forearms, and prominent veins from wrists to biceps. He had sharp long nails and wore nothing but sacred strings of white thread, known as *janeyu*, symbolizing spirituality and sacrifice, indicating that a guru had accepted him as a *shishya*. He also wore strings of Rudraksha beads around his neck and wrists. A coat of ash covered his chest, and a messy bun of long dreadlocks crowned his head, symbolizing his spiritual path. His forehead bore a *tripoorna* of sandalwood, symbolizing the tradition of Lord Shiva, consisting of three horizontal lines with a red tilak in the centre. When Ajaa meditated, he was an example of calmness and hope. His eyes were calmly shut in a trance, and when the sun's rays illuminated his figure at sunrise, he seemed like an embodiment of Lord Shiva.

'Ajaa was described as blazing like gold, calm like silver, resilient like iron, sharp like a sword, with the sight of an eagle, the strength of a bull and the fiery spirit of a pirate. He was cool like the ashes of a sacred fire, embodying the balance of the *trishul* and *trinetra*. He remained still like a mountain when his eyes were closed and volatile like an earthquake when they were open. When seen with love, he appeared as an innocent child, but when looked at with anger, he could awaken the beast within.

'Ajaa resembled Shiva, with a crescent adorning his hair, and his presence was akin to Lord Shiva himself, descending from Kailash Parbat. He was at his best when he reciprocated the Naga sadhus, the protectors of dharma, with a respectful bow of his head.'

Princess said, 'It's hard to imagine him, especially now that he's gone. People say he was a great warrior.'

With pride, I said, 'Yes, he was, but more than that, he was a leader, someone people could rally behind. His words could move mountains, and his speeches—oh, how he inspired the men. It wasn't what he said, it was the way he said it. His voice carried confidence and conviction. When Ajaa spoke, it was as if the very air around him also listened and followed. He had this way of making you believe that anything was possible, and victory was always within reach.'

The princess was more curious, listening to me intently.

Lost in the admiration of Ajaa, I continued without even thinking that I was describing him to a princess. I just carried on. 'Ajaa was Shambhu ji's creation, his life's work, the embodiment of all his visions and dreams of a united and strong kingdom. They were inseparable in spirit—one could not exist without the other. If Ajaa was the light that guided us through the darkest times, Shambhu ji was the source from which that light sprang. Shambhu ji was the sword, and Ajaa was the blade that cut through our enemies. Ajaa was more than just Shambhu ji's son.'

'I wish I could've met him at least once in life,' the Princess responded.

'But Ajaa was no less of a giant in his own right. He proved that during the battle with the ruthless and unforgiving Sardar Khan, the commander-in-chief of Ahmed Shah Abdali,' I said in a voice more intense.

'I cannot get over that fight. Sardar Khan was a master strategist with an army that seemed unconquerable. The odds were against us, but Ajaa . . . he refused to back down and led the charge himself, right into the heart of the enemy lines and the eyes of the enemy, Sardar Khan himself.

'I remember seeing his sword flashing in the sunlight, fighting like a lion with every move precise and calculated. But it wasn't just his skill with the sword that won the battle, it was his mind. He bypassed Sardar Khan, anticipated his every move, and turned the tide of the battle towards him when everything was looking lost. There were three witnesses to it. A bird, an animal and me, standing right in front of you, while one is playing with my shankh and the third keeps hovering above us, Shiva knows what it is waiting for,' I replied while pointing towards Gajraaj and then showing Neelkanth to the princess.

The princess was in awe after knowing all this about Ajaa, her brother. She asked, 'What happened next?'

I replied, 'It wasn't easy. Rather, it was a struggle, a fight that pushed Ajaa to his limits. He was wounded, exhausted, but he never gave up.'

'And that's how I want to be remembered too—strong, compassionate, and a leader who inspires,' said Princess Chandrika, looking at Neelkanth that, by then, went and sat on Gajraaj's back.

'You have the strength, spirit and valour of your parents and brother Ajaa,' I said, looking at the princess with a knowing expression. 'The light that shines on you and the command you have makes you the leader you were born to be.'

She deserved to be the leader not only because of her deceased father, Shambhu ji, and her departed brother, Ajaa, but also because of her mother, the queen, who began preparing for the war the moment Krishna stepped in to her kingdom with the heartbreaking news of her honoured king and spirited son.

In the distance, Krishna was digging an underground tunnel behind a temple in Gokul and the female warriors were working on preparing a wooden machine that had many sleek long holes to place arrows in it. The machine they were trying to prepare, according to a design made by Krishna, was to shoot tens of arrows in every shot. Some others were requested to collect as much dry grass and leaves as possible and prepare huge stacks of them.

'Why was Krishna digging a tunnel and collecting dry grass and leaves?' asked Madhav.

The nameless Naga smiled thinking of Krishna and said, 'Nobody knew that till the war started.'

The queen stood atop the fort, watching the allied forces and cavalry advancing steadily from different directions, as if converging on the horizon. It was an amalgamation of various troops: horse riders with their armour shining under the sun, steel helmets and chest plates adorned with their royal crest, and spears, swords and shields strapped to their backs. Their horses were decorated in blue and silver, the colours of their kingdom. The archers, clad in green and brown leather armour that blended with the earth, carried bows slung across their shoulders, with arrows and daggers, ready for combat. Another infantry marched towards the queen's kingdom in unison, holding their spears high. Clad in dark leather uniforms studded with metal, they carried large shields emblazoned with the emblem of a rising sun, which tinkled with every step. Draped in crimson sashes, the artillery units brought forth five massive cannons, pulled by oxen. Their iron barrels added to the ominous sense of an impending battle.

With all the kingdoms that had sent a contingent of their armies to support the queen, she now commanded an allied force of 3000 soldiers, 250 horsemen and five cannons, in addition to her own Shakti Sena comprising 1000 female warriors, 250 women horse riders and two cannons.

Seeing the forces approaching, she whispered, 'Together we will face everything no matter what comes our way.'

'How many are they and where is Ahmed Shah Abdali heading to?' asked the queen, full of valour, as she sat astride her horse, leading the combined force of 4000 soldiers, 500 horse riders, fifty elephants and seven cannons from the front.

The army headed by Abdali himself had 10,000 soldiers, 1000 horsemen, 1000 camels and fifty cannons. With the additional troops headed by Sarfaraz Khan, Azharuddin, Malik Akhtar and Zoravar, his dangerous army seemed unconquerable. By this time, Sarfaraz's ruthless and destructive troops had already ruined Haripur. Abdali's army would be invisible if he reached his destination and merged all his troops heading to Gokul from different directions.

Jugal Kishore was riding with Neymat in the most secured circle prepared for her on the orders of Abdali. He knew that the best way to win was to know the competition in and out.

'It's a long journey, Neymat. Because we are on the same side, let's get to know each other better. When I left with Sardar Khan on the orders of my king, you did not exist in the registered names of the troops. When I returned, you are the confidante, and you are kept secure as a jewel. Who are you and where did you come from?'

Neymat heard it all, riding her horse, tightly flanked on all sides by members of Abdali's royal fleet. She smiled and looked at Jugal Kishore and then at a soldier.

'She is chanting, and her chants cannot be broken in between. She is in silence, and she is obligated to answer only Shehenshah.'

Neymat looked deep into Jugal Kishore's eyes and smiled again before advancing her horse, leaving Jugal behind and out of the periphery of the royal fleet. Her smile clearly conveyed that she knew what Jugal was trying to do.

A horse rider came parallel to Jugal Kishore and said, pointing towards Neymat, 'She gave me this piece of cloth and ordered me to give it to you after your failed attempt at breaking the ice with her.'

The rider gave Jugal a piece of cloth that read, 'You will never know how, why and when the children of the traitor were sacrificed.'

As he read the words and looked forward towards Neymat in frustration, she turned back and cunningly smiled at him again as if mocking him for his moves that were perfectly anticipated.

Jugal realized again that he was not in the secure circle of the royal fleet of Abdali any more.

7

Shiva's Regal

Torn by guilt for leaving the man to die at the hands of the unknown, angry, inhuman-looking figure, yet driven by his mission given by Ajaa to deliver the message to the chief Mathadhish, Dhruv continued his journey in search of the matha. He fully understood that the message he carried was more important than his own life, and confronting his attacker could have jeopardized his resolve to reach the chief Mathadhish alive. He knew that if he died before reaching his destination, he would not only be the cause of the death of the stranger who emerged from nowhere to defend him in the snow but also the countless lives following dharma, hopelessly waiting in the plains for their protectors to intervene. It was ironic that he had to escape for his life, not die in the snow, to save countless lives in the plains below. Walking tirelessly, Dhruv reached a point where he saw a massive structure atop the next mountain.

'Maybe I am just a cliff away from my search and if I am right, it won't take me more than three days to knock on the doors of that megalith structure,' Dhruv thought. Just at the sight of the structure, hoping it was the abode of the chief Mathadhish, he felt blessed and an aura of antiquity was infused in him.

Dhruv sought to reach it as quickly as possible. But before he could even take a step towards it, the ground beneath him quivered. He looked around for the source of the unexpected disturbance and found an enormous figure, larger than a lion in both strength and ferocity, greater than an elephant in sheer bulk. It rose before him and roared, shaking Dhruv's soul. It was an enormous eight-legged being that was half-bird, half-lion and seemed more powerful than any beast on Earth. Its long tail was strong enough to throw somebody like Dhruv off his stand. He had never imagined a creature so immense, larger than any animal, and as ferocious as a mad beast. With eyes that burned like coals, the creature charged at Dhruv with the intention to kill.

Despite Dhruv's unwavering determination, it was difficult for him to overcome the being's enormous strength. However, Dhruv's fear was working as his strength. He knew that a single opportunity for the beast would mean his last moment on Earth. A vicious chase ensued, with Dhruv evading the attacker's beast-like movements. The conflict of will and valour was palpable in the air. Dhruv was weak, worn out and hungry. He kept dodging, but how long could he keep it up? He tried to leap past the beast's tail but failed to notice the claws closing in on him. In the blink of an eye, Dhruv was caged between two sharp nails of a paw. Helpless and hopeless, he looked in to the eyes of his death. The beast's eye sockets were bigger than Dhruv's face. It came closer to Dhruv's face to snatch his head off his body and splash his blood on the white snow. But just as it was about to open its mouth and devour Dhruv's head in one bite, the beast paused and sniffed an aroma coming from him. Instantly, it released Dhruv and moved aside. It fluttered its wings, causing the snow around Dhruv to swirl in the air from the pressure he created before flying into the sky and vanishing. 'What just happened? Why did he leave me alive?' thought Dhruv, looking up at the sky and watching the elephant-sized lion fly away and vanish.

The exhausting attempt to save himself from the beast drained the last ounce of Dhruv's energy. As the beast vanished in the sky, he blacked out and collapsed in the snow, still one cliff away from the shelter. The sun rapidly set and the chilling darkness engulfed Dhruv.

The night was just as cold beneath the starry sky, where Thomas continued to read the mysterious book about the unusual powers of the Nagas. One of the pages described the fire-breathing Nagas.

In the treacherous mountains, where pointed peaks touched the clouds, lived a solitary community of Nagas who had mastered the ancient art of fire-breathing.

While their abilities are often covered in myth, elements of their practice find roots in real-world traditions and spiritualism. These Nagas, ardent followers of Lord Shiva— the Destroyer in the Hindu trinity, often associated with the cosmic fire that can both create and destroy—were chosen by Shiva for their wisdom to protect sacred places in the Himalayas. Their role was to maintain the balance between creation and destruction, mastering the mystical skill of fire-breathing.

In Bharat, fire has always held a place of reverence, often used in rituals and ceremonies as a symbol of purity and divine presence. The Nagas, with their deep ties to Shiva, took this reverence a step further by integrating fire into their combat and spiritual practices. Fire-breathing was originally performed by ritual practitioners. Over time, it was adopted by certain dance and art forms, eventually becoming a spectacle used by entertainers. The act involved emitting a fine mist of fuel from the mouth and igniting it with an open flame to produce a fireball. The technique required significant skill and precision, as well as an understanding of the fuels used to lessen the risk of injury. The Nagas believed the fire they exerted was not just a physical wonder, but a manifestation of Shiva's cosmic energy.

For the Nagas, fire-breathing was not merely a performance, but a spiritual practice, deeply rooted in their connection to Shiva and the elements. A mixture made from natural oils and herbal extract was carefully prepared using ingredients naturally available in the Himalayan region, such as the 'Chir pine' resin used for polishing woods, obtained from nature, and oils derived from medicinal plants. They were also explosive experts who had great knowledge of ancient chemistry, its elements, properties, proportions, mixtures and reactions. When preparing for a ritual or battle, the Nagas would perform a sacred ceremony, invoking Shiva's protection and guidance. They would then take a mouthful of this oil, using their breath to project the mist into the flame, creating a burst of fire. This fire-breathing was not only a display of their martial prowess, but also a symbolic act of purification and protection.

Apart from worshipping Shiva, they engaged in practices that pushed the boundaries of ordinary human experience. The Nagas used their fire-breathing abilities to protect their sacred lands and people during warfare as it was a weapon and a psychological tool that could implant fear in their enemies. Armies approaching territories controlled by the Nagas would encounter walls of flames erupting from the mouths of the warriors, a sight powerful enough to shatter the morale of any looming threat.

By spewing fire into the air, they could send signals visible from miles away, communicating warnings to their forces or alerting opponents of their presence. This use of fire as both a weapon and a communication tool highlighted the Nagas' cleverness and their deep understanding of their environment. Their legacy endures in the practices of certain ascetic groups and performers who seek to keep the ancient art alive.

Whether seen through the eyes of myth or reality, the Nagas and their fire-breathing art remain a powerful symbol of the stable connection between humans, nature and the divine.

At night, while Thomas was reading about the fire-emitting Nagas in the light of the fire that kept him warm and protected, the same stars in the sky were witnessing the nameless Naga and his follower lying on snow, unprotected and looking back at them.

'If you are not sleepy, may I ask, what happened to Vedant after he left Haripur? Was he caught and killed?' asked Madhav, unable to contain his curiosity to know more.

Still looking at the stars, the nameless Naga replied, 'Vedant was tirelessly travelling back to Gokul with some women and children of royal blood, chased by Sarfaraz's soldiers. A few of his brave and loyal men, including his new commander appointed by Krishna himself, stopped on the way.'

Looking at them, Vedant stopped. He turned his horse and came back asking, 'Why have you stopped? We still have hours to cover before the Afghans reach us. We need to hurry.'

The commander humbly replied, 'My king! Krishna was not just my senior. He was also my mentor who trusted me with your life in his absence. I cannot risk your life for mine. This is not what my former commander expects of me. He expects and deserves bravery and courage from his protégés. These men who have stopped midway with me are all trained under Krishna, and we can't let him down by putting your life at stake, my king. We'll stay here, set up a trap and face the Afghans so that they cannot chase you. We will either kill them or delay them, depending on our fighting skills and their numbers.'

'But I need you!' said Vedant, almost pleadingly.

'No, my king! You don't need me. You just need to learn to make decisions, and I just need to prove Krishna right,' said Vedant's commander with all due respect, his head bowed.

Vedant felt embarrassed and guilty, his eyes low, his selfishness crushed.

'But you are too few in numbers. Let me stay and fight with you all,' said Vedant, showing courage for the first time.

'My king, numbers don't win wars, the will to win and courage to go for it does. If you stay here and fight with us, our purpose of stopping them here and delaying their chase fails as we are staying here so that you reach Gokul alive. These Afghans will not be able to chase you, irrespective of their numbers. You have my word, my king. Now go ahead and reach Gokul safely,' requested the protégé of Krishna.

'Anything that I can do for you?' asked Vedant, as if inquiring about their last wish.

'Yes. Just say goodbye to my commander-in-chief, Krishna, on behalf of all of us. Tell him that he trained us well,' replied the commander with a satisfied smile, his men standing proudly behind him.

The commander appointed by Krishna decided to stand selflessly and face the Afghan soldiers. Vedant was about to lose around fifty of his best men out of two hundred.

On one hand, fifty brave men were about to close their eyes forever, and on the other, Dhruv woke up inside an enormous structure. As he opened his eyes, he found himself standing in a grand hall that displayed an air of timeless wisdom and serenity. The walls were adorned with intricate carvings, depicting scenes from ancient scriptures such as *Sagar Manthan*, Shiva holding Sati's body, Shiva with his eyes closed and his third eye open, his cosmic dance of destruction and all the other gods praying to him. Tall pillars, carved with elaborate motifs of serpents, rose to support the high curved ceiling. Soft, golden light filtered in on a gigantic Shivalinga through accurately placed windows. The air carried a subtle trace of tension, mingling with the earthy aroma of aged wood and stone. Dhruv marvelled at the serene beauty and profound silence that enveloped the place. It was as if he had stepped into another world, far removed from the chaos and turmoil he had left behind. He looked around in awe before his eyes met a fierce old Naga standing in front of him. He was an extraordinary man with a presence that radiated both wisdom and strength. His long white hair flowed like a river down his back, and his beard was as thick and wild as a lion's mane. His eyes, deep and penetrating, seemed to hold the secrets of the ages, while his forehead bore the mark of a trident and was adorned with a tilak. He exuded an aura of power and mystique that captivated all who beheld him. Long beard, deep eyes, wrinkled skin but firm in his voice and clear in his thought, the tall white-haired old man spoke, 'Who are you and why are you here?'

Dhruv put his hand in his bag kept beside him and took out the parchment that the Naga warrior in Gokul gave him to deliver. The old man took it from Dhruv's hand and asked, opening it, 'Who gave you this?'

'Ajaa and Shambhu ji,' replied Dhruv, wondering who he was talking to.

'Come with me,' said the old man as he started walking while reading the parchment that said, 'By the time you receive this letter, we would have attained salvation. The condition on land is worse than we were expecting. We are fighting, but if we lose, Gokul will be lost forever. If we win, they will attack Gokul again, next time with a bigger force. Other sacred places—Somnath, Ayodhya, Ujjain, Kashi, Rishikesh are all under threat. If you don't order the Naga sadhus from all the mathas to come and fight for these places now, we will have nothing left to defend in the future. It will take us hundreds of years to collect the ruins of our temples, break the tomb of their hate and rebuild the shattered belief of Hindutva. Less is the time, and more are the enemies. Gokul is waiting for your weapons and warriors. Yours—Ajaa and Shambhu.'

The old man's eyes, once filled with suspicion and doubt, now had answers and clarity.

Following the wise old man, Dhruv moved deeper into the matha, passing through a series of interconnected chambers, each more awe-inspiring than the last. Statues of revered sages and warriors stood watchful, their eyes seeming to follow his every move. Finally, Dhruv entered a vast chamber at the heart of the matha. The room was dominated by a towering statue of Shiva seated on a raised platform.

'I am who you came this far searching for. How did you reach here despite being an ordinary man?' asked the chief Mathadhish.

Dhruv, though still overwhelmed by the vastness and emptiness of the place with the imposing presence of the chief Mathadhish, gathered his thoughts and bowed down to him with the utmost respect. He recounted his journey in detail, right from the moment he left Gokul. He spoke of the tribal hunter who saved him from a ferocious snowman and had given Dhruv a bow and some arrows and guided him towards his destination. He had also warned him of the dangers ahead. Dhruv then explained how a gigantic human tried to tear him apart and how a crawling man came from nowhere, helping him get by the almost-invincible creature. Additionally, Dhruv described his encounter with the gigantic entity, who had attacked him fiercely as he neared his destination.

The chief Mathadhish realized that Dhruv was destined to lead them to Gokul. Dhruv felt a surge of emotion as he spoke, 'I have come to seek your help and that of the Nagas,' he said with resolve. 'Ajaa, the valiant Naga warrior had sent me to gather your strength and wisdom. We must unite to save our lands and our people.'

While Dhruv was speaking to the chief Mathadhish in solitude, another Naga, with his eyes closed, sat miles away on the steep peak of a snow-covered mountain in the Himalayas. Despite the distance from the Matha, he knew everything—from Dhruv's arrival to the discussion taking place. This mysterious Naga, all alone, opened his mouth and, as if expecting many to follow his command, shouted into the air, 'I want to know every word spoken, every decision made, every movement within the Matha.' He closed his eyes again, while the chief Mathadhish continued addressing Dhruv.

'I cannot refuse you, young man, no Naga can. Because whether you know it or not, we know now that you are godsent,' said the chief Mathadhish.

'What makes you think that? I was an ordinary *gurukul* teacher before reaching Gokul and just a messenger who brought you this message,' said Dhruv while trying to understand why the chief Mathadhish was trusting him.

The chief Mathadhish smiled at his innocence and said, 'The first one you met when you started the climb . . .'

'The beggar . . . Varya!' interrupted Dhruv, confused.

'His full name is Bhikshu Varya and he is one of the nineteen avatars of Lord Shiva,' said chief Mathadhish, completing his statement.

Dhruv could not believe what he was hearing. 'I am just an ordinary man and the one I met was just an ordinary beggar,' he said.

'This undoubtedly is an overexaggeration of his devotion-turned-obsession. Gods don't live on Earth any more,' thought Dhruv, doubting the chief Mathadhish while he silently listened.

'To protect humans, Lord Shiva once assumed the appearance of a beggar—Bhikshu Varya. King Satyavrata of Vidarbha was a valiant warrior who lost his life in a fierce fight. In an attempt to defend herself, his pregnant wife fled into the wilderness. There, she gave birth to her child, but tragically, a crocodile attacked and killed her, leaving the child crying and abandoned. The infant's screams were heard by Lord Shiva. He took the form of a beggar and approached a poor Brahmin woman and led her to the infant. He requested her to look after the child and went on to reveal his true being. The baby was named Pandya by the beggar. Pandya, who was later known as dharma Gupta, grew up strong and wise under the watchful eye of Lord Shiva. Dharma Gupta married a Gandharva princess and reclaimed his kingdom with the help and blessings of Bhikshu Varya.'

The chief Mathadhish then picked up an arrow given to Dhruv by Kirat and said, 'This bow and these arrows that you carried with you are very similar to that of Kirateshwar. The one who saved your life from snow bears was not Kirat, but another avatar of Lord Shiva. Lord Shiva in his appearance as a hunter is referred to as Kirateshwar avatar. His body is well built and powerful, dressed in animal skins with long hair, carrying a bow and arrows.'

Dhruv was now compelled to start believing the wise words of the chief Mathadhish, which had seemed baseless to him at the start. He was more attentive now when the chief Mathadhish further said, 'Arjuna once engaged in intense meditation to manifest Lord Shiva's formidable weapon called the Pashupatastra, during the Pandavas' exile. A demon called Mukha transformed into a wild boar and charged at him, attempting to kill him, while he was meditating. Concurrently, Lord Shiva appeared as a hunter in his incarnated form of Kirateshwar. At the same moment, the hunter and Arjuna both fired arrows at the wild boar. "I shot the boar first; I have the kill!" stated Arjuna. In response, Kirateshwar's avatar said, "No, my arrow hit the boar first. I own the kill!" Arjuna then challenged the hunter to resolve their disagreement. He was astounded by the hunter's power and ability during their intense battle. Arjuna tried his hardest, but he was unable to defeat the hunter. At last, Kirateshwar's avatar grinned and remarked, "Arjuna, you have showed incredible bravery and tenacity. I appreciate your bravery." It dawned on Arjuna then that the one he fought was no common hunter. "Please pardon me, Lord Shiva, I failed to identify you," he begged, bowing his head. Happy with Arjuna's valour and dedication, Lord Shiva bestowed upon him the Pashupatastra. His temple is in Sikkim, known by the name of Kirateshwar Mahadev temple.'

Dhruv recalled that Kirat had told him he was the resident of Lepakshi. 'Was he talking about his abode in Sikkim?' Dhruv wondered.

He could now visualize every word the chief Mathadhish had spoken, as it resonated with his own encounter with Kirat, who he now learnt was Kirateshwar.

'The one angry man who attacked me. Who was he?' asked Dhruv, wanting to know more.

The chief Mathadhish continued, 'The third you met and the one who attacked you was one of the most furious avatars of Lord Shiva—Veerbhadra, renowned for being extremely tall and possessing a muscular physique. His eyes are like fire and he looks like a dark, gloomy cloud. He has strong weapons in his hands and a garland of skulls hanging around his neck.

'The tale of Veerbhadra goes back to Daksha Prajapati, a king who ruled long ago. He was the father of Sati and one of Lord Brahma's sons. While growing up, Sati was an earnest devotee of Lord Shiva and aspired to be his wife. Later,

Shiva and Sati married but her father, Daksha, was never in favour of this union. Daksha decided to arrange a *yagna* and invited everyone except Lord Shiva and Sati. When Sati learnt about the yagna, she urged Lord Shiva to join her. Shiva refused, but he allowed Sati and Nandi to attend the yagna. During the proceedings, Daksha insulted Lord Shiva in front of all the gods gathered. Unable to tolerate the insult to her beloved husband, Sati set herself on fire, driven by her inner *yog agni*. Despite their best efforts, none of the gods present were able to save her from the flames.

When Lord Shiva learnt about Sati's demise, he was furious. Out of intense grief and rage, he tore out a strand of his hair and threw it to the ground. What emerged from it was Veerbhadra, Shiva's most vicious incarnation. Driven by wrath and passion for Sati, he commanded Veerbhadra to destroy Daksha's army and kingdom. Veerbhadra destroyed all that stood in his path. At the end, he cut off Daksha's head. Brahma pleaded with Lord Shiva for his son's life and expressed regret for his actions. Lord Shiva spared Daksha's life and replaced his head with that of a goat. Finally, Lord Shiva gathered Sati's body and left.

It was an impossible task to stand against Veerbhadra. Only Lord Shiva or his avatars could face him, and the one who saved you from Veerbhadra's avatar, taking Veerbhadra's never-ending anger upon his own unending body, was the cursed immortal Ashwatthama, who is also a Shiva avatar.'

Dhruv was shell-shocked to realize that the chief Mathadhish was right. He also relieved himself of the guilt of leaving the man to die at the hands of the brutal and enraged foe, for he now knew that the man he left behind was Ashwatthama, who cannot die. Since Ashwatthama is one of the seven Chiranjeevis, he is renowned for having an endless life. It is known that he is still living today. Ashwatthama was born with a jewel on his forehead, which bestowed upon him the ability to ward off fatigue, hunger, thirst, diseases, natural calamities and animal attacks. Known as Drauni, he is the son of Drona and Kripi. During the Kurukshetra War, he fought alongside the Kauravas against the Pandavas. Feeling betrayed by his father's false demise, Ashwatthama unleashed the potent Narayanastra to contend with the Pandavas. He was left to roam until the end of the Kaliyuga when Lord Krishna afflicted him with eternal leprosy and took away his protection jewel due to his wicked deeds. The temples of Veerbhadra and Ashwatthama are in Lepakshi and Ananth Padmanabhaswamy, respectively.

Dhruv could now remember a few more names of avatars that he read about in his childhood, one of which was the Sharabha avatar. And so he said, 'And the last flying beast must be . . .'

'The Sharabha avatar, the one who caught you under his paws and later released you alive because of this,' said the chief Mathadhish, showing a strand of hair that Varya had kept in his bag.

'This is Bhikshu Varya's hair. Sharabha sniffed it and learned that you are a friend, not an enemy. Only the one that Bhikshu Varya allows can have this hair and without this, nobody, not even gods, can pass by the Sharabha avatar,' added the chief Mathadhish.

'In our ancient scriptures, the Sharabha avatar is known to be an eight-legged deity who is half-bird, half-lion, and is said to be more powerful than an elephant and a lion. His long tail allows him to travel quickly. Sharabha uses his divine gift to display incredible bravery and strength. Lord Vishnu's ferocious avatar, Narasimha, was meant to be subdued by Sharabha. After killing the demon named Hiranya Kashyap, Narasimha's rage was so excessive that it started causing cosmic disruption. "O Lord Shiva, please find a way to stop Narasimha's uncontrollable anger. Now we're all afraid," requested the gods to Shiva. Two of Lord Shiva's avatars, Veerbhadra and Bhairava, initially attempted to calm Narasimha, but they were unsuccessful. They were ignored by Narasimha, who even attacked Veerbhadra. Consequently, Lord Shiva assumed the shape of Sharabha avatar and went to the palace of Hiranya Kashyap, where he met Narasimha. Sharabha summoned all his might and bravery to attack Narasimha after several previous attempts had failed. The Sharabha avatar immobilized Narasimha by gripping his tail, slashing at him with his wings, and swiftly carrying him away. Narasimha lost consciousness and was defeated. After expressing his regret to Shiva for his uncontrolled rage, Narasimha left. Sharabha and Narasimha's confrontation illustrates the battle between two opposing forces in Heaven, which leads to the triumph of holy order over chaos.'

The chief Mathadhish looked at Dhruv and said, 'Sharabha understood that you were no ordinary traveller, but one sent with a purpose and so he stepped aside, allowing you to pass.'

Dhruv was shaken and overwhelmed to realize that he had met not one but five Shiva avatars and that Lord Shiva himself was keeping an eye on him. He remembered Ajaa's statement once again with the understanding of the power of faith: 'May my Shiva be with you and guide you through.'

By the time the chief Mathadhish stopped explaining to Dhruv how he reached and who he met, some more Naga sadhus surrounded both of them.

'Who is he, Guru dev?' asked a Naga.

'He is the chosen one, the only messenger who could have delivered the requests of Ajaa and Shambhu.'

Dhruv then realized what Kirat meant when he asked, 'Who are you?' and dismissed Dhruv's answer by saying, 'I did not ask your name, I asked who you are.'

'Kirat wanted me to understand who I am through my purpose and not what I am known as by my name.' Dhruv felt enlightened by this distinction, resonating deeply within his soul as his heart grew larger with a new-found sense of purpose.

While Dhruv reached his destination and the chief Mathadhish prepared for war in Gokul, Abdali and his commanders were still paving their way through the deaths of innocents to reach Gokul. Jugal Kishore, along with him, continued trying to discover the dark secrets of Neymat while she successfully continued hiding what she was capable of.

Vedant continued his journey to Gokul, hoping to find Krishna alive, while Krishna was busy preparing strategies and tactics to confront Abdali's army.

8

Avatars

Standing, the chief Mathadhish's eyes reflected the seriousness of the task at hand. Beside him stood a Naga sadhu, an expert in explosive techniques, his entire presence radiating ferocity. His name was Vidyut. With a voice rich in authority and purpose, the chief turned towards Vidyut and commanded, 'Call Mahakaay.'

Vidyut bowed his head and rushed outside. In a few moments, Dhruv heard the thud of footsteps approaching the hall where he was. The light from the main door dimmed as Mahakaay entered, stooping slightly to pass through the hall's doorway. He then rose to his full height as the chief Mathadhish approached. Dhruv felt a wave of awe and respect wash over him. The giant figure stood at least thrice the height of an average man, his broad shoulders and muscular frame draped in simple yet elegant robes; the essence of his soul reflected on his face. His very presence commanded attention and admiration. Vidyut and

Mahakaay stood beside each other. On one side, Vidyut, the chief Mathadhish and Dhruv stood six feet tall, while Mahakaay loomed over them at more than eighteen feet and weighed over five hundred kilograms. His long beard looked strong enough to tie to a bullock cart and drag it without any effort.

The chief Mathadhish ordered them, 'Send your messengers and tell all the Mathas and their Mathadhish that before the end of Pitra–Paksh Shraadh, every matha must reach Gokul and for that we will all assemble at the temple of Adi Shankaracharya in Kashyapmar.'

'Kashyapmar. Where is this place located in Bharat?' asked Madhav, surprised, as he had never heard the name before.

Kashyapmar is what the world now knows as Kashmir. It was named after Maharishi Kashyap's son and was once called Kashyapmar or Kashymarr. According to the *Matsya Purana*, it is said that the descendants of Sage Kashyap, along with their people, were once known as Sompath, and the land was sacred to their ancestors. It was famously known as Pitru-Agnivatta.

According to the *Rajatarangini* and *Neelam Purana*, Kashmir was once a large lake and Rishi Kashyap worked hard to drain the water, turning it into the beautiful valley we see today, including the famous Dal Lake. This story shows the deep connection between the people, their land and their traditions.

Adding to his order, the chief instructed the giant, 'Mahakaay, take Dhruv along with you.' Mahakaay nodded, realizing the significance of his task. The chief placed a reassuring hand on Dhruv's shoulder.

'You have done well in coming here. We are destined to unite the Nagas from all Mathas who possess unique powers to descend with us for Gokul together. Now go along with them and we shall soon meet again in the days of Shraadh Paksh at Adiguru Shankaracharya's temple,' said the chief.

As Dhruv absorbed the chief Mathadhish's words, he felt a renewed sense of purpose. He understood now that his journey was far from over. It had only just begun, and the path ahead was filled with both challenges and hope. With the chief Mathadhish's guidance and the unity of the Nagas, he was ready to face whatever lay ahead.

Dhruv was still not aware that each matha possessed special abilities and that their gathering would be a display of heavenly forces of mystique and magnificence. Vidyut and Mahakaay walked out, and along walked Dhruv, leaving all the other Naga sadhus and the chief Mathadhish. They were ordered to send out the messages, so Vidyut asked Mahakaay to call his most trusted members and then he started to leave with two other Naga sadhus.

'Where are you going?' asked Dhruv.

Vidyut turned around and replied, 'There are many mathas hidden in the depths of the mountains, Dhruv, and as the chief Mathadhish ordered, all of them have to be informed to reach the Adiguru Shankaracharya's temple. We three are going to three different mathas to deliver the order. I also have to prepare the pots for war.'

'Pots for war! What about the rest of the mathas?' asked Dhruv.

'You will see. Just be with Mahakaay. And Dhruv, stay as close to him as possible. See you soon at the temple of Shankaracharya. Mahakaay will be with you till then,' answered Vidyut with a smile before he turned and started to walk with the other two Naga sadhus. Dhruv turned towards Mahakaay who sat on his knees under the open sky right outside the matha. He went near him and stood as close as possible.

Mahakaay placed both his palms on the ground and started beating it in a rhythmic tempo. Dhruv wondered what he was doing. Then he stood, felt the flow of the wind, turned his body against it, and smashed both his hands together, producing a loud clap. Because of his enormous body and the size of his palms, the clap was so loud that it echoed in the other mountains. He then lifted his face towards the sky and made a peculiar sound. The base of his voice was so heavy that it felt heavenly. Dhruv kept wondering what Mahakaay was doing until he heard the growl of a wild animal right behind him. Even before turning, he realized that a carnivorous animal was staring at him. He looked at Mahakaay to understand what he should do.

'Turn around! It's okay,' said Mahakaay, his voice as heavy as his body.

Dhruv was mesmerized once again. It was a powerful and huge snow leopard. An animal that could cross the highest peaks and deepest valleys without leaving a trace.

Its remarkable speed, awareness of danger and ability to attack would ensure that their messages would be delivered without delay. These leopards were believed to be the holy guardians, born in the frosty regions of the Himalayas. Their spiritual bond with the mountain deities gave them unmatchable strength.

Mahakaay went ahead and sat on his knees. The snow leopard bowed in reciprocation. Mahakaay held its face and pampered it as if playing with a cat. Though this cat was bigger than the modern-day lion. Before Dhruv could absorb the mesmerizing bond between the giant Mahakaay and the snow leopard, a snowbird came and sat on his head. Snowbirds were faster than any other species in flying because they could control the wind. They were pure white with ethereal radiance. These beings were believed to be the children of the wind deity Vayu. They were endowed by their heavenly parents with melodic songs that allowed them to communicate ideas clearly and quickly.

Mahakaay stood on his feet again and the snowbird jumped from Dhruv's head to Mahakaay's wrist, which was parallel to Dhruv's head. After greeting the snowbird, Mahakaay started looking all around as if searching for somebody.

'What are we waiting for?' asked Dhruv, keeping a distance from the snow leopard.

'Shhh! Listen carefully,' replied the giant with excitement and an innocent smile. Dhruv could sense eagerness and enthusiasm in both the snow leopard and the snowbird. The giant Mahakaay bent slightly, as if preparing for a hand-to-hand combat with the approaching figure. Now Dhruv was also able to sense something running and approaching them all.

The third messenger was a Tibetan Mastiff that emerged from nowhere with unmatchable speed and attacked Mahakaay. Dhruv had never seen a dog that massive. In that moment, Dhruv realized that it was a lovable gesture that the giant dog shared with the giant Naga whenever they met. The Tibetan Mastiff was no less than the snow leopard in size and even more in weight and looks. This was a devoted and extraordinarily powerful Tibetan Mastiff that was capable of towing big loads over perilous terrain. With their excellent sense of scent and direction, they could always be relied upon to locate recipients. These canines' astonishing power and devotion are the consequence of heavenly favour, making them steadfast guardians of sanctified spaces.

Within a few minutes of Mahakaay sending three different signals, one through vibration, another from the clap and the last one by the sound of his voice, there were three different species ready to serve, each with the ability to travel across different terrains and quickly arrive at far-off locations to convey the messages across all the sacred mathas.

Dhruv could now see four heavenly creatures standing together, the giant Mahakaay and his three mesmerizing messengers. Seeing the awe on Dhruv's face, Mahakaay said, 'The snowbird can fly so high, it's as if they are invisible in these snow mountains. Being invisible serves as a blessing to keep them safe from pursuers and adversaries, which make them ideal defenders of heavenly communications. Their ability to become invisible and traverse any terrain at any time of the day or night makes them ideal messengers for dangerous areas. The snow leopard bounds soundlessly across the landscape and the Tibetan Mastiff trots steadily along old paths, each creature taking its own message and moving towards different allotted destinations.'

Right then, a Naga sadhu came with the parchments and handed them over to Mahakaay, who gave them to his three unique messengers, saying, 'Make it to the mathas as quickly as possible.' They bid goodbye to each other in their own ways and left immediately, as if understanding the gravity and importance of the situation.

'How do you all understand each other?' Dhruv asked.

'Trust' was the only word Mahakaay said in response to Dhruv's question.

'Come! We also must move quickly now,' he said and started walking with huge strides.

'Where are we going?' asked Dhruv quietly, following Mahakaay.

'To my matha to gather the other giant Naga warriors to protect dharma and preserve the sanctity of Gokul from the approaching shadows of tyranny and violence,' said Mahakaay with measured words and steadfast commitment.

Dhruv had to keep jogging to match his walking speed.

A new era of hope and unity began as all the four messengers prepared to journey to their assigned mathas. Just as sacred as the message itself were the chosen messengers for this critical mission.

Somewhere in a cave in the Himalayas, an invisible, choking voice informed the lone mysterious Naga, 'Kaaldhwaj! They are gathering in Kashyapmar . . . all of them.'

The mysterious Naga commanded the choking voice, 'Who is the chief Mathadhish's enemy?'

Thomas could now feel that he was getting closer to the plains as the oxygen levels were higher and the cold was comparatively bearable. However, the exhaustion acted as a barrier, hindering his ability to maintain speed and cover long distances. He sat down, panting. The book of the nameless Naga calmed his nerves whenever he read it. He turned another page, and this time it was about another group of Naga sadhus who possess a unique and powerful gift: the ability to communicate with plants. The Nagas, the holy guardians of nature, are attuned to the rhythms and secrets of the plant kingdom and the earth through years of meditation and devotion. The Naga Sadhus move through the forest like shadows, their feet barely touching the ground, as they listen to the whispers of the trees and the songs of the flowers. Every branch, every root, every bark holds a story, and the Nagas have the power to communicate with and understand these stories through their wisdom and practice. Whenever danger threatened the sacred land, the Naga Sadhus called upon their leafy allies. Using their chants, they awakened the spirits of the trees, which stood tall like guards, their branches creating a protective canopy over the land. The roots beneath the earth twisted and turned to avoid any underground threats, making the forest a living, rigid fort. During war, the Naga sadhus and their plant allies unleashed their full power.

Trees uprooted themselves, their massive trunks becoming living hammers that could crush the enemy. Creepers, as strong as iron, snaked through the battlefield, binding invaders and dragging them into the heart of the forest, where they disappeared without a trace. On the orders of the Nagas, the ground itself swallowed the enemies, pulling them into the depths of the earth, never to be seen again. These trees and plants were not just used in battle, but also healed the wounded, providing medicines to treat even the most grievous injuries. In return, the Nagas nurtured the plants, ensuring that the balance of the forest was maintained.

Thomas had lines of tension on his forehead while reading about the tree controllers while somewhere else in the mountains, Madhav, following the nameless Naga, was also in tension listening to the true story that was leading towards the final battle of Gokul.

'Any news about the approaching army?' the princess asked Krishna.

'We don't have much time before we face them,' Krishna said, his voice tense with stress.

'Is there anything that you are hesitant to speak about, Krishna?' the princess asked, reading the expression on Krishna's face.

'There are four armies approaching us from four different directions, Princess. A total of 30,000 foot soldiers, 2000 horse riders, 1500 camels and seventy cannons,' said Krishna.

'What's our strength?' the princess asked, her expression resolute.

'Not more than 500 men and women including 100-odd untrained villagers, Adhiraj, you and me,' replied Krishna.

It felt as if Gokul had been stained anew, just so Abdali could return and play his game of destruction once again.

'Send a messenger to the queen. Tell her we need reinforcements at the earliest,' said the princess in a commanding tone.

'But Princess, including the whole army of Surajgarh, we will still be less than half of their strength,' said Krishna.

'Yes, but we will be more than double what we are now, and you don't know the queen well. You have just seen the Durga Defence Forces that I am leading, you have not met the Shakti Sena that follows my mother. Send her the message and let's hope that my mother reaches before the father of the Afghan army,' said the princess confidently.

'Yes, Princess!' Krishna replied before leaving.

'Where are you, Mother?' murmured the princess.

Her mother, the queen, was on her way to attack and break the overall morale of the Afghan forces by killing Shehenshah Ahmed Shah Abdali before he could reach Gokul.

On the other hand, advancing towards Gokul, Abdali encountered a distressing sight which made him clueless of the happenings. His soldiers were falling seriously ill with some mysterious ailments. Many were vomiting uncontrollably, and those who slept to rest, never woke up again. The camps were filled with the stench of sickness and death seemed to be present in every corner. Even the cavalry arriving from different directions faced the same fate, much to Abdali's misfortune. Abdali was confused and anxious as he could not understand why his massive force was decaying before his eyes. The journey towards Gokul was turning into despair because of the fear and confusion that spread through the ranks.

Getting the news of his soldiers dying, Abdali suddenly got up from his seat and walked out of the tent towards Neymat's abode. As he entered, he learnt that Neymat was not there.

'Where is she?' a desperate Abdali asked the soldiers guarding her tent. But it was Jugal Kishore who answered him.

'She left in the dark of the night, my king, and took around 100 horsemen and some camel carts without your authorization. Maybe she was uncertain of your plan of war and victory, but I am here, and I have gathered men from all around who understand the reason why our men are falling.' Jugal was trying to win Abdali's trust and get back his control and position, but he failed again, when both Jugal and Abdali turned towards Neymat's voice. 'While you were assembling healers, I was collecting poison from herbs for the dying,' said Neymat.

Neymat was back with the camel carts full of poisonous herbs and Jugal was clearly terrified by her presence. She walked to Abdali, took his hand and bowed down to put her eyes on it, showing her respect and trust in him.

'What's all this?' asked Abdali.

'Our troops are poisoned by herbs, my king, and these are the medicines that will save their lives and assure your victory,' said Neymat confidently.

'Explain!' ordered Abdali while trying to understand why she wished to poison his troops.

'A small, diluted dose of this potion mixture will immunize our men against the larger doses mixed into almost all the water sources on our way to Gokul. They will feel dizzy and sick for a while but won't die. This may slow our speed by one day, but it's better to be slow and sick than dead and lose the war,' said Neymat.

'They will all die if you serve them with this poison,' said Jugal hastily.

'They are already dying. Neymat, do whatever you think is right. Jugal Kishore, do what she says,' said Abdali, still uncertain, as he walked back to his camp, leaving Jugal and Neymat staring at each other.

'Let's start with you!' said Neymat to Jugal with a smirk on her face. Jugal Kishore was now having the taste of his own medicine with the same kind of cunning smile and double-meaning lines he toyed with before Sardar Khan's death. While Abdali's troops were slowing down in the plains, Dhruv was nearly running in the snowy mountains to keep pace with the walking Mahakaay.

'You are blessed to have met five out of the nineteen avatars of Shiva. His blessings are bestowed upon you,' said Mahakaay.

'What about the other fourteen that the chief Mathadhish did not enlighten me about?' asked Dhruv as he panted and shivered in the cold.

The giant Mahakaay said, 'Sage Dadhichi and his wife Suvarcha were expecting a child a long time ago. The son Suvarcha gave birth to was a Shiva avatar named Pipalad. But to help Lord Indra in conquering the evil demon Vritra, Sage Dadhichi donated his bones and died as a result before Pipalad's birth. After learning of her husband's death, Suvarcha, too, left her body. Before she died, she left her son Pipalad beneath a *peepal* tree. Dadhimati, the sister of Pipalad's father, then took care of him. As Pipalad got older, the fact that his father had passed away before his birth caused him great distress. Pipalad learnt that his father's demise was caused by Shani Dev, the God of Saturn. In rage, Pipalad cursed Shani Dev to be cast out of the universe. The other gods rushed and requested Pipalad to forgive Shani Dev. While he agreed, he had one condition for Shani Dev: that children under sixteen years of age should not be affected by him. Shani Dev agreed to the condition to save his life. People who have trouble because of Shani Dev pray to the Pipalad avatar of Shiva. They believe Pipalad can help them overcome the bad effects of Shani Dev.'

Shiva rides on Nandi, a creature that is half-human and half-bull, possessing the head of a powerful bull and the body of a human. He has four arms in human form, two are folded in respect while the other two hold an axe. This form of Nandi is known as 'Nandi Eshwar'. It was from a particular yagna conducted by Sage Shilada that Nandi was born. Lord Shiva was pleased with the yagna and bestowed on Sage Shilada an eternal child, Nandi, who was clad in diamond armour that covered his entire body. Growing up, Nandi loved and obeyed Lord Shiva. He is the representation of power, loyalty and affection. Nandi, who is shown with a bull's face, is revered as a herd protector. He guards Lord Shiva's residence atop Mount Kailash and always remains by his side. Lord Shiva taught Nandi yoga and meditation. Nandi's statue is often built outside the main temple area of Shiva temples. People believe that if they pray to Nandi, Lord Shiva will hear their prayers quickly. The tale of Nandi imparts lessons to us about faithfulness, strength and love and teaches us to have a firm faith and to be modest.

When Lord Vishnu formally assumed human form to defeat Ravana, Lord Brahma requested Lord Shiva to show up as an avatar to aid Vishnu. Anjani was an *apsara* who was married to Kesari, a *Vanara* chief and Brihaspati's son. She was born on Earth as a princess of the Vanara race. Kesari and Anjana prayed to the wind god Vayu to be born as their child. At last, Shiva was born to Anjani as Hanuman. Hanuman came into existence as their son after Vayu, the god of wind, was moved by their devotion and granted their wish. Consequently, Hanuman is referred to as Anjani Putra or Anjaneya, which means Anjana's son. As an incarnation of Lord Shiva, Hanuman was born to Anjani and Kesari with a powerful physique, having a muscular build that highlighted his strength and vitality. With a mace (*gada*) in one hand, Hanuman demonstrated his might and capacity for self-defence. One obvious characteristic of Hanuman that demonstrated his rapid speed was his long tail. He had the ability to grow both to enormous sizes and to microscopic dimensions. He was able to lift mountains with his bare hands and soar through the heavens. Feeling hungry upon waking up one morning, he flew up to catch and devour the rising sun, believing it to be some fruit. Lord Indra punished Hanuman for his mistake of grabbing the sun from the sky by striking him with a thunderbolt when he saw him do it. Hanuman was struck on the chin, falling to Earth and losing consciousness. This explains how he received the name 'Hanuman', which translates to 'disfigured jaw'. Upon learning of this, Vayu, the god of wind, became enraged and resolved to remove all air from Earth. Due to the threat to life posed to all living things, Lord Shiva had to bring Hanuman to his senses. After Indra struck him with his thunderbolt, or the Vajra weapon, Hanuman was blessed, becoming just as strong and powerful as Indra. Hanuman was also gifted with various abilities and protections by numerous other gods. He was gifted by Lord Brahma with the power to expand or contract in size as needed. Hanuman was told by Lord Agni that he would never be harmed by fire. Varuna granted him the protection that water could never harm him. In order to enable him to travel at the speed of wind, Vayu bestowed upon him the ability to fly. According to Hindu literature, Hanuman is also regarded as one of the seven Chiranjeevis who will remain on Earth until the end of the Kaliyuga.

Shiva's Bhairava avatar appears to be angry, holding his weapons alongside a dog with protruding teeth, a frightening expression and a garland of skulls. Bhairava is also referred to as 'Dandapani', who is known to punish greedy and arrogant offenders. The beginning of Bhairava's tale was an argument between Brahma and Vishnu over who is the greatest god of them all. 'Who do you believe to be the universe's greatest creator?' Vishnu asked Brahma. Brahma arrogantly replied, 'I am the one who created all living things. As the almighty creator, it is me who is worthy of adoration.' Vishnu calmly looked towards Brahma and said that true beauty lies in humility, but people who fail to recognize this become blind to the truth because of pride. With Brahma listening, Vishnu arrogantly said again, 'I created the universe and so I am the most powerful and should be revered by all.' This arrogance enraged Lord Shiva, transforming him into an avatar known as Bhairava. 'Brahma, you have become so arrogant and self-centred that you have lost sight of who you really are,' said Bhairava. He punished Brahma for his arrogance by cutting off one of his five heads. After realizing his mistake, Brahma prayed to Lord Shiva and asked for forgiveness. He said, 'I finally recognize the consequences of my conduct.' Following this, Bhairava too regretted his actions and eventually carried the skull of Brahma as a reminder of his mistake. Before being pardoned, he spent twelve years wandering about with the skull. The life of Bhairava teaches us the value of forgiveness and humility.

Bhairava is also renowned for protecting fifty-two locations named Shakti Peetha. The goddess Shakti holds great significance for these locations. At each Shakti Peetha, there is a temple dedicated to Bhairava, where he keeps watch over and protects his followers.

Long ago, during the churning of the ocean by *devas* and asuras, numerous treasures that came out included the nectar of immortality called *amrit*. Later, a fierce battle broke out for amrit between the devas and asuras. Unfortunately, the devas started losing the battle because of Sage Durvasa's curse on them. Lord Vishnu then took the form of an enticing apsara named Mohini to distract the asuras and assist the devas in obtaining the nectar. The asuras got attracted to the mesmerizing beauty of Mohini, allowing the devas to take the amrit. Once the asuras realized this betrayal, their anger created chaos everywhere. Concerned, Lord Brahma then requested Lord Shiva for help. Shiva took the form of Vrishabha, a powerful avatar and defeated the asuras to restore balance.

After the devas were given amrit, they became proud and arrogant. When Lord Shiva realized this, he was furious and resolved to discipline them. Yaksheshwar was the form that Lord Shiva assumed. He had a demonic–human appearance. His eyes shone brightly, his complexion was dark and he, too, wore a garland of skulls. Yaksheshwar issued a challenge to the devas and requested them to chop a bunch of grass that he had shown them. The devas attempted to cut the grass, but they were unable to do so. They knew that their arrogance was unwise. Finally, after many failed attempts, the devas apologized to Lord Shiva, learnt humility and adored Yaksheshwar.

Durvasa was a wise sage born to Sage Atri and Anusuya. His name meant 'someone difficult to live with'. He possessed the anger of Lord Shiva and was known for giving both blessings and curses. It is said that Lord Shiva, in a fit of rage during the conflict with Brahma, scared even the gods away. Parvati, Lord Shiva's wife, also expressed her annoyance for his temper. And from this anger, Anusuya conceived Durvasa. Being intense, Durvasa is a key figure in both balance and disorder and has the power to change lives with his blessings and anger.

Goddess Parvati's desire was to wed Lord Shiva. Through her worship and prayers, she proved her love and devotion to him. But Lord Shiva made the decision to test her one day. He manifested as a Brahmahchari, a guru, before her, presenting an appearance that was far removed from his true self. Parvati was questioned by the Brahmahchari, 'Why do you love Lord Shiva so much? He resides in the mountains and practices yoga.' Parvati listened quietly with firm determination and later responded to the Brahmahchari form of Lord Shiva: 'I love Lord Shiva for who he is, not where he lives.' The Brahmahchari persisted in challenging her. He even made disapproving remarks about Lord Shiva. Parvati's love, however, remained unwavering. She remained resolute and strong before the sage. When the Brahmahchari saw her undying devotion and love, he disclosed who he really was. All along, he was Lord Shiva. 'You have demonstrated true love and devotion,' he remarked, smiling at Parvati. Parvati burst into a grin. We can learn lessons from this narrative about commitment, true love and the value of maintaining our spiritual path's dedication.

On the banks of the Narmada River once lived a Brahmin whose name was Vishwanath and his wife Shuchismita. They fervently prayed for a son as strong and knowledgeable as the gods, being devoted admirers of Lord Shiva. They were granted their wish when Shuchismita gave birth to a child who was named Grihpati in honour of Lord Brahma. Vishwanath once told his wife with love, 'Our prayers have been heard. Lord Shiva himself will bestow blessings on to our son.' Shuchismita replied, 'Indeed, Grihpati will grow up to be as wise and strong as the gods.' From an early age, Grihpati imbibed extraordinary knowledge of the Vedas and other holy books. When he was nine, Narad Muni visited his parents and discussed the health difficulties he would face as a result of poor astrological placements. Muni said Grihpati would face difficulties ahead. 'He needs to ask Lord Shiva for help.' Upon learning of his destiny, Grihpati decided to travel to Kashi to pray to Lord Shiva and seek protection for his life. 'Dear parents, I will go to Kashi and pray to Lord Shiva,' declared Grihpati with determination. He devoted himself to the worship of Lord Shiva, who, impressed by Grihpati's unwavering devotion, appeared before him and said, 'Grihpati, I am pleased with your devotion. You can ask me any wish and it will be granted.' In humility, Grihpati replied, 'My Lord, I have no wish to ask for. Please keep blessing me, that's all I desire.'

Grihpati was blessed with a long life. Lord Shiva told him, 'Grihpati, you are going to be called the Lord of All Directions in future. You deserve this honour because of your dedication.' Grihpati thanked Lord Shiva.

The Agneshwar Linga, which represents Lord Shiva's defence against fire, originated from the Shiva Linga that Grihpati had placed and venerated at Kashi.

Krishna Darshan, an avatar of Lord Shiva, teaches us about the significance of yagna and wisdom in an individual's life. This avatar of Shiva appeared before Nabhag, a prince who left his family as a child to study in Gurukul. But when he returned, all the wealth of the kingdom was distributed amongst his brothers, leaving him with nothing. He was told by his brothers to ask their father about his portion. Nabhag, upon reaching his father, narrated the whole story.

But was advised to help Sage Angira to complete the yagna as a solution. Later, when the yagna was successfully completed, Sage Angira offered the remaining wealth to Nabhag. But suddenly, at that moment, Lord Shiva, in the form of Krishna Darshan, appeared before Nabhag and claimed it. Nabhag argued with Krishna Darshan as the wealth belonged to him. In response, Krishna Darshan asked him to go back to his father and ask whom the wealth belonged to. Nabhag's father explained that the wealth belonged to Krishna Darshan, who was Lord Shiva himself. Finally, Shiva blessed Nabhag and taught him that true prosperity lies in wisdom and spirituality and not materialistic riches.

Once there was a young sage, Upamanyu. He was Sage Vyagrapa's son. Upamanyu adored Lord Shiva and offered daily prayers to him. Lord Shiva and Goddess Parvati made the decision to put his devotion to the test one day. They took on the forms of the god Indra and his wife Indrani and attempted to discourage Upamanyu from praying to Lord Shiva when they arrived. If he stopped loving Lord Shiva, they would grant him all his wishes. Upamanyu was a true devotee with strong determination and a powerful heart. He continued to adore Lord Shiva. He kept praying despite what Indra and Indrani stated. Impressed by his unwavering faith, Lord Shiva and Parvati revealed their true forms and introduced themselves to Upamanyu. They bestowed upon him blessings and assured him that he and Goddess Parvati would always be close to their forest home. Upamanyu's affection for Lord Shiva only became deeper after that day. Because of his devotion, he came to be known as Sureshwar.

Lord Shiva once took on an avatar of a dancer and showed up at Parvati's father's kingdom. He danced like Nataraja while carrying a *damru* in the king's court. After receiving praise from the courtiers, when asked what he desired in return, Shiva requested King Himachal for Parvati's hand in marriage, which enraged the king. Shiva later showed Parvati his full form while still in his avatar form before departing. As a result of this deed, Parvati's father and his minister gained a divine understanding, which inspired them to get Parvati married to Shiva.

Yatinath avatar was a sage of wisdom who exuded a dazzling glow and wore robes adorned with holy emblems of Lord Shiva. His bamboo stick served as a symbol of his divine presence and his eyes shone with wisdom and kindness. Ahuka was a tribal man who lived in a jungle. He and his spouse were recognized for their exceptional hospitality and were deeply committed to Lord Shiva. They also performed Shiva *sanskar*. One day, Lord Shiva made the decision to come see them in the guise of a guru called Yatinath to assess their genuine devotion and hospitality. As he returned from the forest, Ahuka exclaimed, 'Oh, who is this sage waiting near our hut?'

'I am Yatinath and I am looking for shelter for the night,' Yatinath responded.

'Dear sage, our hut is very small,' Ahuka said with concern. 'It's not even enough for my spouse and me,' he added.

'I understand and shall not trouble you,' Yatinath replied.

Ahuka's wife hurried outside and exclaimed, 'Wait! How can we deny a guest, Ahuka? Please let him in.' Ahuka invited Yatinath, promising him a good night's sleep. 'Thank you, kind soul,' Yatinath said to Ahuka.

During the night, when everyone was asleep, Ahuka was attacked and killed by a wild beast. Ahuka's wife later stated with sadness yet pride in her voice, 'My husband gave his life for our guest. I shall also follow him by giving up my life.' When Lord Shiva (Yatinath) revealed himself in his true form and saw Ahuka's wife in grief, he replied, 'I am pleased by your dedication and hospitality. You will be Nala and Damayanti in your next lives, meant to be reunited by my grace.' After enduring numerous hardships in their subsequent incarnations as Nala and Damayanti, they were reunited with the aid of Lord Shiva, who manifested as Hansa, a swan.

To shatter the ego of Lord Indra, the god of gods, Lord Shiva took on the form of Avadhuta avatar. As Indra and Brihaspati moved towards Mount Kailash, Lord Shiva suddenly appeared as a beggar and stood in their path. Indra halted and asked Avadhuta to clear the way for them to pass. Lord Shiva, in his Avadhuta avatar, stood motionless, gazing at them without saying a word.

Brihaspati then again requested, 'Get out of our way, beggar!' Lord Shiva's Avadhuta avatar kept quiet. Indra, becoming agitated, angrily warned, 'I'm going to put you down if you don't clear our way.' In response, Lord Shiva's avatar instantly immobilized Indra with a gaze from his third eye.

Indra was now aware of his mistake and realized that it was Lord Shiva. He and Brihaspati apologized for their mistreatment. And that is how the avatar Avadhuta taught a lesson to Indra and Brihaspati. The Avadhuta avatar imparts valuable knowledge to humans. It demonstrates the way to liberty, self-awareness, endurance and transformation. By realizing the sacred presence in every living thing and teaching us to let go of the outside world, this avatar helps us to let go of our pride.

By the time Mahakaay finished explaining all the remaining fourteen avatars of Lord Shiva, their journey too came to an end, and they were standing at a massive gate of another matha. Dhruv looked at Mahakaay and instantly realized that the door was so tall and wide because he was about to meet more beings like Mahakaay.

Dhruv bravely entered the door with Mahakaay and saw other giants. At nearly six feet tall, Dhruv appeared like a dwarf surrounded by the members of this clan. Although their numbers were fewer compared to other mathas, Dhruv realized that while a regular Naga could fight and kill ten enemies, these giant Nagas could crush fifty or more due to their immense size.

9

Hopeless Case of Excellence

Upon receiving their communications from the creatures of the snow, every matha reacted with urgency and respect, commencing their movements to reach the Adiguru Shankaracharya temple in Shraadh Paksh.

'What is the importance of Shraadh Paksh?' asked Madhav, interrupting the nameless Naga.

The nameless Naga explained, 'The word "Shraadh" comes from the Sanskrit word "shraddha", meaning "faith" or "devotion".'

Shraadh is an annual ancestral ritual in our culture and belief that is performed to pay homage and provide spiritual sustenance to deceased parents, grandparents and other family members.

Shraadh ceremonies usually coincide with the death anniversary according to the Hindu lunar calendar, known as 'Tithi'. Alternatively, it can also be done during the Pitru Paksha period, a fortnight dedicated to honouring ancestors that ends on a no-moon night. The ritual signifies the Hindu belief in the cycle of birth and death, encapsulating the philosophical aspects of life.

The central aim of Shraadh is to ensure the well-being of the ancestors in the afterlife. It is a way of showing respect and gratitude to the forefathers, and it is believed that the blessings of the ancestors protect the family.

Preparing the deceased's favourite foods, making offerings of pinda (rice balls), and chanting mantras are integral parts of the ceremony. The food is vegetarian and often excludes certain ingredients like onions and garlic, which are considered to induce passion and therefore are avoided in many ritualistic contexts.

The *Garuda Purana* is the primary source of guidance for Shraadh rituals. It is one of the eighteen *Mahapuranas*, a genre of ancient Hindu literature. It is in the form of a dialogue between Lord Vishnu and his mount, Garuda. The *Garuda Purana* and other Hindu scriptures deeply root the concept of Shraadh in the belief that there is a spiritual link between the living and the deceased.

One of the most well-known parts of the *Garuda Purana* is the section that deals with death, the afterlife, and the rituals surrounding them. This includes a detailed account of what happens to the soul after death, the concept of heaven and hell, and the path that the soul takes after leaving the body.

It lays out specific procedures for Shraadh, explaining how the rituals are to be performed, who should perform them, and what materials should be used. The text stresses the importance of Shraadh for the deceased soul's well-being and outlines how neglecting to perform these rituals can adversely affect both the departed soul and their living relatives. These ancestral rites, according to the text, can also have an impact on one's karma.

The rituals performed during Shraadh aim to assist the soul of the deceased in its journey through the afterlife. According to Hindu cosmology, the soul may traverse various realms (known as *lokas*) after death, and these rituals aim to ensure a smoother passage.

The presence of a knowledgeable priest is considered essential. He chants mantras and guides the ceremony as well as the offerings to the departed soul. The meal prepared typically consists of the deceased's favourite foods. This involves the offering of water mixed with black sesame seeds, with the utterance of specific mantras. Some people also add items like honey, milk, ghee and jaggery. After the ceremony, the food offered to the deceased is often distributed to priests, ants, cows, dogs and crows, assuming that it will reach the ancestors in whatever form they will be in then, an insect, a vegetarian mammal, a carnivorous animal or a bird, respectively. The ritualistic offerings are believed to be received by the ancestors to attain peace and are considered as sustenance for the departed souls, aiding them in their transition between realms or even helping them attain salvation (moksha). The ceremony is believed to bestow blessings and positive energies upon younger generations and living members of the family.

Family members are encouraged to participate in the ceremony. Their involvement adds value to the ritual, increasing its effectiveness. A *sankalp* (vow) is made, stating the purpose of the Shraadh, the name of the deceased and the relationship to the performer.

The *Garuda Purana* suggests that failing to perform these rituals can adversely affect the deceased soul's well-being. The soul may become a 'preta' or 'restless spirit', wandering between realms without peace. This notion can be distressing for living relatives, who may feel obligated to assist their ancestors in attaining peace.

The Naga sadhus started descending from different mountains towards the plains. They marched in unison towards Adi Shankaracharya's shrine under the full-moon sky towards the fortnight of the Shraadh Paksh period ending at the no-moon night sky. Their numbers spoke of their combined might. The Himalayas were filled with the sounds chanting of 'Bum Bum Bhole'. The noise echoed through the valleys and mountains like a powerful avalanche, but it did not reach Abdali's asura army, as they still had a long distance to cover before terror could pierce their deaf ears of indifference. Instead of snow and ice cascading down, what was falling was a torrent of dedicated Naga sadhus generating a substantial force of nature.

Dhruv witnessed in awe the grand procession as streams of different mathas flowed towards their sacred destination, Adi Shankaracharya's temple at Kashyapmar. From the periphery of the vast Himalayan ranges, these streams arose, each with its unique essence and power, converging in a harmonious dance of purpose and devotion. The chants of 'Har Har Mahadev' and 'Bum Bum Bole', echoed through the rugged landscape as these streams engaged in the misleading paths and snowy stretches. Dhruv saw and experienced what these mystical Naga warriors could do if needed. He witnessed first-hand how the tree controllers requested food from apple trees near Adiguru Shankaracharya's temple in Kashmir, and the trees grew apples in abundance for every Naga present. The members from every matha gathered at a prearranged spot to form a magnificent parade before travelling down from Kashyapmar to Gokul.

As more Nagas arrived at the Adiguru Shankaracharya temple in Kashyapmar from diverse mathas, rich in special powers and abilities, the Nagas started transforming the temple assembly into a convergence of extraordinary skills. A sense of holy energy and anticipation filled the air. The grounds of the temple were transformed into a tapestry of mystical force and age-old customs, as each group contributed their own aura.

Dhruv, along with the group of giant Nagas, also reached the temple where he was witnessing everything that Thomas was reading about the Nagas and their spiritual powers.

The gathering at the temple was a display of heavenly power, supernatural strength and divine ability.

While everyone settled and ate apples and other fruits, the chief Mathadhish ordered the bird whisperer, 'Send some birds for the ground report of Gokul and the progression of Abdali's troops.'

Dhruv felt as though he was in a mystical land when he saw the bird whisperer taking orders from the chief Mathadhish and then passing them on to the birds. His name was Mayuran. He tended to the birds after speaking, and they soared off towards Gokul

Dhruv then noticed a Naga in the crowd who, despite being exposed to the sun, did not have a shadow. Dhruv could not resist walking up to him and asking, 'Who are you?'

The Naga looked at him and said, 'I am alone and that's my strength.'

'Alone!' said Dhruv with a confused face. The Naga showed him the ground where Dhruv could see his shadow, but the Naga had no shadow at all.

'How do you do that? Where is your shadow?' asked Dhruv out of curiosity.

'I keep it hidden so that nobody else can control it. I control it myself,' replied the Naga.

'What do you mean?' asked Dhruv, expecting a straight explanation.

'I am a shadow catcher and there are more like me in this camp. You shield yourself before attacking. We could become vulnerable if someone else gets control of our shadows. The outcome could be devastating, so Nagas like me keep our shadows hidden to ensure that we cannot be controlled through it,' replied the Naga.

'I still do not understand,' said Dhruv.

Suddenly, Dhruv felt as if someone was ripping his skin off his body. He felt unbearable pain along with semi-paralysis that left him unable to scream or react. Dhruv squeezed his eyes shut, trying to endure the source-less pain. And when it suddenly stopped, he opened his eyes to find a shadow standing right in front of him.

'Look below!' the young Naga said.

Dhruv looked down only to learn that his shadow was no longer attached to his body on the ground. There were two men without shadows now and a shadow standing in front of them. It was Dhruv's own shadow that he saw standing in front of his face.

'How many more times do we have to tell you that this is no trick to display for claps,' a strict voice was heard saying. It was from another shadow catcher, much more elderly. The young Naga lost his focus and suddenly Dhruv's shadow went back to its designated space.

'The battlefield will show you what we can do,' said the young Naga with a smile before walking off.

Dhruv noticed another Naga sadhu whose aura felt different. He had many leather bags hanging from his waist. Mahakaay noticed Dhruv speculating about what was in those bags.

'They have a very dangerous fluid that creates fire. They are from the clan of Vidyut, the Naga you met above with the chief Mathadhish. They are the masters of producing fire and creating explosives,' Mahakaay said while walking close to Dhruv, who could also see Vidyut at a distance with many others like him, all carrying earthen pots with them or leather bags tied to their waists.

'Will you please tell me more about them and the shadow catchers?' requested Dhruv. Mahakaay was about to start explaining when, at that moment, everyone in the camp collectively experienced a wave of depression and sadness. It was like a foul smell, one that everybody could sense but no one could decipher or explain in words.

Dhruv suddenly felt the pain of the death of all the children he once taught in the gurukul, and tears rolled down his cheeks. He felt depressed, as if he were experiencing the same painful emotion he would feel if those children were killed right then, in front of him.

With a few seconds, the camp was in chaos, and everybody was failing to fight their past pains.

'What is happening to me?' Dhruv asked in a very tense voice as pain surfaced on his face and overwhelmed his heart without any context or reference. He looked at Mahakaay for an answer, but Mahakaay was gazing at the chief Mathadhish.

A sole Naga was walking towards the chief Mathadhish and everyone else present there seemed controlled by some invisible dark power. The Naga approached the chief Mathadhish, unquestioned and spoke with firmness. 'Let me participate in this war. We can debate on my conduct later after this crisis. But for now, allow me to stand by my brothers. You know what I can do,' the Naga said.

Everybody listened when he spoke, even the chief Mathadhish.

'Free all the souls. They are not yours to command or carry. If you release all the souls you command and choose to fight as a Naga, I allow you to join us,' the chief Mathadhish said.

'It is as if you are asking me to cut my own hands in order to pick up a weapon. You are asking me to give up all my power to prove that I can be of help in the war. What good am I without the souls I possess and what purpose will I be able to serve in the war without my army of spirits?' questioned the agitated lone Naga.

'He is a soul catcher, maybe the only one left alive, a Naga who walks alone as it seems with naked eyes, but is followed by a large number of invisible souls impacting every living thing in and around him,' explained Mahakaay, his rage and pain flowing through his mouth in words and his eyes in tears simultaneously.

Dhruv realized that every Naga present in the camp had a slave soul shadowing him under the order of the Naga who was debating with the chief Mathadhish.

'You are disturbing the supernatural ecology by capturing these souls. There are souls who deserve salvation, and you are the reason they cannot attain it. We Nagas dedicate our life to dharma and its protection. In return, we hope and pray for salvation. This makes you against dharma and us,' said the chief Mathadhish.

'You think the Afghans are going to fight fair? You need to be dishonest and undignified to win over them. This wrapper of self-respect and morality will lead you to the defeat that will wipe Hindutva from the face of the earth. I would rather choose to be undignified and immoral than become a myth in the future,' replied the soul catcher in rage and frustration. To this, the chief Mathadhish replied, 'Whenever you change your mind and free all these souls you have seized as slaves of your invisible spirit army, I shall announce in front of all my Naga mates that you will be accepted to fight for us and claim your respect in the Naga clan again.'

The soul catcher scanned the faces around him to determine whether it was just the chief Mathadhish's words or a collective decision. He found the same firmness in the expressions of others as he saw on the chief's face.

'Leave them!' he ordered in the air and turned back. Suddenly, Dhruv, Mahakaay and every other Naga felt relieved from a kind of possession that had been feeding on the deepest regrets and unhealed pains of every Naga sadhu. Dhruv learnt that every Naga sadhu had an alien soul that was overpowering their own souls, and none could take any action till they were released by the order of the Naga who emerged from nowhere and walked out in no time.

'What just happened?' asked Dhruv, trying to absorb the sudden appearance and disappearance of the strange Naga sadhu and this overwhelming feeling that came from nowhere.

'That was Kaaldhwaj, the last of the soul catchers alive as per our knowledge,' replied Mahakaay.

'He is excellent in his powers, simply unbeatable but his practices crossed the ethical boundaries, and he failed to follow rules whenever he was put to the test. A hopeless case of excellence,' Mahakaay added.

Dhruv was the witness that these Nagas, known for their extraordinary abilities in both combat and mysticism, moved with disciplined grace in huge numbers, which proved their importance in the gathering. Despite the difficulties of the journey, including challenging terrains and severe, extreme weather, the mathas pressed on with passion. The stream of 981 Nagas from the matha of trained warriors, known for their sheer strength; 207 Nagas from the matha of shadow catchers; 144 Nagas from the matha of hypnotists; 90 Nagas from the matha of fire and explosives including Vidyut, eleven Nagas from the matha of bird communicators, nine giants including Mahakaay and nine tree whisperers. They all flowed like powerful currents, rhythmically chanting as they moved closer to the sacred temple for blessings, from where they would converge to fulfil their divine mission, merging into one powerful river.

The temple stood as a grand dam, holding this powerful river of devotion and strength collectively. From there, the river flows down the mountainside like a majestic waterfall. Its waters, in the form of all the powerful Nagas with their extraordinary skills, roll toward Gokul, ready to fulfil their divine mission and strengthen the bonds of their ancient order.

In the meantime, the Gokul hamlet, which had been reduced to ruins following Sardar Khan's destruction and was a mere shell of its former self, was painstakingly restored by Krishna, Adhiraj, Gajraaj and the Durga Defence Forces, reestablishing the once-devastated terrain to its former glory.

Rebuilding with unwavering determination was their first assignment. Carefully arranged paths led the homecoming locals through the revitalized hamlet.

The villagers, slowly returning in small groups, were in awe of their beautifully restored homes when they came back from their temporary shelters of safety. Upon their return, the villagers were welcomed into homes that exceeded their expectations in beauty, each one bearing witness to the love and labour that went into their rebirth. Not only were the temples at the centre of Gokul reconstructed, but they also underwent a magnificent makeover. Temples that had been little more than rubble were now decorated; the gods and goddesses in there restored to their former grandeur. The great temple sprung up from its former state, from a simple skeleton of stones. Scenes were painted on the walls. The shrines inside had been meticulously maintained and depictions from their holy books were painted on the walls. From the tiniest idol to the largest statue, every deity was cleaned and adorned with flowers and other decorations. After being reduced to rubble, every home was carefully rebuilt. Roofs were thatched and walls were raised. The aroma of incense filled the air, blending with the sounds of hymns and prayers.

They successfully attempted to revitalize Gokul by encouraging the locals' resilience and sense of togetherness. As a result of their unwavering efforts, not just a community transformed, but Gokul became a symbol of strength and hope. It was prepared to meet whatever challenges arose. As life returned to the area, there was an optimistic sense of rejuvenation in the air. A spirit of hopeful regeneration pervaded the air as the village came back to life. The once-baby elephant Golu, now grown into a young elephant named Gajraaj, wandered among the villagers as Krishna, Adhiraj and the others still worked ceaselessly with the residents of Gokul to restore its beauty while Neelkanth kept an eye on all the ground events in Gokul.

Gajraaj was a vibrant and inquisitive representation of the village's revitalized spirit. As a young companion in the arduous process of reconstruction, he had grown taller and stronger physically. Though his obsession with my shankh continued as he still was dependent on me to hear its sound, he wanted to blow it himself so that he could hear the music of it whenever and however many times he wished to. Whenever he had a chance, he noticed me carefully while I blew it for him. He had to learn how to hold it and blow it at the same time. He tried a few different positions with the conch, but nothing seemed to work, and it was always cute and fun to watch Gajraaj try and unsuccessfully practice blowing it like me.

Gokul's returning residents and the united protectors seemed to be in peace till the day some villagers came running from the outskirts of the village to alert the defenders.

'We saw some soldiers on horses approaching us,' said the men, panting.

Everybody was on their toes. The Durga Defence Forces took their positions. The women and children were terrified and were asked to take shelter in the temple. The untrained village men also picked up the weapons left by the dead Afghan soldiers in the previous battle of Gokul. As the men approached, a voice from within the village shouted, 'Don't attack. Let them in.' It was Krishna's voice and the soldiers approaching were in the uniform of Haripur soldiers.

Vedant managed to escape alive from his kingdom Haripur, which had been brutally attacked by Sarfaraz and his army. Running for his life and seeking asylum with around 150 bleeding and tired men, he arrived at Gokul, and the ones standing to stop him and his men were the women of the Durga Defence Forces. Vedant's men drew their swords, unable to distinguish between friends and foes. In response, the Durga army also was charged to cut them dead in moments.

'Stop!' announced Krishna in his authoritative tone, commanding both sides. The princess had an eye on all of that.

Krishna rushed to the clash site on his horse and noticed that, at the centre of a tiny formation, Vedant was trying to deceive the enemy by wearing an ordinary soldier's uniform.

Breathless and broken, Vedant felt relief upon seeing Krishna. Before he could react, however, all his soldiers recognized Krishna's voice and followed the command to lower their weapons.

'Vedant!' said Krishna wondering.

Just hearing his name from an elderly man, who once stood alongside his father, made Vedant feel like a child under the protection of a father-like figure. Krishna had seen Vedant since forever, and before Vedant could utter a word displaying his vulnerability, Krishna requested him to ride with him in private.

The Durga defence and Haripur soldiers, still eyeing each other with suspicion due to the lack of trust and information, continued to stare one another down, while Krishna and Vedant, in a quiet space under the open sky, discussed something.

'Okay, I will take you to the princess. Only she can decide on your request, my dear,' said Krishna to Vedant, giving him hope at the end of their discussion.

In no time, King Vedant and Princess Chandrika stood face to face. 'What brings you here?' asked the princess suspiciously. Krishna stood right behind, just as he used to stand strongly behind Vedant before.

'The fear of my death in Haripur and hoping to find safety in Gokul,' replied Vedant, his eyes lowered in shame and his heart sinking in fear as he remembered his journey and the overwhelming strength of Abdali's army.

'They are coming to Gokul, Krishna!' Vedant continued, his voice firm with seriousness. 'I have seen the army of Abdali. They are enormous and powerful. Abdali is a prophet of doom.' The princess and Krishna exchanged a solemn glance, both realizing how serious the situation was. The tiny army that had laboriously restored Gokul was now faced with a new task that would put their bravery and fortitude to the ultimate test.

Their actions were encouraged by Vedant's warning. They promptly started fortifying the town in anticipation of the impending invasion.

While they were preparing to confront the biggest army Gokul had ever seen, Ahmed Shah Abdali's men had recovered, as he continued destroying everything in his way. He was approaching Avanti Pradesh on his way to Gokul. When Avanti Pradesh was about nine hours away and Gokul around twenty-four hours away, the merciless and unrelenting army of Ahmed Shah Abdali stopped advancing on his orders. Abdali ordered his troops to stop in a valley as it was getting dark.

Their tents stood out sharply against the peaceful surroundings of the mountain range. As the soldiers awaited their next orders, a palpable tension filled the air. The notoriously violent and vicious Ahmed Shah Abdali was restless.

While Abdali still had a day and a night to travel to reach Gokul, Sarfaraz, the commander who attacked Vedant in Haripur, was half a day away from standing at the mouth of Gokul, eager to enter and attack. But Abdali's orders were to wait for his arrival. The Durga Defence Forces, under the command of the princess, guided by Krishna's experience and the labour of the villagers, were busy preparing traps and some locally-made gadgets to attack the Afghan army. Alongside them stood Vedant, feeling low and ashamed of the decisions that had cost him his kingdom, palace and legacy. Krishna, busy in the preparations for the upcoming challenging days, looked at Vedant as he worked like a common soldier and approached him.

'King! I have seen you growing within the royal walls. These laborious tasks under the burning sun are not your duty. Please go and rest in the camp set up for you,' said Krishna generously.

Vedant, sweating with a plough in his hand, replied, 'I am no king. There is no Haripur any more. I am not special. I am as ordinary as everybody else here and I wish to contribute in the fight, the result of which is pre-decided. Gokul will fall. Each and every one you see and know here will die. All who stand against him will be hanged but not by their necks, maybe by their hands or fingers, starving for food and screaming for death. Before Abdali's troops attacked Haripur, my informers told me that he is coming to Gokul with his full strength. He has a total army of more than 30,000 soldiers. He wants to set an example for the other kingdoms and the coming generations to teach them what happens to those who try to stand against him. What is about to happen here is going to be beyond brutality.'

The news compelled Krishna to look around and ponder how those hundred-odd women and fifty untrained villagers, along with himself and me, were going to face an army as vast as that.

He realized that the advancing army would sweep them off just like waves wash off insects.

He kept a hand on Vedant's shoulder and said, 'I suggest you keep moving in the opposite direction and save yourself, Vedant. I may not be your commander-in-chief any more and I may not have any authority to suggest anything after how we departed last time. But I am still a man who loves you as his own son and have seen you grow. I saw Shambhu ji see his son Ajaa die in front of his own eyes, but I am not as brave as him to see you die helplessly.'

Krishna's eyes were moist, as if he could not bear to imagine it but could only see Vedant dying in reality.

Vedant hugged Krishna, saying. 'I have realized that I was a fool to turn a blind eye to others of my own land and religion dying to protect dharma, and I was a fool thinking that running would save me. I was a fool thinking that I could make any kind of peace arrangements with them or that we could co-exist. It's too late to understand that the only way to survive is to fight and not run or hide or expect the unexpected that they may offer peace. I am sorry that I realized this too late. I wish and hope that the coming generations learn it sooner than me before it's too late.'

'It's still not yet late, my king! I am ready once again to fight under your flag,' replied Krishna, bowing to his former king.

'Krishna! I will fight, and this time, I will fight under your command. You challenged me with thirty kills last time. If you are still standing alive, I am sure you kept your word. This time, I challenge you. Let's see who wins between both of us. The one who kills more enemies before falling wins,' said Vedant, bowing in return.

Gokul was not the only land under threat at that point in time. In a not too far-off empire close to the queen's domain, Avanti Pradesh, which was surrounded by a large area of undulating hills and fertile forests, was unaware of the impending storm. But their king was well versed with the looming threat. He and his courtiers were wise enough to notice the gloomy clouds forming over the horizon. By then, Sarfaraz's troops could be heard from Gokul. As he reached the outskirts of Gokul, the first to welcome him was Krishna's strategy to break the morale of the troops and agitate Sarfaraz, making him prone to mistakes in his anger. Sarfaraz and his front line saw a large wooden standee that read, 'Shhhh! This is where Sardar Khan and your other Afghan brothers are asleep.'

It was the trenches dug and then filled with the bodies of Afghan soldiers and Sardar Khan buried. While Sarfaraz was fuming is rage outside Gokul, Abdali himself was about to reach Avanti Pradesh. The king of Avanti Pradesh sent a pigeon post to the queen of Surajgarh that read: 'Need immediate help and reinforcements. Please help!'

There were people in relief, thinking that Surajgarh was not falling in Abdali's path to Gokul. But the king of Avanti Pradesh knew that Surajgarh never turned its back on any kingdom requesting for help.

Closest to the kingdom of Avanti Pradesh, the queen's letters and messengers urged action in all the surrounding empires, inspiring them to set aside their differences and unite against the common, raging enemy. As time went on, monarchs and kings from far and wide began to support the queen's cause, realizing that her resolve to oppose widespread oppression surpassed all previous objections, grievances, complaints and hatred. Different kingdoms sent different aids. Some chose to send men, some decided to facilitate medicines, some managed food for the soldiers and others offered refuge.

On the other hand, the innocent flying messenger was received with a sense of urgency and resolve as soon as it arrived at the queen's royal gates. As the message of help was read to the queen, she paid close attention, furrowing her brow in anxiety at the gravity of the issue. The court was called immediately, and the queen addressed those gathered, saying, 'We will not desert our neighbours in their hour of need.' Her expression was resolute and firm as she accepted the messenger.

Taking an unprecedented step in preparation for the war, her troops summoned all the ladies of the kingdom to fight with them. 'Men possess strength because we give birth to them. We have the power to create life in us and anyone against life is our enemy. Let nobody be mistaken that we creators cannot be destroyers. Stand up and join me in the war that begins with us,' said the queen.

The realm resonated with the queen's words of encouragement.

At the queen's summons, the Shakti Sena roared and soared their horses and chariots, all prepared for combat. The queen's speech was so powerful and moving that it encouraged all the women in the kingdom to take up arms. They had undergone difficult training that enabled them to use swords, shoot arrows, and engage in hand-to-hand combat. Under the strong and unbeatable leadership of the queen, they followed the call to protect the honour and territory of Avanti Pradesh. With an air of complete confidence and power, they marched to defend the weak.

With the roaring hooves of war horses pounding the earth and the intimidating banners of Abdali, the conqueror known for his ruthlessness and ambition, his unrelenting march began. The invading force was approaching the seemingly unaware empire like a tidal wave of destruction. The courageous and honourable king of Avanti Pradesh watched from the top of his fort's walls as an army approached, gazing with a sorrowful heart for he knew that his people were about to confront an unparalleled threat. The citizens of the kingdom began to feel helpless, as they knew that the enemy would descend upon them like a thunderstorm, their numbers overwhelming and their objective only death.

'We will attack tomorrow morning. The blood looks beautiful in broad daylight,' said Abdali, looking at the fort walls of Avanti Pradesh. They had no clue about the unbelievable act of bravery and the queen's daring decision to attack Abdali. Not only was a troop marching from Surajgarh to Avanti Pradesh, but another countless set of warriors was simultaneously marching towards Gokul.

'Will the Naga warriors reach before time? You said that Ahmed Shah Abdali was two days ahead of them and would reach Gokul before the Naga warriors,' asked Madhav, the worried Naga following the nameless one. The nameless Naga could sense the curiosity and nervousness in the follower's eyes.

10

Shakti

'I want them dead and cleared before the sun reaches its peak. By evening, I want to proceed to Gokul,' ordered Abdali to Azharuddin, one of his commanders who joined him with his troops one night before the attack on Avanti Pradesh. Now, Abdali's strength had grown significantly, with a formidable army of over 10,000 soldiers, 1000 horsemen, 1000 camels, and fifty cannons, up from nearly 15,000 soldiers, 1000 horses, 1300 camels and sixty cannons. It was still only half of his total strength. The remaining half was to join him outside Gokul.

The first light of dawn broke as his forces stood at the doors of Avanti Pradesh. Azharuddin was sure they would destroy the whole kingdom by noon. It was horrifying how they unleashed their terror upon the small villages on their way before reaching the gates of Avanti Pradesh. Abdali's men, under the command of Azharuddin, launched the attack on Avanti Pradesh.

Meanwhile, the courageous queen, who never backed down from a fight, was on her way despite knowing that their numbers combined with allied forces were still not even half of Abdali's troops outside Avanti Pradesh.

'I hope you know the risk, the danger and the consequence of our participation, my queen!' cried one of her strategy consultants while they were travelling to Avanti Pradesh. With unwavering resolve, the queen replied, 'Yes! I know, and I also know that I can skip this war today but not forever. Sooner or later, as they stand at Avanti Pradesh's door today, they will be at ours too. I would rather choose to die brave today than live as a coward tomorrow.'

The queen led her 1000 women warriors, 250 horses, fifty elephants and two cannons in battle, but she also had the army of 3000 men, 250 horses, fifty more elephants and five more cannons from the surrounding empires fighting alongside her. To maximize their combined strength and resistance, the queen and her allies from several adjacent empires coordinated their movements and attacks. Under her command, the Shakti Sena and the allies joined forces and intensified a strong defence against Abdali's advancing forces. In terms of strategy, the queen tactically positioned her allied forces to take advantage of the terrain's ability to hamper Abdali's progress. With thousands of arrows, her skilled archers were ready to ambush and restrain Abdali's army in order to weaken their morale and supply routes. With courage and determination in her heart, the queen rode out to confront Abdali's army head-on, preparing to charge with her Shakti Sena.

Joining arms with the allied forces, she gave her allies the reassuring news that the way to victory over the oppressors was now clear, and that hope was shining brightly. Assuring them that the period of gloom and hopelessness would soon pass, she emphasized that this would be no ordinary battle but a real fight for people and their pride in the face of insurmountable obstacles. With this conviction, the bold queen and her army, believing that their courage and strength would lead them to victory, marched on.

Right before fight, the queen motivated the women soldiers of her Shakti Sena by reminding them of the resilient 1111 Naga warriors, the strong beasts who had previously resisted Abdali's ruthless army.

Inspiring her Shakti Sena, she said, 'Thousands of Nagas could emerge only from the bravery of thousands of strong women if every Naga is born from the strength of a single woman. Just realize the power you possess. My sisters, you are strong and resilient; fight till the last breath, cling to your courage and never give up.'

The queen infused her warriors with a strong sense of purpose, motivating them to confront their adversaries with unwavering resolve, understanding that their fight is not just for triumph, but also for honour and dignity to the very end. As she faced her female army, the queen evaluated Abdali's mental state.

It was an army of about 4000 men and women under the queen's banner, facing Abdali's formidable force of 15,000. They had 500 horses against his 1000, 100 elephants against his 1300 camels and seven cannons standing against his sixty.

In a display of bravery and aggression, the queen, her allies and the surrounding empires charged towards the opposing army, swords glinting in the sunlight as they tore through the lines. The queen and her female warriors fought valiantly and made a bold tactical move that ultimately surprised Abdali and his army.

The shocker was entirely unexpected for Abdali and his army, much to his amazement. He never imagined that somebody would dare to attack him. A different kind of army that Abdali had never seen before loomed across the battlefield: the queen and her women army were strong, well-prepared and as merciless as Abdali's men. Abdali was interested by the sight, not frightened. Observing the women's bravery and strength in battle, he grew inquisitive. Wearing a smirk on his face, he gave orders to call Azharuddin.

Abdali observed the women's army fighting valiantly and delivering a counter-punch with great appreciation. In no time, Azharuddin was standing at his service.

'Catch all the women alive without injuring them,' Abdali ordered, his mind filled with dark fantasies and wild thoughts.

'It will take us more effort, time and loss of men to do so, Shehenshah. Many of our soldiers will lose their lives trying to capture them alive and unharmed,' said Azharuddin, tense from the order.

'I know, but we have enough soldiers to spare, and there are more standing at the gates of Gokul under the command of Sarfaraz. Thousands more are on the way, following Malik Akhtar, and Zorawar will join Sarfaraz's troops in Gokul. Let some men die so that these women can be caught alive. In the years to come, these women will reproduce more men than you lose today. They are so resilient and strong that with the best and bravest of our soldiers, they could bear powerful men to fight and girls to have more fearless children.'

'That might take a day more, Shehenshah,' urged Azharuddin.

'Hmm! Can you hear what I hear?' asked Abdali, smiling with his eyes closed.

'No, Sire! What do you hear?' asked Azharuddin, trying to understand what he missed.

'I hear Gokul whispering in my ears. It says, "I can wait one more day to be ruined by your pious feet."'

His voice and madness were terrifying to even Azharuddin and the soldiers around him.

'I am going to my tent. It shall end by tomorrow noon. Get back to your task,' said Abdali before returning to his camp.

Taken aback, Azharuddin and his troops dutifully followed the directive.

Abdali knew that he would defeat these allied forces. What he didn't know was that the queen readied her women warriors not just for the actual combat but also for the psychological threats that their adversaries harboured. The army was extremely well-trained to be watchful and ready for any situation in which their fortitude and resolution would be put to test outside of the battlefield. Along with their weapons, they carried the enigmatic essence of their queen's leadership as they marched towards the battlefield. As a last line of offence against invaders who would degrade and disgrace them, they had this secret weapon. They would not have hesitated to commit themselves if they had ever been unable to fight or were in danger of being captured, preferring martyrdom over surrender.

The swords clashed and war shouts echoed across the battlefield. Knowing that her female warriors would rather die as martyrs than surrender, the valiant queen commanded her troops with courage.

Azharuddin, the merciless Commander-in-Chief of Abdali, stood at the centre and yelled, 'You are going to fail, old bitch and so will your army of whores. And now, we will make you realize your real purpose. You all are merely the vessels for breeding; the whores and you will bear our babies inside your pretty bellies. Now face it as your purpose in this world is going to change today forever. You will just be for the pleasure of not one but many of us.'

The queen's eyes narrowed and were uncompromising. 'Dreams of a child. You need to be taught manners, something your father certainly failed to do,' she responded. Riding her white stallion, she galloped forward towards Azharuddin, her devoted warriors fighting by her side followed with equal ferocity and determination. It was expected that they would meet, and when they did, the ground shook.

With a sharp clang, their swords collided, sparks flew as they struck repeatedly, neither giving an inch of space to the other. The queen dodged Azharuddin's powerful blows with grace. Her response to him was so quick that her blade seemed to blur. Fierce Azharuddin attacked forward, his blade sliced through the air and brushed the queen's shoulder. It was a narrow escape. But the queen remained resolute. She struck back with a ferocious shout, landing a blow directly on Azharuddin's arm.

A junior commander ran to Abdali's tent, breathless and announced, 'My king! Our Commander-in-Chief is wounded and may lose his life at the hands of the queen.'

Both Abdali and Azharuddin were surprised for a moment, one in the tent and another on the battlefield. Azharuddin howled and moved forward again. The queen was prepared, her blade smashing his weapon to the ground, eventually disarming him with a quick and decisive move. When Azharuddin's armour was penetrated by the queen's blade, his eyes grew wide with horror. He collapsed to the floor, breathless as his strength failed him. Despite the fierce struggle around her, the queen stood triumphantly over him, her breath steady. Abdali watched the result of his careless command: the courageous queen, with one of her boots planted the blade firmly on Azharuddin's still-breathing body, appearing as if Goddess Durga herself was standing over Mahishasur.

'In our land, when children make mistakes and misbehave, we pull their ears hard . . . but unfortunately, you are not a child and what you said was not a mistake but beyond it,' said the queen. She then took her dagger and chopped off one of Azharuddin's ears. He screamed in pain, loud enough to reach the ears of Abdali.

'Shhhh!' said the queen calmly, adding, 'I told you that you are not a child, you are man grown enough to produce babies, stop screaming and crying like one. Now comes the lesson for you. In our land, we are not called "bitches" and "whores", we are called Shakti and Devi, which means Goddess. We decide who enters the world, and not even our male gods can come to earth without our permission. Lord Rama came to earth when Kaushalya allowed him, Lord Krishna came into existence when Devki permitted him to. You think you can enter my land and rule my people without the permission of these women warriors . . .'

She then looked at Abdali who was looking at the fate of one of his most trusted and capable commanders. Their eyes met while she finished her statement. 'No, you are not welcome here,' she said and then looked back at Azharuddin and declared, 'And this was the last lesson for your purposeless life.' And then, without warning, she slashed his neck. Once a scene of bloodshed, the battlefield fell silent as her armies achieved their ultimate victory. Once again, the queen stood tall, sun shining through her armour and her eyes gleaming. She had proved to be a hero before her people.

Abdali was prepared to lose men to capture the beautiful and fierce women of the Shakti Sena alive, but never in his wildest anticipation, did he imagine losing his trusted commander, Azharuddin, on a small speed breaker in his journey to Gokul.

Assassinating the ferocious supreme commander ignited a spark of optimism and the prospect of success among the troops and the allied armies of the neighbouring countries. This potent symbol gave them hope and a renewed motivation to battle on since it showed that success was well within grasp. Some witnessed a spectacle to behold as Shakti Sena fiercely battled the unrelenting advance of Abdali's armies, raising the banners of their adjacent empires with greater fervour and excitement. This was a demonstration of strength and solidarity in the face of difficulty. However, Abdali was not so easily defeated because his goal was not only to win but also to eliminate any opposition in his path to Gokul, leaving no trace of their existence behind.

However, the queen, along with her highly skilled and resilient army, knew that they were battling for more than just their own survival—they were fighting for the future of the land's soul and dharma. With each Afghan killed, their determination grew stronger, and they were ready to face whatever came ahead and win the battle that would shape the future of many kingdoms of central Bharat.

The queen, standing amid all the chaos, knew that merely killing Abdali's commanders would not be enough now as she could see the Shakti Sena and the horsemen falling alongside their men. Along with this, of the fifty elephants that charged, a few had already collapsed under the cruel assault. Victory seemed impossible now. Meanwhile, arrogant Abdali, sure of his achievement, underestimated the situation. What he didn't know—what nobody knew— was that the queen possessed a secret weapon, a true power that neither Abdali nor his forces had yet discovered. A hidden and mysterious weapon that could turn the tides of war when all seemed lost.

As the conflict wore on, it became evident that the queen had foreseen Abdali's wish to seize her female warriors alive, even if it would cost him more dead men to achieve this goal. During this pursuit, Abdali's army lost men and gave their lives trying to apprehend the female warriors alive. The loss might have been smaller if Abdali had not been so determined to capture the female soldiers alive, admitting the awful truth of their loss. Despite their greatest efforts and sacrifices, they had failed to fulfil Abdali's goal, as the women, fueled by their determination, undermined every attempt at capture.

On the orders of the queen, hundreds of arrows began to rain down relentlessly on the Afghanis. Surprisingly, with even a prick from the arrows shot by the queen's army, Abdali's men started falling to their deaths. Abdali was confused. It left him furious and unable to understand the source of such lethal accuracy.

'How is it possible? A mere scratch from the arrows on hands and legs is killing my men like flies!' Abdali barely tried to contain himself. Neymat called some medics gathered by Jugal Kishore to inspect the dead soldiers. They examined a few of them.

'This is no ordinary arrow, Shehenshah! The tips of all these arrows are filled with the venom of the deadliest snake ever known. It not only kills men but animals within seconds, and there is no cure for it,' said the medic while drawing a blank expression.

Abdali was surprised to hear the words 'snake's venom'.

Knowing this, it becomes more evident that Vasuki, the huge snake that coils around Lord Shiva, was blessing and contributing his bit to the battle for saving dharma. In the absence of the guardians of dharma, the Naga sadhus, it felt as if Vasuki himself had stepped forward to stop those who threatened to destroy the sacred. This disrupted the tempo of the advancing Afghans toward Gokul, causing their strength to slowly wane.

Furious, Abdali yelled at his men, 'No more games now. Kill the queen. She will continue to harm my men while she keeps leading. Get her dead.' In response, one man from his force hesitantly replied, 'Shehenshah, reaching her seems impossible as she is surrounded and secured by her elite force of warriors who are well-equipped. It is just like an impenetrable fortress.'

'A well-aimed arrow can bring down even the bravest lioness. You don't need to reach her. Call all your royal archers and get this task done,' said Abdali. As the command echoed through the field, the royal archers assembled with their bows, ready and aiming arrows at the queen. With pinpoint precision, each arrow was aimed directly at her. The contingency was ordered to strike and with a single command, ten arrows were released in a storm of death, all aiming at the one brave queen fighting the enemies on the ground, unaware of the strike from sky. Unfortunately, one arrow, more precise than the rest, struck the queen on her chest. The strength that had carried her through so many battles suddenly began to wane, and she struggled to keep standing firm. This was a painful and heartbreaking sight for all the warriors of the Shakti Sena.

She struggled to stay upright, her strength failing due to the severity of the attack. Some cried and some laughed, some screamed and some smiled, but under the genuine leadership of her master, a young warrior, no older than sixteen, decided to spare the queen from the pain she would endure before her death. With grief in her heart and resolve in her eyes, the young girl in the armour and logo of Shakti Sena stepped ahead, lifted her sword, and with a single blow, put an end to her master's misery. The carrier of courage died. The act left everyone witnessing the scene stunned in silence.

'She secretly ordered me to do that before entering the battle,' said the crying, proud little warrior, the youngest in the Shakti Sena. The queen and her warriors had an unshakable relationship, which was demonstrated during this moment of mercy.

'What's your name, soldier?' asked one of the older warriors, but before she could speak, an Afghan soldier beheaded her too. Although everyone who knew her cried and screamed, her spirit lived on in everyone's hearts. The thrill of slaying the queen with his own hands was fleeting for Abdali.

'What was the queen's name?' asked Abdali.

'I heard everybody called her Shakti, my king,' replied Jugal.

Even after her death, the battle continued with intense fury. The queen's army, now fueled by anger, was more determined than ever to defeat Abdali's army at any cost.

Abdali was renowned for his brutality throughout the territories he sought. His harsh and vicious personality, which thrived on violence, dominance, cold-heartedness, and an unquenchable ambition for power, made him a figure of fear and a bearer of brutality. He grew more fearful and merciless after witnessing his soldiers fall. Driven by cruelty, he devised a horrific scheme to demoralize the remnants of the queen's army. This proved to be a successful demonstration as the commanders, both male and female, decided to continue fighting, but the soldiers in the allied forces decided to retreat and return to their respective kingdoms. After the queen's demise, there was no one who could keep the forces and their determination intact to continue the stand against the demon who looked like a man.

Those who decided to march forward, were mutilated and the others who turned their backs to their own made peace by being called cowards. They chose to dwell in disgrace rather than perish in flames. But those who decided to die fighting had more to suffer before their sacrifice.

Abdali gave orders to his men to shave the dead queen's head. But the ruthless king found this insufficient and told his troops surrounding him to tie the heads of hundreds of dead female warriors, with their hair clutched to the tails of the horses they rode. The heads swayed vigorously as did the tails of the horses', when they galloped. The decapitated heads of Shakti Sena warriors were either fixed on the javelins or tied to horse tails.

This was an act of blatant violence and cruelty performed by Abdali's forces. The battlefield, which had once been a site of honour, had turned into a horrifying and disgraceful exhibition of brutality and cruelty that left a lasting scar of fear and hopelessness in its wake. This horrific deed was intended to break the hearts and morale of the defenders of Gokul and solidify Abdali's merciless rule over them.

With a heavy heart, the nameless Naga described the terrifying scene to Madhav, warning him that the worst is still to come. With a sombre expression and a firm look, the Naga muttered to his junior, 'The war is still ongoing. Women are still cut into pieces and won as trophies.' With dawn approaching, the Mathadhish spoke to all the groups of the Nagas in a voice full of conviction and authority. 'We have gathered here to honour the Nagas who fought against the invaders. We are here to guard Gokul. We don't know their numbers and they don't know our devotions. With our combined array of abilities, we are an unstoppable force. Our stand will decide the future of this Godland. Get ready to show them who we are and what we can do. Let's prove to them that Shiva exists. Get ready to define the meaning of wrath. Get ready to display your powers against the army of asuras. Get ready to perform Shiva's dance of destruction.'

All the Naga sadhus roared 'Har Har Mahadev' as if challenging the asuras to stand in front of them if they had the courage to face the powers of these Naga warriors.

Mathadhish finished his words with: 'As Dhruv is familiar with the quickest routes, he will lead us to Gokul. We shall march as a group and engage in combat.'

Among them stood Dhruv, prepared to lead 1451 Nagas along the path, their bodies covered in holy ash and armed with tridents and other dangerous weapons. Their hearts were full of heavenly purpose, while each had special talents and abilities. With the strength of their combined forces and Dhruv's wisdom leading them, they marched for Gokul, prepared to meet any obstacles head-on with bravery and determination.

Nobody knew that a set of eyes was silent yet closely following this avalanche of sadhus as they progressed. The eyes were of Kaaldhwaj, the mysterious Naga.

'Was he following them so that he could capture their souls too as and when they fall?' asked Madhav following the nameless Naga. Dodging the question, the nameless Naga continued with his narration.

Inspired and unified, the sadhus set about preparing their hearts full of determination to protect Gokul and uphold the sanctity of dharma. A new chapter in the fable of the Naga warriors was about to open with the start of the journey from Shankaracharya Temple at Kashyapmar to Gokul. A sea of tridents and saffron robes started moving in unison and their purpose was an amazing sight. From the heights of the Himalayas to the plains of Gokul, their chants of 'Har Har Mahadev' and 'Bum Bum Bhole' grew louder and their presence more potent.

They would soon have to put their combined might and extraordinary powers to the test as they set out to protect Gokul and uphold the holiness of dharma. However, they were not aware that they needed more time than Abdali in reaching Gokul.

Conversely, the period of Shraadh Paksh continued as Dhruv and all the Nagas, numbering in the hundreds, travelled from Adiguru Shankaracharya temple towards Gokul.

'The stench of smoke and despair along with the anguish and sorrow of the individuals who had lost everything to Abdali's brutality was infused in the air. Mortal remains were scattered across the burnt ground, bearing witness to the slaughter of not only men but also women and castles,' a bird whisperer informed the nagas moving towards Gokul, having received this information from his purple-rumped sunbird—a small bird, four to five inches in size, that typically feeds on flower nectar. The sunbird was sent to fly over Abdali's army to manoeuvre around and assess the numbers of his cavalry.

'And the children?' asked Dhruv, who felt as though he were reliving his own past horrors from when his village was attacked.

'Converted and misused,' replied another bird whisperer whose old-world sparrows returned in a group from the other direction and saw the army that was led by Zorawar. All eyes turned on him as he continued speaking. 'The houses are burning, the injured are screaming, rats and other animals are feeding on human flesh and blood,' he said.

'What are they up to?' asked the chief Mathadhish to compare their numbers with that of Abdali's.

The answer came from the third bird whisperer, whose mynah returned after seeing the battle between the queen and Azharuddin. The mynah is a black bird with a yellow and orange beak and claws, capable of mimicking human speech and understanding human languages if trained well. 'Abdali's soldiers have tied women's heads on the tails of their horses that are dragging on the mud's surface, the other heads are on their javelins. They have hung the bodies of the dead men on wooden planks that are now serving as symbols of their brutal intentions and a recall of the pain endured by the Gokul defenders. Some of the men hanging on both side of roads are still alive under the harsh sun without any food, water, medical aid and clothes. It feels like the road to hell. Every road that Abdali is covering to reach Gokul has the same visuals. This was done in an attempt to make a strong statement to everyone who survived or is still living or those who are trying to oppose him.'

The chief Mathadhish said, 'It is a warning to us all. Abdali is ensuring that by sparing a few, these couriers will spread word of his ruthless campaign and warn anyone who might still consider opposing him that his army is on its way to Gokul. How many soldiers are heading towards Gokul?'

Mayuran, one of the bird whisperers, made different sounds, and in no time, a mynah and an old-world sparrow came and sat on both his shoulders and one on his palm, making sounds as if talking to him. The Naga then spoke after the birds stopped. 'They are in thousands, coming from three different directions, the biggest fleet from one side, I believe they are led by Abdali himself as some queen killed his commander but died afterwards. Overall, they have hundreds of horses and camels, thousands of soldiers and many huge guns that emit fireballs when shot. Every gun needs around five men to operate it.'

'They are called cannons and they are the weapons of mass destruction. I saw them in the last battle with Sardar Khan.' Mahakaay was absorbing the information while Dhruv asked, 'Any news on the Nagas at Gokul, Ajaa and Shambhu ji?' Dhruv asked curiously after educating them about the cannons.

'No bird has news about them,' said the whisperer. The news was disappointing for Dhruv, but also hopeful as he still was not ready to hear that they were dead.

'How far are they from Gokul?' asked the chief Mathadhish.

'One of his fleets is standing at the mouth of Gokul, but they have stopped as if they are waiting for something. The other two armies will not take more than two days max,' replied Mayuran.

'There will be nothing left to save if we fail to reach before them. We must speed up. We will now not stop unless we reach Gokul,' the chief Mathadhish ordered.

A few miles away from these united Nagas, the lonely Kaaldhwaj, as an outcast also, stood and continued to follow them all. The united Nagas didn't know that Kaaldhwaj had an eye and ear on everything said and done among them. Some dark souls serving Kaaldhwaj were among the Nagas invisibly.

Abdali's army was approaching Gokul from three southward directions, while the Nagas were urgently advancing from the north. The Nagas now, for the first time, knew the size of the enemy's army, the situation at hand and the urgency of the moment. They realized that they had to reach Gokul as quickly as possible to prevent its destruction.

The failed attempt to imprison the women warriors cost Abdali a commander, nearly 5000 soldiers, 400 camels, 600 horses, twenty-five cannons and an additional day to reach Gokul. However, the 1451 Nagas descending from the Himalayas still needed one day more in comparison to Abdali.

11

We–Men

With birds bringing word from all directions, Dhruv and the other Naga warriors soon realized that Gokul was in imminent danger, as the birds flew above the paths of Abdali's destruction. Dhruv and the Nagas quickened their pace, anxious to reach Gokul before Abdali's forces could do further damage. They were determined to safeguard Gokul. Dhruv reflected on a time when the Naga warriors were unprepared and poorly equipped in the battle of Gokul. They were a formidable force to be reckoned with, marching with warriors from many Mathas who were armed with strong mystical talents and lethal weapons. Their resolve grew with each step, knowing that Gokul's fate rested on their preparation and unwavering courage.

It was during this period of planning and manoeuvring that Princess Chandrika was informed of the queen's defeat and death. She was devastated when the news eventually reached her. Despite her unbearable anguish and sense of orphanhood, she refrained from crying and felt empty inside.

Her mother was a symbol of compassion and strength. Krishna approached her to offer comfort, recognizing her struggle in adversity. 'Princess, I can feel the pain in your heart. Your mother was not only a guiding light to you but to us all. She had left her body, but her love and wisdom remain in you.'

The princess, feeling drained of strength, was overwhelmed with a sense of loss and despair. Krishna reassured her by saying, 'It's important to transform your pain and turn it into your strength, princess. The queen would have always wanted you to carry her legacy forward and become a strong and wise ruler. Living through you would be her legacy.'

I walked forward and reassured the princess. 'The pain of losing someone you love can feel overwhelming but know that her spirit and essence will always endure you with love and guidance. You should take comfort in knowing that your mother, the queen, your father, King Dhyanendra and your brother Ajaa, are all unified and are with you right now, right here, blessing, watching and protecting you. It's time to make them proud.'

The princess replied sorrowfully, her voice trembling, 'It's hard to think that they are not here anymore.'

I continued, 'They aren't really gone, princess, as they live on through you. Rather than mourning their loss, embrace the love and unity they share now. You should feel their presence and let it give you strength.'

The nameless Naga told Madhav in a serious tone, 'The princess was soothed and supported by Krishna and me as we guided her through the depths of her grief with concern and sympathy. Women of our soil possess hearts of gold and embody the essence of our goddesses in the truest sense.'

The nameless Naga paused, turned and asked Madhav, 'Do you know, why our ancestors held the women of our land in such high respect?'

Madhav replied curiously, 'I have heard stories but I'm not sure why they were held in such high regards.'

The nameless Naga explained, 'It's because they were far from being delicate and weak, their tales are not just about their beauty, but of grace and strength too. They were warriors, fearless and formidable in battle. These women, especially the Rajkumaris, were trained in swordplay, warfare and other fighting techniques. Their strength was unmatched both in spirit and body, as they were raised strong and resilient. These extraordinary women served as symbols of resistance to oppression, and their bravery and strength are remembered throughout history. Till date, there are hundreds of examples to validate my words, some of which people have heard and read like Rani Lakshmibai, the Queen of Jhansi who was born on 19 November 1828 in Kashi and died on 17 June 1858 at the age of twenty-nine because she refused to surrender Jhansi to the British. Lakshmibai was proclaimed the custodian and caretaker of Jhansi, and she ruled on behalf of her successor who was an infant then. Upon joining the revolution against the British forces, she quickly mobilized her troops and rebels from nearby areas rallied to support her. Under Gen. Hugh Rose, the British forces encircled the fort of Jhansi, and a fierce battle ensued. Lakshmibai decided not to surrender even after her troops faced heavy casualties. However, Lakshmibai managed to escape from the fort with a group of palace guards and headed east, where more rebels joined her. She then mounted a successful assault on the city fortress of Gwalior. After taking Gwalior, she marched east to confront a British counter-attack. In the disguise of a man, she fought a brutal battle and was murdered in battle.

'People have also heard about Ahilyabai Holkar, a highly respected commander of the Maratha Empire, born on 31 May 1725 in the village of Chondi in Maharashtra. She moved to Maheshwar, now located in the state of Madhya Pradesh, on the banks of the Narmada River.

'She took over the throne of the Holkar dynasty after her husband, Shree Khanderao Holkar, was killed during the Battle of Kumbher in 1754. Her father-in-law Malhar Rao Holkar also died twelve years later. Having Tukoji Rao Holkar as her army chief, she personally led the troops in battle against the invaders. More than her commanding skills, she is known and respected for building Hindu temples and *dharamshala*s across Bharat.

'She personally inherited a fund estimated at about sixteen crore rupees, which was dedicated to charity and building temples. In today's value, this would amount to billions. Some of her notable works include Shri Vishweshwar Temple in Amarkantak, Shri Ram Temple, Shri Treta Ram Temple, Shri Bhairav Temple and

Nageshwar/Siddhnath Temple. She also contributed to the Sharayu Ghat and various dharamshalas in Ayodhya, Badrinath Temple in Badrinath, the Garden and Warm Water Kund at Dev Prayag, as well as numerous temples and ghats in Ganpati, Pandurang, Jaleshwar, Khandoba and Tirthraj. Additionally, her projects encompassed fire temples at Belur, Pranpratishta of Shri Ramchandra at Chitrakoot, Vishwanath, Kedarnath, Annapurna and Bhairav; many dharmashalas at Gangotri, numerous temples, ghats and dharmashalas in Maheshwar, including Mamaleshwar Mahadev and Amaleshwar, Trimbakeshwar Temples, Gauri Somnath Temple and dharmashalas with water resources in Omkareshwar. Shri Ram Temple, Gora Mahadev Temple, dharmashalas, Vishweshwar Temple, and Ramghat in Panchvati; Hanuman Temple, Shri Radha Krishna Temple in Rameshwaram; Shri Ramchandra Temple in Puri, alongside its dharmashala and garden; many temples including Shrinathji and Govardhan Ram Temples in Rishikesh; Chintaman Ganapati, Janardhan, and various Shiva temples and ghats in Ujjain; Kashi Vishwanath Temple, Shri Tarakeshwar, Shri Gangaji, and many Shiva temples and ghats, including Manikarnika Ghat and Sheetla Ghat in Kashi.

'But there are many more equally great names that have either been lost to history or have not received the recognition they deserve. Names like Rani Talash Kunwari, also known as Purvanchal's Rani Lakshmibai, a Durgvanshi Dikhit princess married to Raja Jung Bahadur Singh Kalhans of Amroha, Basti in present-day Uttar Pradesh.

After the demise of her husband, Raja Jung Bahadur Singh, she took control of the estate in 1853. She protested and stood heroically against British forces in the Revolt of 1857 and sacrificed herself with her own dagger before being captured by her enemies.

'Another name that is lesser known in present-day Bharat is Nak-Kati Rani, whose real name was Rani Karnavati Parmar. After losing her husband, King Mahipati Shah Parmar of the Garhwal kingdom, in 1631, Rani Karnavati, ruled the kingdom on behalf of her seven-year-old son, Prithvipati Shah. She successfully defended the kingdom against invaders and ruled for many years to come, during which she resisted an invasion by the Mughal army led by Najabat Khan in 1640. She started the trend of cutting the noses of the Mughal invaders and other enemies who attacked her kingdom. In time, she earned the nickname Nak-Kati Rani.

'Imagine a Rajkumari back in 1730, fluent in Urdu, English and French. Trained in the art of warfare and martial arts. Rani Velu Nachiyar was a rare woman of the seventeenth century. When British forces seized the kingdom after her husband's death, she was resolute to reclaim it. She planned and assembled allies for an attack and trained an army of females for warfare known as "Udaiyaat" and defeated the British forces to reclaim her throne. Due to her courage and determination, the queen is fondly remembered as "Veeramangai". Sadly, only a few people know about her today.

'It's just not about the Rajkumaris and the queens of my soil, it's about the hidden fearlessness and devotion in every woman towards the duties of their dharma. Hada Rani Chauhan is a testament to history, like thousands of other women who chose to sacrifice themselves rather than become the playthings and pleasures of their enemies. Hada Rani is a familiar name in Mewar, but the rest of the Bharat is ignorant about her deeds. She was the daughter of a Hada Chauhan Rajput, married to a Chundawat ruler of Salumbar in Mewar who sacrificed herself to motivate her husband to go to war.

'It so happened that when the King of Mewar, Maharana Raj Singh, ordered his commander to join the battle against Aurangzeb. The commander was hesitant to do so because he was married just a few days earlier, and his love for his wife was overshadowing his duty to his motherland and the honour of the Rajputs. He shared this with his wife Hada Rani and requested a memento from her to take along to the battlefield. Realizing that the obstacle to his duties for Mewar was her love, she cut off her own head and asked her guards to put it on a plate. It was covered with a cloth after her death and presented it to her husband. Devastated by her actions but realizing his duty and feeling proud of his love, the commander hung her head on his neck and fought courageously.

'We have all heard and sung for Chhatrapati Shivaji Maharaj, but people hardly know about his daughter-in-law, Maharani Tarabai Bhonsle, a bold and challenging substitute of the Maratha Empire during a crucial period of the land's history. After the death of her husband, Chhatrapati Rajaram in 1700, Tarabai took charge as a caretaker for her young son, Shivaji II. She was known for her daring and gutsy decisions during the Maratha resistance against the Mughals. Tarabai was a skilled strategist who successfully mobilized the Maratha forces, ensuring the empire remained united and did not fracture under her command. Her leadership towered over her image and stature as one of the most formidable lady rulers in Maratha history.

'This country and its generations owe a debt to these remarkable women, and they should be celebrated as fervently as cricketers and actors.'

The nameless Naga wished that this story would encourage the generations of today, instilling in them the courage, tenacity and defiance of these remarkable ladies. As he considered the passing of time, he saw the stark differences in the roles, perspectives and observations of women in modern society.

'Nowadays, it's common to see women driving vehicles with decals that read "papa's princess" or "daddy's darling". But in the past, women were more likely to ride horses and fight with swords to be priceless treasures,' said the nameless Naga.

'But doesn't the word princess and rajkumari mean the same?' asked the confused follower.

'No, it does not. The wordly meaning may be the same, but the depth of both is entirely different. Close your eyes and imagine what you see when I say "princess" and tell me what changes in your imagination when I say "Rajkumari".'

The young Naga opened his eyes in amazement as if he had discovered it all, and the nameless Naga put his thoughts into words.

'They were not as delicate as a princess, wearing a pink frock and a light tiara on their heads, waiting for a prince as the final goals of their lives, to be married and dependent. They were strong as a Rajkumari who led their troops and fought like Durga and Kali. They were not confined to just love, above that was their land that they treated as their mother. Their culture was their pride and respect were their jewels. Their culture, their motherland and their respect came above their love and were non-negotiable. The shift from a warrior's role to that of a beloved daughter within societal norms highlights the evolving times. The resilient spirit, however, endures and inspires the next generation despite these changes.'

Upon discovering the queen's death, the princess felt a deep compulsion to return to her realm out of the sense of duty. She told Krishna with a heavy heart, 'I have to go back to reassure and uplift my people and tell them of the sad news.'

The princess landed in Gokul with a contingent of Durga Defence Forces, consisting of about 300 warriors and 100 female horse riders. Whereas the queen's Shakti Sena, that had a strength of 1000 women warriors, 250 horses, fifty elephants and two cannons, suffered heavy losses and was reduced to around 250 soldiers, 100 horse riders and five elephants, who returned to reunite with the army back in the kingdom. Around 400 more warriors, comprising both Shakti Sena and Durga Defence Forces still stood ready, having stayed behind to defend their own walls if need be. It was challenging for the princess to balance her responsibility towards Gokul and her kingdom with the forthcoming threat from Abdali and his forces at the same time.

The princess found it difficult to simultaneously manage her duty to her country and the impending threat posed by Abdali and his army. Krishna knew that she would have to return to her kingdom at Surajgarh at once to regroup her strength and assure her people that the kingdom is not orphaned, and she is still alive to lead and protect them.

Seeing her struggle, Krishna offered the princess some encouragement and hope. Before she departed for her kingdom, Krishna gathered everyone, including me, and revealed a long-kept secret about the silent meeting with the masked men that had long distressed everyone's interest and suspicion. Krishna desired to be honest with them.

'The men in masks that you all noticed a few days back on the outskirts of Gokul, they were my agents, my confidants. Their mission was to set up barriers and obstacles so that they slow down Abdali's force. I deployed them to lay traps, poison wells and produce distractions aimed at impeding Abdali's progress in order to give us more time to fortify our defences and get ready for the looming storm,' he said.

Everyone looked at each other, their doubts gave way to gratitude and understanding.

The princess was worried that Abdali's journey would cross the quickest path back to her country, but Krishna reassured her by saying, 'Princess, you don't have to worry as all necessary steps have already been taken to block their progress towards Surajgarh. By now, they must have understood that going towards Surajgarh would need the sacrifice of more men as the wells to the route are poisoned. The queen's courage and strategies underlined that she has not left her forts defenceless, and now Abdali has to choose if his priority is to destroy Gokul or break the defences of Surajgarh and delay his original mission to reach us here. I am sure he will leave Surajgarh later and attack Gokul now, though Abdali's army will need more time than they expected to reach here too. Your path is safe, and you can move without any blockades.'

This diversion would impede their advancement even more, giving the princess additional time to return securely to her realm and for Gokul's defences to be reinforced. As Princess Chandrika was getting ready to go to Surajgarh, the tension in Gokul was almost at its highest point. She was aware that it was her responsibility to tell her people about the queen's passing and reassure them of her leadership and presence.

Princess Chandrika was reassured by Krishna once more. He gave her a map of a safe passage to Surajgarh and back. She gave him a nod in appreciation of his brilliant strategy and forethought.

She then got on her horse, trailed by her tiny group of eleven horse-women. 'I will be back, and I will be back with more soldiers. Till then, you have to hold your ground. I was the princess and the commander-in-chief to my queen. Now when I am compelled to take her seat, I have a request to make to you,' she said.

'Please order, Princess,' said Krishna.

'It will be my honour if you accept the position of my commander-in-chief and lead the army. I request you to bless me and Surajgarh by leading us all,' said the princess.

Krishna had tears in his eyes. He was overwhelmed and his throat choked while he was trying to express his gratitude verbally. That was enough for the princess to understand that Krishna was ready to serve.

'Commander-in-chief, I order you to hold your ground till I return. You are not allowed to die till my return.'

Krishna's eyes were shining with the power of the new command from his queen, energizing everyone present and making them feel invigorated.

With a handful of soldiers, the new queen left Krishna and the remaining defenders, who redirected their focus to the impending threat.

With every second that passed, the sense of seriousness and impending battle increased as Abdali's massive invasion seemed to get bigger.

Krishna was right as Abdali's massive army, still estimated to be 25,000 strong, advanced relentlessly towards Gokul from all three cardinal directions. In the meantime, hundreds of Abdali's soldiers perished at the poisoned wells along their path and hundreds of other men were too sick to even stand. It was not just the soldiers who were falling ill. As many as 250 horses were also suffering and dying. The count of dead men and animals was climbing, but Abdali kept pressing forward, approaching Gokul from three directions. Seven thousand warriors from the east, commanded by Sarfaraz, were standing on the outskirts of Gokul. There were another eight thousand from the south, under the command of Zoravar and Malik Akhtar, and ten thousand from the west directly walking under the banner of Abdali himself. Their strength was frightening and scary.

They moved like a tsunami, their purpose singular and obvious, and the sun's reflection on their weapons created a brilliant glow that signalled their approach with an air of strength. However, as these three tremendous armies moved towards Gokul at lightning speed, a second, equally powerful movement emerged from the north. The warrior Naga sadhus, numbering in hundreds, were moving in unison. They broke out of the Himalayas, a group of 1451 Nagas, falling down like an avalanche. With their unwavering conviction and resolve as identification and armed with magically powered weapons, they embodied a spirit that defied defeat and would not submit.

As the troops converged, there was a sense of an impending epic battle, as if all the powerful forces were gathering at one central location to oppose one another. The weight of approaching forces caused the ground to quake and shiver. The shadow of the battle seemed to descend from the sky.

'Har Har Mahadev! Har Har Mahadev' echoed the promise of bravery and retribution. This enormous conflict was certain to be a spectacular display of bravery and strategy, one that would go down in history. Everything was ready for a titanic battle that would determine Gokul's future.

After arriving at Gokul initially with his regiment from one side of the nation, Sarfaraz, the brother of Sardar Khan observed the situation and concluded that Gokul had very limited defenders.

'Everyone who gets in our way must move aside. Let us launch an attack and show the king this victory as a sign of our triumph,' stated Commander Sarfaraz.

'However, the king hasn't issued such an order,' his underling warned.

'What relevance does it have? By eliminating these individuals and demolishing Gokul, we will lessen the king's task. Rather than being upset, he will be happy when you give him a gift—Gokul,' Commander Sarfaraz answered, with ambition in his eyes, and chose to assault Gokul the next morning.

Gokul was now on the verge of a huge struggle with enormous stakes and predictable results of defeat and destruction. The defenders, resolute and fierce, prepared for the inevitable clash without knowing what the next morning was about to bring them. The Naga warriors still needed more time to reach Gokul, but time was up.

The outcome teetered on the brink of fate, and what would happen next remained a mystery. The residents of Gokul, their hearts racing, imagining the storm of death moving in, knowing that their cherished home might not survive.

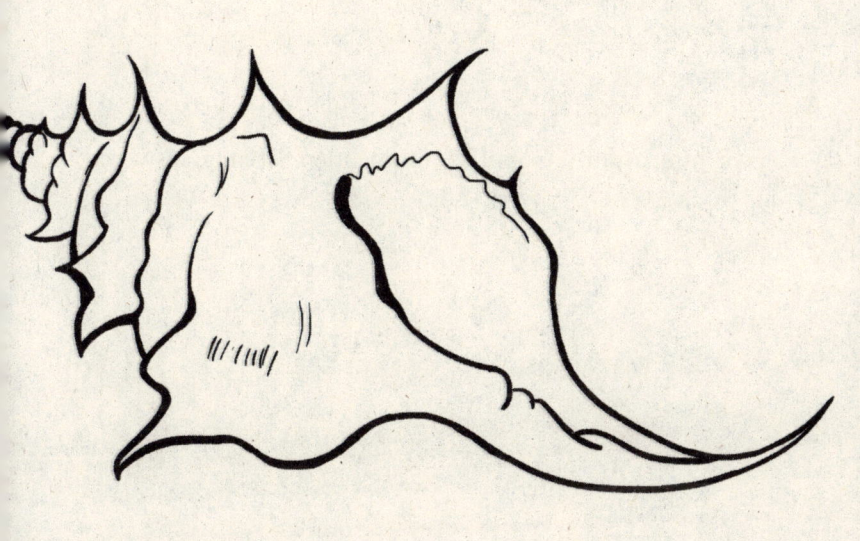

12

Why Not Fight?

At sunset, Krishna gathered the villagers and everyone else, including Vedant and his soldiers, myself, and the female warriors of the Durga Defence Forces, and spoke to us all: 'Brothers and sisters, I can see the fear in your eyes which ought to be there because we are humans made up with the elements of nature. But those men coming to ruin our mud and blood are unnatural and inhumane. They will not spare you and your children even if they find you harmless and innocent. And if they choose to keep you alive, you will be stripped of your beliefs, your family, your dharma, your clothes, your self-respect, your dignity, your will to live and your right to freedom. It will be worse than death for you all. We must choose to be fearless; be courageous enough to fight against these enemies of humanity. They are powerful and ruthless, but they are not unbeatable. You all need to realize one thing that you are no mere villagers, but soldiers who are going to battle hard against them to save your homes, your families and your honour. And above all, your dharma. Isn't it your duty to protect it? Our fate in this war is uncertain, but our actions and determination must not waver.'

Krishna looked around, making eye contact with the doubtful villagers, and continued, 'If you will trade your land, your dharma and your beliefs for food, clothes and shelter, they will one day snatch your bread, strip you off your clothes and burn your homes. It's not the time to fly away in fear, it's the time to be faithful and bear what comes ahead as a huge joint family. I ask you now, what do you choose? To live in fear or to fight for your freedom?'

'Krishna was absolutely right then, and his words resonate with the present as well. If today's generation does not wake up to his statement, the genocide in Kashmir will repeat itself across the country. They will starve us as slaves, nude us as animals and burn us as corpses. Our society is collectively suffering from dementia. They need to wake up to reality and learn from history. Today's generation needs to be unforgiving and unforgetting to such heinous incidents that happened in the past if they don't want to be repeated with their own women and children.' The nameless Naga appeared to be seething with anger. He took a pause to calm himself down and spoke further.

With a mix of sorrow and pride, Krishna continued, 'Before you make your decision, just think of the fierce and valiant Naga sadhus who fought until their last breath against these ruthless invaders and sacrificed their lives for you all and Gokul. Why should I or Adhiraj or the

Durga Defence Forces or any Naga fight for you when you don't have the spine to stand for your own women and children? In the battle of Gokul, Ajaa and Shambhu ji will be remembered forever for holding the frontline until their last breath, never once considering their own lives, even for a moment. Think about Dulari, a mere animal in the eyes of some; she gave up her life protecting your sacred land. Vanraaj, who never belonged to Gokul, fought with all his might without considering where he came from but where his heart lay—with us, with our land. For Gokul, for dharma.'

Krishna's voice grew louder and louder now. It was filled with admiration and determination. 'Look at these women of the Durga Defence Forces. Women who have stepped forward to fight, not because they were asked to but because they chose willingly to lay down their lives for Gokul without even thinking of their own safety. They are equally your responsibility as much as you are theirs. If they can fight, then so can you. They all have shown us their love for our land, our dharma. Now it's our chance!'

Vedant took a step forward and spoke, 'Krishna is right. We cannot choose to live forever, but we can choose how we die. Do you all want to die like cowards or with heads held high, dying and fighting for our land and our loved ones? When we know that we are all going to die one day then why not die with respect and dignity rather than in fear? Because if we fall, we will be remembered in history as those who did not bow to oppression. Think!'

There was a pause in the conversation between Krishna and the villagers. Suddenly, an old man with excess wrinkles that proved his experience and understanding about life, stepped forward and said in a trembling voice, 'Why die in fright? Why not fight?'

There was a change in the attitude, expressions and body language of all the villagers, as the headman's words ignited a spark in them.

'The gods are with us, and we are strong. So, as commander-in-chief of our army, I ask you again, my warriors, will you stand with me and fight?' screamed Vedant, backing Krishna.

The villagers nodded in agreement and raised their weapons, ready to stand by Krishna and fight for their land.

'Tell us what you want us to do,' said a young villager, taking the authority on behalf of the villagers.

'We strike them in the dark,' replied Krishna with confidence as if he already had a plan in place for Afghans.

It was finally decided that Gokul would attack the Afghan forces before the first light of the sun touched the land.

Krishna and his troops decided to strike the enemy when they least expected it. With the advantage of darkness, every move had to be precise, as each strike would be critical. He divided the roles of each of his allies. The main force would create chaos and attack guards silently, ensuring that no alarm is raised while circling the camp. The Durga Defence warriors would play a vital role by destroying the enemy's water supplies, food reserves and other important resources.

The Durga Sena split into small groups, targeting different sections of the camp on orders.

In the spur of the moment, Krishna's men started taking down the first line of soldiers at the peripheries silently like a group of ghosts. The first of them was Vedant who moved like a shadow, cheating detection.

Villagers were given the responsibility of setting fire to the camp. They ignited the tents of the Afghan soldiers, who slept clueless. Although the motive was to eliminate the high ranks of the opponent's army, no one knew their exact location. Therefore, the best strategy was to set everything ablaze, leaving no one alive.

As the tents started to burn, there was utter confusion among the Afghan army. To save themselves at that moment, they ran as quickly as they could out of the chaos. It looked like a swarm of bees fleeing their hives when they were set aflame. As one of the Afghans ran for water reserves to extinguish the fire, many of their burning soldiers screamed and ran for their lives. But all the water reserves were emptied before the fire started. The visuals of burning soldiers were haunting and terrorizing for everyone, including the villagers and the Durga Defence Forces who, orchestrated the entire scene. Sarfaraz Khan, who thought he would have an easy day the next morning, was devastated with the visuals in the dark.

When everybody unarmed ran out of the burning tents, Krishna was ready with his people to kill them with swords. A small group of women archers was positioned at a distance to target the Afghans, using the fire of the burning soldiers that helped them identify and aim at their enemies easily and quickly. Vedant and his men charged through them on horseback, cutting and slicing the men like dry bushes, testing the sharpness of their blades in preparation for the real battle in the morning.

As the sky showed a little light and the sun showed signs of rising, Krishna ordered everyone to return to their base, as they were becoming visible at the break of dawn. As all of them ran back to the Gokul camps, some Afghan soldiers saw a few old men who could not keep up with the rest. The Afghans spotted them running towards their fellow soldiers and decided to chase the unarmed villagers by any means possible. They ran behind them without their armours and shields. Some even rode their horses bare-chested, having just woken up to chaos everywhere. They chased the villagers, thinking they could easily kill them in the vast barren lands that the barefoot and untrained villagers had to cross to reach their camp. The villagers ran as fast as they could, while the Afghans on horseback, followed by men running with swords in hand, chased them at full speed and with fierce rage. The last few villagers ran past a marker and raised their hands. The Afghans were left wondering why they had done so. There were many sacks of hay placed at equal distance from each other. Before the Afghans could understand anything, they noticed the marks on the ground and a shower of arrows rained on them. The villagers raised their hands to signal that they had reached on the safer side and everyone behind them were now in the shooters' ranges. The arrows struck the horses and the unarmoured, shieldless, provoked and disorganized Afghans from above. The darts sent by the queen were launched from the multiple arrow-launching machines that Krishna had prepared with the help of the village carpenters while preparing for the battle. The hand-operated wooden shooters showered arrows in such quantities that it was nearly impossible to keep an eye out and dodge them. Many horsemen fell, broke their bones and necks. Others behind them on foot were struck to death. A few tried to run back towards their camps but were too late. The few Afghan troops who crossed the mark to safety and entered the terrain with sacks of hay, were attacked by the same villagers who ran before them to lure them into the trap planned by Krishna. The villagers and soldiers cheered in a sense of victory, though they knew it was not even ten per cent of the total army they had to face.

The commander gathered all his soldiers. They still numbered more than a thousand against barely a hundred men and women, both trained and untrained. They got into a formation, this time with their shields covering their bodies from the front as they marched. They successfully reached and crossed the safety marks, still wondering why hay sacks were placed in a formation. Some of the soldiers walked to the sacks and stabbed them to check if any enemies were hiding inside, but no bodies bled beneath the sacks.

Krishna fitted an arrow to his bow and ignited its tip. Looking at him, the women warriors too nocked the burning arrows. Together, all of them shot arrows on the hay sacks. They started burning immediately, producing thick and dense smoke all around that obscured the vision of the Afghan army. This thick smoke filled the air and restricted them from moving with their commander. The soldiers lifted their shields in front of them to be protected from the wooden arrow shooters. However, they did not anticipate that Vedant's archers were hiding on both their sides.

An announcement signalled death for the formation marching towards Gokul. The announcement was in the voice of Krishna and the word was: 'Shoot!' This time, the arrows flew from both sides, piercing the bodies and heads of the soldiers. The formation broke as they could hardly see anything in the smoke. Many started choking and coughing. The others, anticipating arrows from their sides, turned left and right with their shields. Many fell in the first wave of arrows, creating gaps and breaking the formations. The Afghans then heard the sound of hooves pounding from both sides. Five horses from both sides came rushing, breaking their shields and faces with the weapons held by the riders. Before they could see or do something, the horse riders emerged from the left and right and vanished again in opposite directions, aided by the smoke that continued to choke the men.

The remaining hundreds prepared themselves for another attack of horse riders and archers from both sides, but Krishna's intelligence and strategy proved them wrong again.

By this time, the wooden arrow shooters were reloaded and ready to fire again. All that the Afghan soldiers could hear before facing their deaths was the sound of arrows slicing through the air before striking them.

When the smoke produced by the fire vanished, the count of the dead was clear. Krishna's commanding skills killed nearly 500 Afghan soldiers without losing even one of his. Everybody on the side of saving Gokul realized how right the princess was to appoint Krishna as her commander-in-chief.

The fire, along with its smoke, provided a momentary advantage for the Gokul defenders, lasting only until the ground was cleared of dry bushes to burn and the fresh morning air dispersed the smoke. As it happened, fierce one-on-one battles erupted. Krishna and his troop still had an upper hand as the Afghan soldiers were unprepared, unarmed and disoriented. Arrows flew from both sides and the villagers were prepared. But as the battle stormed on, another Afghan commander, Zoravar, followed by Malik Akhtar, joined the fight with another 8000 soldiers and now the villagers were trapped between two forces. Surrounded, the villagers saw the size of the Afghan army that was several times larger than their own numbers. Acknowledging the urgency of the situation, Krishna's battle-hardened men rushed into action with haste. Standing steadfast with his soldiers, Krishna ordered them to continue fighting and striking their adversaries, instinctively reminding them that one soldier could take down one man.

All of them trembled when they saw the first villager fall to the ground in two halves, struck down by the simultaneous slashes of many swords aimed at the man standing at the front of the line. With this brutal death, they all knew that it wouldn't be long before the last of them standing would fall before the massive army that looked like a sea ready to swallow a well. Now the villagers, along with the Durga Defence army and everyone fighting for Gokul, were surrounded from all sides. The faces of the villagers held the terror of death and both sides stopped fighting. The Afghans were smiling, waiting for the surrender. The villagers were frightened and waiting to die. Seeing that Krishna and his troops were surrounded by a merciless army, Vedant, with terror in his eyes, said, 'Krishna, we are surrounded. It is better we surrender than die. It's hopeless to continue fighting from here on. We stand no chance.'

As both sides waited for the first blow, Krishna turned back with a calm smirk and replied, 'This is not a hopeless situation, rather it's a blessing.' Vedant and everybody hearing Krishna were surprised by the statement, trying to understand what he meant.

'There is no doubt that we are surrounded from all sides, which means that we don't have to aim for our targets precisely anymore. Instead, now we can strike our weapons in any direction without aiming and thinking and an enemy will be hit and fall certainly. What better can happen? Feel blessed by this situation of luck and strike with full force till either they fall, or you do. At least ten of their army's men should fall before you fall. That must be the target for each one of us.'

Krishna's bravery motivated the villagers, including Vedant. They realized that surrendering was not an option, so everyone prepared to face their surroundings.

Krishna further continued, 'Forget about your lives, simply keep pounding and battling. Keep in mind that every hit you land reduces one soldier of Abdali's army.' Even the army commander-in-chief of Abdali's army and their soldiers felt challenged by Krishna's strong voice. 'Allow them to fall because of our bravery.'

Krishna had encountered situations similar to this in previous fights, remembering how a handful of Nagas battled the army of Sardar Khan with courage and determination.

Listening to Krishna's words of encouragement, a mocking laughter erupted among the ranks of the Afghan soldiers. The opposing soldiers knew they had the upper hand and there was no way they could be defeated by a bunch of inexperienced and untrained civilians backed by trained and seasoned women. The laughter grew louder, mocking the little but stubborn defenders. Their giggles echoed through the village to the temples where the women and children were hidden in. I was the only Naga who survived the bloody battle of Gokul under the trident of Ajaa and Shambhu ji, and I was about to see the same bloodshed again. I tightened my grip on the sword and axe and murmured 'Har Har Mahadev' while their hoots continued mocking the little group of defenders of Gokul. However, this moment didn't last long for them.

Just when they felt as if death was looming over them, shaking the foundation of their determination and bravery under the demonic laugh of the Afghans, a loud noise suddenly filled the air, drowning out the mocking laughter.

It was cut short by a powerful, resonant sound of a conch being blown with a crescendo of power and purity, reverberating across the land. It grew louder with each

passing moment, sending shivers down the spines of all
who heard it. The sound pierced through the battlefield and
echoed in the air. Everyone turned toward the source of
the sound, and while all were surprised, the most astonished
of all was I, then known as Adhiraj, upon discovering the
source of the sound.

It was Gajraaj, the son of brave Dulari, raising his trunk
high as he blew the conch for the very first time in his life.
It was as if the earth was responding to the call of the divine.

The Afghan soldiers, who had been hooting and
laughing at the surrounded defenders, now stood frozen.
They sensed the arrival of something far greater than they
had anticipated.

It felt like the air was charged with the electric energy
of looming payback. That was through the blurred vision
of figures appearing with dust swirling in the air. There
were trembling movements with the thunderous sound of
approaching footsteps, as if the beasts of war themselves were
showing up. Slowly, the blurred figures became clear, and the
sight was awe-inspiring. It was the army of Naga sadhus led by
Dhruv and Mathadhish. They were the defenders of dharma,
coming to the aid of the defenders of Gokul. The fierce
warriors, advanced towards the battlefield with their bare
chests smeared with ash, and their wild, matted hair flowed
like the mane of a lion. They chanted 'Har Har Mahadev'
loudly. Later, the sound grew louder and more powerful than
the laughs of the enemies of humankind. As the Naga sadhus
drew nearer, the chant transformed into a forceful crescendo
that seemed to alter every heartbeat throbbing within the

chests, but also filling the hearts of villagers, Krishna's soldiers and others with a sense of hope and strength.

That was the day I learned the actual meaning of 'Har Har Mahadev'.

Madhav following the nameless Naga, clueless of where they were heading. He couldn't contain his urge to know what Adhiraj learned about 'Har Har Mahadev'. And so, he asked, 'What did you learn?'

'"Har Har Mahadev" means "O Mahadev, come and destroy the darkness and negate the negativity". "Har" means "eradicate" or "terminate". It felt as if Shiva truly heard my appeal of "Har Har Mahadev".'

A sonorous shout of 'Har Har Mahadev' grew louder and louder in the distance. The mocking soldiers suddenly halted, their features changing from haughtiness to bewilderment and terror.

Dhruv emerged from the northern outskirts of the settlement, leading a large group of Naga sadhus. With unflinching determination, these soldiers advanced—fierce and otherworldly.

The sun glinted on their bodies, decorated with symbols of authority and sacred ash. They possessed a variety of deadly weapons, each more potent than the other. The Naga sadhus combined their varied magical abilities, creating a powerful force that sent shivers down the spine of Abdali's troops led by Sarfaraz Khan.

The Afghan soldiers, who moments before had felt victorious, were now in the grip of total uncertainty and instability, as realization dawned on them that they were not just fighting with men, but against the forces of nature. The ones surrounding Krishna and his people were suddenly surrounded from both sides. Krishna, along with his defenders from within and Dhruv, leading his forces from the outside, were ready to reduce the Afghans to nothing.

Eyes shining with the light of truth, Krishna looked at Vedant and said, 'Do you see? This is not just a battle of Gokul anymore, but of the army of gods against asuras, and we, as humans, must choose which side we stand with. We are not here to just fight for our lives, but for the truth, for the very soul of our land and the sound of our heart.'

Seemingly, the tides of battle had turned, and the dark forces of the invaders were stunned by the light of dharma.

13

Death Traps

The battleground changed in a matter of minutes. The ruthless army of Abdali, once the hunters, were suddenly the prey. They found themselves imprisoned in a lethal formation called *chakravyuh*, a configuration evocative of the old battlefield. Neelkanth, still flying above the battleground, had an aerial view of the chakravyuh. It looked magnificent as if choreographed by some perfectionist. With thousands of Abdali's warriors encircling them, Krishna and his soldiers stood in the middle, facing the onslaught. However, the formidable Naga sadhus, under the command of the chief Mathadhish following Dhruv, had now surrounded this core group of enemies led by Sarfaraz Khan, who thought of gifting the heads of the Gokul residents to Abdali on his arrival.

With the arrival of Dhruv and the Naga sadhus, Krishna and his men were at the peak of their strength. The opponents who had appeared unbeatable were now under attack from both inside and outside their circle. From the outer side, the Naga sadhus surged with the force of a hurricane, while Krishna's resolute defenders struck with the ferocity of a volcano attempting to break through the mountain.

The moment served as a tribute to the strength of human solidarity and the unbreakable spirit of devotees of Shiva. The tide began to turn as the chants of 'Har Har Mahadev' reverberated throughout the battlefield. Once bold and merciless, Abdali's soldiers now trembled at the sight of death staring them in the eyes.

The struggle of strength and weaponry outside Gokul turned into a symphony of courage and combat. An epic battle ensued, where faith shaped the fate of the defenders, and devotion transformed defeat into the death of the demolishers. Like a heavenly response, the Nagas had shown up at the right time to save them, just as I called Mahadev when they were in need. But there was so much more to unfold in the battle of Gokul to transform it into a war of the worshipers.

An alarming image shattered the calm of the early morning as the sun rose above Gokul, casting a powerful glow with its golden rays that made the weapons of Nagas gleam dangerously, as if they were not ordinary weapons but the very arms of the gods. Gajraaj was looking at all of it, and the seriousness of the situation made his heart race. He picked up my antique shankh again and blew into it, producing a sound that reverberated with the echoes of ancient battles, all with a decisive urgency. The first shankh that he blew served as a welcome for the Nagas and a warning for the Afghans. This time, it was an announcement of war, prompting Krishna to address his warriors with resolute and self-assured intent. 'Sons of Gokul, get your weapons ready. Your targets have changed now. Each one of your new targets today is to eliminate fifty enemy soldiers. Let each hit be precise and unflinching. With the Naga sadhus at our back, we carve our path out of the mouth of death to victory with every strike.'

This time, no Afghan dared laugh at Krishna's words; instead, they shattered their morale into a thousand pieces.

Encircled on all sides, Krishna reflected on previous conflicts. He remembered the fierce and heroic battle the Nagas had waged under the beacon of Ajaa and Shambhu ji, with the one and only idea that they must prevail at any cost.

As the Afghan soldiers found themselves trapped between the powerful Nagas from the outside and Krishna with his army from within, panic spread amongst their ranks. They realized there seemed to be no escape. To their surprise, they felt the presence of dominating towering figures—the giant Nagas—who were crushing enemies under the leadership of Mahakaay. The giants were crushing the horses and camels while lifting the Afghan soldiers and tossing them through the air like mere toys. These soldiers who were thrown from one side of the battlefield to the other were falling right into the waiting gaze of the hypnotizing Nagas. These hypnotists wasted no time in locking their glowing eyes on the soldiers, disorienting them and transforming them into mindless allies. Those hypnotized men began to move calmly and silently towards Gokul like obedient slaves following one Naga sadhu.

Looking at this unbelievable view, a female warrior asked, 'What will these Naga do with all these Afghan soldiers?'

The other soldier of Durga Defence replied, 'Whatever they wish to.'

'What do you mean?' asked the warrior again. The respondent gestured towards the hypnotized Afghans. The Naga walking ahead of the hypontized Afghans said, 'Say together, Bum Bum Bhole.'

All of them in sync followed and repeated 'Bum Bum Bhole' as ordered.

Witnessing the otherworldly powers of the Nagas, Krishna and his army were now filled with hope and determination. The battlefield, once filled with the clashing of swords and battle cries, now echoed with terror and utter confusion.

The Afghan soldiers, who had initially been confident about their strength, both in numbers and tactics, were now totally devastated by their rapidly dwindling ranks. The reason were the fearsome Nagas and their supernatural powers.

Seeing the tables turning against him, Sarfaraz impatiently charged on one of the giants in anger with a small group of horsemen. It was surely a hasty and anxious move, resulting in Sarfaraz and his horse falling to the ground. Many more of his men following him were tossed like toys by the giants. Some of them were crushed under heavy feet, shattering rib cages and spines, while Sarfaraz could only watch helplessly. Now, he knew what his brother might have faced in the battle of Gokul. He tried to stand back to regroup his scattered men and shouted, 'Hear me out, soldiers!' But before the soldiers around him could react to his voice, he caught the attention of a giant who picked him up and threw him far away to the masters of hypnotism. By shouting just before being thrown away, Sarfaraz unintentionally garnered an audience that witnessed his fate as he was tossed into the air, shattering the dying morale of the Afghans completely.

Panic gripped the soldiers to the extent that they began to flee back to their burnt camps, charred by the fires of war. Few villagers and Krishna's soldiers chased them and were eager to finish what they started. Krishna, the very next moment, yelled for the men to stop chasing the Afghans and warned them, 'You all need to stop right away as you don't know what awaits you on the other side!'

He was right once again, as the soldiers were running towards the reinforcement brought by the two commanders—Zoravar and Malik Akhtar—leading the troop. They intended to crush any resistance in Gokul. The battleground had blood and dead bodies, fire and smoke, screams of the dying and cheers of 'Har Har Mahadev'. On one side stood around 8000 foot soldiers, 600 horsemen, ten cannons and the remaining soldiers, horsemen and camels of Sarfaraz Khan's troops who were ready to kill under the command of the two commanders crueler than Sardar Khan and his brother. On the other side were around 1450 remaining Naga warriors, including me, wielding supernatural powers, along with some villagers under Krishna, Durga Defence Forces, and Vedant with his limited men—all the defenders of Gokul ready to die.

'We wait for Shehenshah's arrival! Till then, we will keep our distance from them and only use our cannons to bombard them so that we keep them engaged without engaging in face-to-face combat with these troops. Call all who have returned alive and get the cannons prepared for tomorrow morning. We need to know what we are fighting against before we face them again,' Commander Zoravar ordered after consulting with Malik Akhtar.

On the other hand, Neelkanth, manoeuvring in the sky, gathered information about the strength of the opposing forces they would encounter the next day, including the largest army led by Abdali himself, one that Gokul had never seen before, and reported back to one of the bird whisperers. This was the first time Neelkanth met the bird whisperer. The bird whisperer listened intently as Neelkanth recounted everything he had witnessed during the battle of Gokul, including the deaths of Vanraaj and Dulari, along with all the other Nagas. It gave a pretty good picture to all the other Naga sadhus when the same was narrated by the bird whisperer to all the others on his side.

Now was the time when all the forces in favour of Gokul met. The Nagas met the villagers while the women of the village prepared meals for everyone. The warriors of Durga Defence bowed and greeted the Naga warriors trained in all forms of fights.

Krishna and I met Dhruv and the chief Mathadhish.

'Ajaa was sure that you will reach and bring them all here to defend Gokul. You proved him right,' I spoke.

Dhruv, with hope in his eyes, asked, 'Where is Ajaa? And Shambhu ji? And how did you all manage to defend Gokul against Sardar Khan after I was sent to Himalayan ranges?'

Krishna and I exchanged glances, deciding how best to convey the message to him. I decided to be the voice, though it seemed from Dhruv's eyes that he was anticipating my unfortunate answer even before I started speaking. I broke the news of the demise of Ajaa and Shambhu ji to Dhruv and the chief Mathadhish. A silence filled with pure respect enveloped the temple we were in.

The silence was then broken by the chief Mathadhish, who said, 'I once met Shambhu and his Mathadhish was one of my best prodigies, extremely devoted and highly skilled in the mastery of hypnotism.'

'They all died a very proud and respectful death, chief. It is for them that Gokul still stands alive,' said Krishna.

'We shall save the village that they died for at any cost. Gather all heads! We need a plan,' said the chief Mathadhish.

'Plan! I have one,' replied Krishna.

'Defenders had fought bravely, still the greatest of all challenges was yet to come the next day—a day of reckoning—victory or defeat—depends on our synchronization,' said the chief.

'Today we saw the moment their commander fell; the soldiers were clueless and started running for their lives.

What if we kill Abdali before he reaches here?' asked Krishna.

The chief Mathadhish said, 'First strike will be ours. The tree talkers will take a safe passage tonight with the help of the villagers who know the path and some soldiers of the Durga Defence Forces will ensure that they reach the jungle safely. Tomorrow morning you will all ambush Abdali and his army, as and when they cross the jungle to reach Gokul.'

The tree talkers had their orders and so they immediately left the temple to prepare for the jungles.

'Abdali's army numbers in thousands. How can these nine Nagas possibly engage them?' Vedant cautiously voiced. The chief replied confidently, 'These tree talkers are not ordinary Naga sadhus, they are the commanders of the roots, trees and jungle itself. They can trap Abdali and his men. And for us all, nature will fight on their request. They have a strong bond with the plants and would use them as their weapons.'

Two of the villagers who were acquainted with the jungle and its surroundings volunteered to guide the special community along the path that Abdali was supposed to take. Four female warriors were chosen to escort them safely through the jungle and fight alongside them. As darkness was an added advantage, they slipped into the woods and used its canopy, twisted creepers and climbers to their favour and prepared for the ambush.

At the first light of dawn, the commanders ordered the mouths of the cannon to open and the booming sound echoed through the jungle for miles. The ground shook, and suddenly, hundreds of birds burst into the sky from all sides. They were of different species, sizes and colours. The bird whisperers, who could communicate with these aerial creatures, watched in awe as the birds flew towards the jungles, where the tree controllers were preparing to ambush Abdali.

Two giants tried to run and reach the cannons, dodging many attacks until one of them was struck in the chest and exploded. He began bleeding but managed to reach the first line of defence, which consisted of horses. The second line held soldiers, and the cannons were set in the third line, behind the horse cavalry and foot soldiers.

The giants killed many horses and soldiers while being attacked from all sides, causing the Afghans to fall before they could destroy the cannons.

'We have to destroy the cannons at all costs, or they will ensure the defeat and destruction of Gokul,' the chief said, his voice tense.

'We are ready to go in,' said the young commander of Durga Defence Forces. At this juncture, Krishna shared his experience, saying, 'That is exactly what they want. That is why they are not marching forward. They have archers waiting for us all. We will die without even killing a single Afghan, and the less we will be, the less time they will need to defeat us.'

'We can't just sit here waiting,' said the young female commander.

'No, we won't sit! We will walk,' replied Krishna. Everyone looked at him with confusion after this statement.

Krishna informed them about the underground trenches he had prepared in anticipation of the events of this day. He took Dhruv, the chief Mathadhish and the Durga Defence commander to the temple, behind which lay a large pit leading underground.

Krishna said, 'It divides into ten branches further. All of them have a dead end but if dug upwards, it will all vent out around different cannons placed strategically against us.'

'How did you know where to dig trenches according to the cannons?' Dhruv asked.

'I have fought many wars, and I have learned with my experience about the strategic placement of cannons for maximum destruction and minimum threat of the enemy reaching the cannons to destroy them. That is why it is never kept in the first line of defence. Those horsemen and foot soldiers are standing before it to ensure the safety of those cannons that can decide the victor of any war. Their strategy is clear and so is our counterattack.'

In no time, around fifty well trained fighter Nagas with fire torches in their hands entered the underground tunnel, which was wide open at the entrance and had enough space to walk side-by-side. However, as they advanced deeper, the tunnel narrowed, forcing them to move in a single line before splitting into ten different narrow routes. The Nagas divided themselves into groups of five before entering each tunnel. The villagers guiding them inside the tunnel instructed them all to extinguish their torches after a point. In the pitch-black darkness, the Nagas were unable to see even their hands while walking through the deep tunnel.

They could only feel the vibrations caused due by the firing of the cannons up the ground and the warmth of the earth under their feet. To help one another navigate, they placed their hands on each other's shoulders and marched forward in silence. The sound of the cannons constantly reminded them of the devastation happening in Gokul.

Reaching close to the junction, the Nagas experienced trembles and vibrations of the walls of the tunnels, making the urgency more intense. Each of them wanted to hurry, as time was of the essence, and with each cannon shot, more of Gokul was being reduced to ruins.

Meanwhile, above ground, Krishna stood helplessly, watching the cannons fire upon Gokul, destroying the spaces that I and Gajraaj along with him and Durga Defence Forces had remade. At the same time, the tree talkers, hidden in the dense jungle along with the Durga Defence soldiers and villagers, were also waiting to ambush and strike Abdali's forces. Neelkanth soared through the sky, using its sharp eyes to monitor the advancing and unstoppable army approaching the jungle with thunderous force.

The Nagas walking underground passed beneath the horse cavalry and the vast army of men standing above. They reached the dead end of the tunnel and began to dig upward with utmost caution, creating a vent through which they could emerge to the surface. In no time, they could see light as the last layer of mud fell right on their faces, and unhesitatingly, one of them erupted into the air from the pit, slicing the soldiers around him with the sword he carried in both grips. This act of unbelievable bravery occurred at nine more places, where each hole in the ground saw a Naga erupting from the ground, creating space and time for the others to crawl out. Like shadows, the first of every pit rushed towards the nearest cannon, and the other four protected the one in the centre as shields around them.

Slowly, all the groups of four protected the fifth in the centre with their swords clashing in the light. The fifth position at the centre in all formations was occupied by the flame emitters, who used a liquid stored in their mouths to unleash fire powerful enough to incinerate everything in its path. The warriors moved toward the cannons, and one by one, the cannonballs stacked near them were set alight by the fire breathers. Within a fraction of a second, flames erupted and engulfed the nearby cannons.

The Nagas died, some in battle and others due to the blast from the nearby cannonballs, but many Afghans perished alongside them as well. While some were killed by the Naga swords, others died due to the selfless determination of the Nagas fighting for their temples, religion and the brothers still alive on the other side with the chief Mathadhish. Several blasts occurred, each near a cannon, but the biggest explosion was yet to come.

The most daring group out of all captured a nearby tent filled with more cannonballs. The Afghan soldiers from all sides rushed towards the cannonball storage tent and found four Nagas guarding it from four sides.

'Kill them all and capture it back. That tent has all the cannonballs we need,' screamed a senior soldier. Every

Afghan soldier who heard the command ran towards one of the four Nagas.

'Not now! Hold your ground,' screamed the oldest Naga. They were more than two hundred Afghans running towards the tent, screaming in hatred and ready to chop the four Nagas into small pieces. The Nagas, with no shields or armours and only two weapons in hand, stood on all four sides of the tent walls, ready to face more than fifty Afghan soldiers each.

'Now?' shouted the fifth Naga from inside the tent, questioning the timing.

'Not yet,' came the reply from outside.

The Afghans attacked and the Nagas defended, but they were too many in number against each one of them. Many Afghan throats were slashed, while the Nagas suffered cuts across various parts of their bodies from the blades.

'Moksh Mahadev,' yelled a Naga warrior. Those were his last words before he died. The other three Nagas, lying on the ground yet still cutting and slashing the Afghans, heard it.

Within a few moments, two more Nagas heard the same line from another dying Naga: 'Moksh Mahadev.'

Now the remaining two Nagas had fallen on the ground, their souls ready to leave their bodies at any moment, and the tent walls were defenceless. The Afghans rushed towards the entrance of the tent, and then they heard the last word of the last dying Naga. 'Now!' he screamed, blood gushing from his mouth as a smile spread across his face. Before the soldiers could understand why he screamed 'now', the last

Naga set himself on fire, shouted 'Har Har Mahadev' and jumped on the stock of cannonballs, creating an explosion unlike anything anyone on earth had ever seen before that day, killing every soldier surrounding and entering the tent. Many bodies were seen flying by the force of the explosion. The sound of the explosion made hundreds of Afghans deaf, and many sustained injuries by the particles that shot like bullets from the tent.

The massive explosion rocked the battlefield, and the blast echoed miles away, creating a shockwave that reached Abdali, Neymat and Jugal Kishore in the jungle. The battlefield was in sheer chaos with cacophonous birds circling the sky, flames rising high and cries of soldiers echoing far and wide, proving the fight had only just begun. The sound made Ahmed Shah Abdali halt, puzzled. His eyes narrowed in confusion, thinking how his army could start the war without his permission. He had no idea that the ones to start the war were not the huge army of offenders, but the little clans of defenders brought together. Abdali's speed increased and he entered the jungle.

Nobody on the side of the Nagas cheered for this big victory, of destroying nearly all the cannons and killing nearly 400 Afghan soldiers, as they knew that it had cost fifty Naga lives. Now the Afghans still had some cannons operational, but no cannonballs left to shoot. But on the other hand, seeing the open pits on the ground, the Afghans discovered the underground route to reach the other side, crossing the whole battleground from under the surface. The massive explosion broke the tunnel's upper layer from many places and the sunlight was bright enough at uneven intervals to walk inside without fire torches. Though the crest of the tunnel was broken from many places, it was still a lengthy trench to reach the other side. Many Afghan soldiers entered all the ten trenches and started walking. Inside, they could smell something but couldn't identify what it was. They walked in line and in no time the trenches were packed with Afghans walking in line, progressing underground to Gokul. As they reached near the other side that had a wider opening, they all found me standing with some other Naga warriors and a fire torch.

What they could smell was kerosene, and I held the thread of their lives, connected to the flammable oil and explosive powder hidden beneath their feet. As they were visible from all the vents, I lit the thread. The sparks diverged and entered every underground tunnel. There was no place for them to run back and no time to run forward. All the tunnels burned and exploded, killing the Afghans trapped beneath them. As hundreds of soldiers were killed instantly, the tunnel transformed into a burning grave, leaving ashes behind.

Not too far away, the nine tree controllers along with two villagers and four female fighters, were waiting for Abdali's army to reach the jungle. With the advancement of the Afghan soldiers, there was an eerie silence in the jungle. As Abdali entered the jungle, the tree controllers kept an eye on his soldiers. When the army reached the middle of the jungle, one of the controllers whispered to the trees at the entrance and exit to close the way by creating a wall around the jungle so that nobody could run out. The trees obeyed, and the moment the last Afghan soldier entered the jungle, the gigantic trees began to stir. Their roots dug into the soil, twisting and curling like snakes. Their branches started bending low which made the jungle come alive. Together, all the trees on all the sides started sealing the army's paths.

Abdali's army was suddenly targeted. The villagers and some of the female warriors shot arrows and spears from the high branches of the trees, showering down as the tree controllers whispered orders to strike. The trees became allies, hurling branches and roots to trip and drag soldiers down. Confused but determined, the Afghans started spotting the Nagas and began climbing the branches. The women of the Durga Defence Forces started aiming at the Afghans to keep the tree talkers safe and alive.

Though furious, Abdali's mind still raced with plots, and he knew he had to attack as soon as possible. 'Surround Neymat and do whatever it takes to keep her safe,' ordered Abdali in his highest pitch.

Neymat was surrounded by soldiers, and many began cutting down every branch that tried to reach her. Some soldiers were dragged and thrown by the trees, but others quickly replaced them to protect Neymat.

The Afghan army was carrying an inflammable liquid that they needed to cook food, light torches and start campfires at night for safety. The quantity of the liquid was enough to burn the whole jungle down.

Abdali commanded his men to pour the liquid on the barks and dried leaves scattered across the ground. The order was immediately executed. The huge lids kept on the carts were opened, and the horses and camels were made to run wherever they could. The liquid started pouring on the ground as they ran in different directions. The other group of soldiers began splashing the liquid on the massive trees around them.

Abdali lit a fire torch in his hands and threw it into the centre, where all the horses and camels tied to the carts were forced to run. The fire spread faster than the animals and soon reached the containers that still held half of the liquid. The containers exploded along with the carts. As a result, the fire reached the highest branches of the trees. Many Afghan soldiers perished in the fire, but it also forced the Nagas and others to fall one by one to save their lives, though death awaited them all on the ground. Some fell on the burning ground and others were brutally killed and sliced by swords all at once. Some female warriors fought bravely, but they were too less in numbers against the brutal numbers of Afghans. While some of them were killed by the soldiers, others chose to take their own lives rather be captured alive. Those trees which were the protectors a moment ago were now turning into death traps. The animals and birds fled in panic, leaving their homes behind. The jungle had now become the battlefield of flames. Amid this, Abdali was successful in capturing the main tree controller, who tried to whisper to the trees once more. But before he could speak, Abdali cut out his tongue. The jungle was burnt to the ground, with the fire and smoke rising high into the air. The birds lost their permanent habitat and didn't know where to fly for shelter at night. As the day drew to a close, many animals, burning alive, fled from the flaming jungle towards Gokul in search of help. However, they were still too far away to cover the ground and survive. Neelkanth and the other birds who lost their loved ones and their homes flew above the burning jungle, experiencing the viciousness of men in green.

In the distance, the Nagas saw fire and understood that the tree talkers had failed. Seeing the fire and smoke, the Afghan Commanders at the gates of Gokul knew that Abdali was near and would reach in a few hours. This gave them back their lost confidence and strength.

The army that entered the jungle had more than 10,000 men, 1000 horsemen and 1000 camels. But the army that walked out was reduced to around 3000 men, 400 horsemen and 500 camels. The cannons with Abdali were still safe and ready to serve.

Nine tree controllers killed nearly 4000 Afghans in the forest. By nightfall, Abdali's army had cleared the way, and the defenders of Gokul knew that the final confrontation was near.

14

Ifrit

The jungles burned through the night, lighting up the sky above. This light gave hope of victory to the dark forces of the Afghans, casting a silhouette of sorrow and slaughter over the protectors of dharma.

The homeless birds, flying at night, watched the burning animals run for rescue, unaware they were suffering for the greed and vengeance of men. There was no one to save the rabbits, deers, the burning peacocks or the baby bears. The air reeked of burning hair and skin, filled with painful screams that could shake even the hardest hearts and the bravest brains. All that the defenders of Gokul could do was to feel the burn in their hearts that ignited more rage in them against Abdali and his soldiers.

The night passed somehow, and morning brought more challenges for the men of Gokul. The Afghan army was reinforced once again. This time, the largest force arrived with their Shehenshah—Ahmed Shah Abdali himself. The

Nagas saw Ahmed Shah Abdali for the first time. Now, they knew the face of the enemy. The defenders of Gokul had been reduced, while the forces aiming to destroy it were reinforced once again.

There were now around 1200 defenders against the collective remaining army of nearly 16,000 men. Adding to their strength were forty operational cannons, 900 horses and 1200 camels.

The cannons roared once more as the foot soldiers advanced with the shield formation to be saved from the arrow-shooting machines prepared by the defenders under the leadership of Krishna.

A villager in fear, gazing at the vast army standing right in front of Gokul, said, 'We can't win over them in a direct fight.'

'Yes! But we can fight,' replied the chief Mathadhish. By now, Krishna too felt hopeless as all his preparation and strategies were exhausted. He was left with no more traps and tricks down his sleeves.

'I don't have any more strategic advancements,' murmured Krishna, disappointed in himself.

'You did well, Krishna. You are the best army commander that I have ever come across and the credit that Gokul still stands in this war is well deserved by you. You have done your duty at your best. And if we die, it will be our honour to die fighting beside you,' said the chief Mathadhish, motivating Krishna.

Realizing that his murmuring reached the chief's ears, Krishna said, 'I am sorry that I couldn't prepare more than this for Gokul.' His voice trembled in the pain of helplessness.

The chief, along with me and Dhruv, walked near Krishna and said, 'Krishna, we are fighting for Gokul because we have sworn to defend and protect the dharma. The villagers fight for Gokul because it is their home. These soldiers, both men and women, are fighting for Gokul because their duty is to follow orders of their kings and queens. But Vanraaj and you stood and fought for Gokul with Ajaa, Shambhu and other Naga warriors selflessly because you followed your heart. You were not bound by any duty; this is not your home. Neither are you a Naga, and yet here you are standing by our side. Tell me who is the greatest among us all?' asked the chief, making Krishna realize what he did.

Krishna was surprised and overwhelmed, wondering how the chief knew all of that. Mathadhish read the question in his eyes and said, 'The greatest among us all are Vanraaj, Dulari and you.' Gajraaj had tears in his eyes, remembering how his mother Dulari fought and died alongside Vanraaj.

'Adhiraj told me all about your valour, your determination and your dedication. If you even kill one more of these asuras, it will help Krishna. Don't be disheartened,' continued the chief.

Krishna bowed in response to the chief. All the other Nagas had gratitude and blessings in their eyes for Krishna. Right then, Neelkanth came and sat on the shoulder of Mayuran, the head of the bird talkers, and whispered something. Everybody calmly waited for the bird talker to share the news.

'There's another troop of Afghans army approaching,' informed Mayuran.

'It's the final day then,' replied the chief firmly.

The chief turned towards his warriors and ordered in a strict tone, 'The sole purpose of the giants must be to destroy the cannons at any cost. The firefighters must take their fuel bags and fire torches. Half of the remaining Nagas alive must fight with the remaining Durga defenders and Vedant's men. Krishna will lead you all.'

'Me?' asked Krishna, feeling respectful.

'Yes, Krishna. You,' said Dhruv on behalf of the chief.

Krishna was overwhelmed but determined at the same time. He joined both his hands in gratitude.

'Try to kill as many as possible before the approaching troops can join them. It may be our last day on earth but for them it must be the longest and most painful,' said the chief, filled with anger and determination.

'What are the orders for the remaining half Naga sadhus, chief?' asked Dhruv while standing beside me.

'The remaining Nagas, including you, will wait till the sun reaches our heads. We will then attack with the shadow catchers secured between our formation.'

'The shadow catchers must be protected at any cost. The sun is behind them now. The shadow stealers will only be taken forward post twelve, when their shadows will be ahead of them. Each shadow stealer will be encircled by the protective layer of Nagas defending them from the blades and arrows of Afghans. Also keep Sarfaraz Khan and his men ready for their king,' added Mathadhish with certainty in his eyes for the plan.

'Sarfaraz Khan ready? What does that mean?' asked Madhav climbing the final mountain with his feet sunk till his knees in the thick layers of ice, making every step difficult.

The nameless Naga smiled at the question and continued narrating without answering his follower's question.

The first layer of defenders were the giants who ran at full speed towards the Afghan foot soldiers, wielding shields to keep them as far as possible from the cannons. The idea was to break their formation, make them vulnerable and reach the cannons to destroy them. Every step they took was thumping in the chest of every man present near the battleground. Their mission was clear—to break the enemy's formation, making them easy targets for what was to come following the giants. The hallucinators rushed back to open ground, where Sarfaraz Khan and the other Afghan soldiers lay sleeping in the open. Under the open sky, all the Afghans, including Sarfaraz Khan, were in deep sleep as if put into unconsciousness or coma, where they couldn't hear even the cannons roaring. Sarfaraz Khan and other Afghans appeared like harmless innocent men.

'Bum Bum Bhole!' a hallucinator shouted, causing all the possessed Afghans to open their eyes and wake up for their orders.

A hallucinator Naga ordered them to take their position and wait for orders. As ordered, the hallucinated Afghans, including Sarfaraz Khan, swiftly took their positions, waiting for further orders.

Behind the giants, as the second layer of defence, ran the horses and foot soldiers of Durga Defence Forces, with Vedant and Krishna leading them from the front. They ran together in perfect formation, prepared to take advantage of the giants' disruption and drive the enemies further back. The giant Nagas began throwing Afghans from one side to the hallucinators on the other side of the terrain.

The third layer consisted of firefighters, holding fire torches in one hand and leather bags filled with flammable liquid strapped across their waist. The liquid inside swayed, ready to unleash fiery destruction. Each firefighter had seven to nine bags covering their waists. They seemed like live bombs running. Their presence on the battlefield was like a walking storm of flames—a symbol of their willingness to sacrifice everything to protect their homeland.

Behind the rocks, the other hallucinator Nagas were casting illusions into the minds of more Afghan soldiers who were thrown to them, while the giants, led by Mahakaay, were trying to reach the cannons. Their struggle was clearing the path for other defenders of Gokul. The soldiers thrown by giant Nagas toward these hallucinators were disoriented and trapped by these mental tricks, losing all sense of reality. This was adding more Afghan soldiers to the new set of Sarfaraz Khan's fleet, ready to take orders from the Nagas and execute them blindly.

In between smoke and shouts, the firefighters relentlessly turned the battlefield into a nightmare by taking the fuel in their mouths and spewing fire all around, even setting the Afghans ablaze. They were burning tens of soldiers with each sip of fuel. Abdali was losing hundreds of men with every single flame-throw. However, this move proved to be very costly for the Naga warriors. The brave souls spewing fire and burning their faces were also struck by arrows and javelins from all sides. Still with their trembling hands they opened the fuel bags and burned them all. The ignited flames exploded, engulfing the Afghans around them. They killed many more with their last breaths before being consumed themselves. As flames engulfed the battlefield, only one firefighter remained, watching death consume both sides. Vidyut, the expert in explosives, stood beside the chief helplessly as his orders were to be on standby.

The firefighters were falling and so were the giants. The women warriors were slaughtered as were the men of Gokul. Each of them had numerous Afghan soldiers to handle and take blows from. It resembled a mob lynching, with every defender and protector were surrounded by thirty to fifty odd soldiers, taking their rage on the dead bodies, beating, slaying and flaunting their body parts while trying to prove their supremacy.

With Krishna down and women soldiers falling, their strength fading with each passing moment, hope also seemed to diminish. It was almost announced that we have lost the war, and with it, Gokul would soon perish. But then, in a burst of unexpected power and strength, the Shakti Sena and allied forces with princess Chandrika leading them entered the war. 'Har Har Mahadev' and 'Jai Maata Di' echoed together from the Naga warriors and the Durga Defence Forces as they witnessed the Shakti Sena sweeping through the Afghan army, slicing anybody who seemed to be an obstruction in the grand meeting of disciples of Shiva and Shakti.

'Nagas, the battle is far from over. Their arrival is a sign. Kali came to Ajaa and Shambhu ji . . . Durga comes to us. We fight on,' asserted the chief, uniting the exhausted.

The princess and her force attacked Abdali's army with all their mightiness, giving Mathadhish more time to hold the shadow catchers before they finally entered the war.

Amid all this chaos, the Mathadhish kept looking up at the sky and then back at his own shadow formation again and again. He was waiting for the sun to move westward enough for the shadows to start falling in front of Afghans.

'But what were these shadow catchers going to do?' the impatient Madhav questioned while still walking upwards. With his feet sunk in ice, the nameless Naga replied, 'Think what will happen if your shadow leaves the ground and stands right in front of you as your mirror image fighting against you.'

Madhav stopped walking as he started imagining what the view would be like while the nameless Naga continued, 'These mysterious shadow catchers possessed a power that few can comprehend, a mastery overshadows, a gift bestowed upon them by Lord Shiva himself. But through intense meditation and firm devotion, these Naga sadhus have widely opened the secrets of the shadow empire using the shadows as a weapon against their own bodies on those who wish to harm the land of dharma. They had the mastery of shadows which reflected the duality of existence that is 'the light and dark, good and evil, creation and destruction'. The shadow catchers were often seen only at dusk or dawn when shadows were the longest. They moved like spirits with bodies wrapped in dark robes that blended with the shadows around them. Their glowing eyes could see beyond the physical realm, using supreme power to manipulate shadows, shaping them into forms that could match their own physical form with the same strength and move till they destroy their enemies, the bodies that created the shadows. Once the body is murdered, the shadow has no existence. It vanishes as if it never existed, and you never get to know who killed the body because the shadow of the body cannot be blamed, caught or punished. The shadow dies with the body.

Later, the sun tilted towards the west. Mathadhish, along with the remaining Nagas, me and Dhruv, joined the battleground. The firefighters met their salvation, and it was the shadow catchers this time who were kept in the centre, secured from all sides.

With a mere gesture, these shadow catchers seized the shadow of the soldiers that reached them before the bodies and turned them against their creators. That day was the biggest display of how the sun could help protect our dharma when hundreds of Afghan soldiers fought in fear against their own shadows that neither got tired nor killed until their real bodies fell on ground.

The villagers and the allied forces of Surajgarh saw the real power of the Nagas that day.

'They are still double that of us in numbers,' Dhruv addressed.

'Unleash the captured commander and his men on Abdali's forces,' ordered the chief Mathadhish.

'Bum Bum Bhole! Attack!' said a hallucinator to Sardar Khan and other possessed Afghans. Sarfaraz Khan charged with his men at Abdali's army, this time fighting for the Nagas instead, chanting 'Bum Bum Bhole'. Their swords were now raised against the army they had sworn to fight for. The Afghan soldiers, who had not yet fallen prey to any of these giants and other tricks, were traumatized as they were fighting against their own men. Their expressions started transforming from shock to terror and disbelief to helplessness as all the hallucinated men ran and blended into the Afghan army. Mistaking their allies for enemies, these deceptive soldiers attacked them in confusion. No one knew who was on whose side, as they were also dressed as Afghan soldiers, following the Nagas' orders. It was not only a striking moment for the opponents but also for the villagers who were watching this event from a distance.

With their mouths and eyes wide open in awe and fear, the villagers witnessed the unbelievable event they had heard about—the powerful Nagas possessing supernatural skills. The female warriors, who always stood with strong determination, were astonished and hesitant, sharing clueless glances with one another. Their swords, once steady, now wavered in their hands with unease.

The hypnotized Afghan soldiers shifting to their side were also tipping the balance in their favour, increasing their numbers and breaking the enemy's spirit.

Abdali noticed, much to his disbelief, that the chief Mathadhish, along with all his living warriors, stood at a distance, quietly observing the chaos and death of Afghani soldiers by the hands and weapons of Afghani soldiers. The soldiers carrying out the killings were under the command of their hallucinated commander, Sarfaraz Khan, fighting against the soldiers of Zoravar and Malik Akhtar.

'Catch him alive. We can save the rest in influence if we can bring Sarfaraz back. Every man alive is important,' said Neymat.

Everybody who heard it wondered how Neymat could bring them back. From a distance, Kaaldhwaj, who was keeping an eye on the events of war, noticed Neymat for the first time.

Zoravar decided to counter Sarfaraz and bring him back to his senses, as Sarfaraz was their own. He took charge and reached Sarfaraz. In a battle between them, where everyone else was ordered to be on standby, both the enemies of Gokul showed their skill and strength. They fought courageously, but there was a difference. The difference was that Zoravar was still a man of who would tire and exhaust, while Sarfaraz Khan was not; he was ordered to keep fighting against his will and stamina until his death. It was a sight to behold as we silently stood and watched the enemies kill each other. No matter who lost in the battle between Afghans, we were sure to gain an advantage.

All that we didn't know was that our pawn named Sarfaraz Khan would end up killing one of the last two remaining commanders of Abdali.

Tired to death, panting heavily, Zoravar gave himself a moment to breathe, but senseless Sarfaraz Khan ended it with a single blow, chopping his head off. Abdali's finest commander lay lifeless on the ground. This broke the morale of all the remaining Afghan soldiers. Sarfaraz Khan looked at Abdali and started advancing towards him.

Abdali was perplexed and alarmed while watching this horrifying stance. He gripped one of the captain's shoulders and said, 'What are they doing? Why are they attacking on their own?'

He became clueless and frustrated as he was not able to understand why his soldiers were turning on each other. He sensed his control slipping due to some unseen events behind the rocks in a bizarre way. His soldiers seem to be losing their minds, turning against one another without reason. Clenching his fists in frustration, Abdali tried to make sense of the madness that unfolded before him. 'What is happening?' He felt a sense of helplessness creeping in, realizing that this was an abnormal war. Something threatening was at play, something beyond his watch and control.

The captain, equally puzzled, shook his head and went ahead to carry out the orders. While everybody else was unable to stop the brutal brother of Sardar Khan and he kept advancing towards Abdali to kill him, the one who emerged as a saviour to this mayhem was Neymat.

Miraculously, the moment Neymat entered the battlefield and looked at Sarfaraz Khan, he got back to his senses. He ordered all the other soldiers under him, who were also hallucinated but still able to hear his commands, to stop.

There was pin-drop silence across the field of death and chaos. Sarfaraz Khan immediately approached Abdali, apologizing for his sins, and explained to him that he was not in his senses, and that he was tricked. He told Abdali that a set of hallucinators hidden behind the rocks were doing the trick. But the anger and frustration of not being able to kill Sardar Khan and the queen all came out on killing Sarfaraz. Abdali ordered his royal soldiers to hold Sarfaraz tightly, and then beheaded Sarfaraz Khan himself.

Abdali then ordered Malik Akhtar to attack the villagers and hallucinators, trapping the Afghans from behind the rocks. Meanwhile, the cannons turned towards the approaching giant Nagas who were continuously being attacked by the enemies. Yet, they were moving towards Abdali. He then realized that the eyes of the giant Nagas were fixed on cannons that were continuously bombing Gokul. He ordered his captains to turn all the cannons towards the approaching giant Nagas and shoot. The captains did as they were ordered. With every blast, the giants stumbled and fell, but they kept moving forward, their eyes were still locked on the cannons. The ground shook with the force of the attacks, yet the determination of the giants was resolute. Abdali watched closely, a mix of rage and worry growing as the giants reached their targets, destroying them to the ground.

Once self-assured of his victory, Ahmad Shah Abdali now found himself at the doorstep of the fear of defeat. Desperation gripped him as he glanced over the bodies of his fallen soldiers scattered on the ground. And with this came the thought of a conversation he had long ago with Neymat. Abdali's eyes moved from one group of soldiers to another. He called out to one of his soldiers standing beside him. 'Call Neymat . . . right now,' Abdali ordered, his gaze fixed on the chaos.

In no time Neymat entered, and without any forewarning, Abdali spoke to her in desperation.

'Neymat, the battle is going against me. I give you the freedom to do whatever it takes to confirm my victory. How long will you need?' asked Abdali. Neymat smirked at his words, knowing that Abdali's order would need a great sacrifice from her. The power she was about to unleash was not to be taken for granted as it could really turn the tides against the Nagas in favour of the Afghans.

'I knew you would need this, which is why without your permission I started the calling already. Just a few hours more,' said Neymat. Jugal Kishore, standing beside Abdali, was still trying to grasp the essence and substance of the talk.

'The no moon night is almost here. The dark forces favour us and are the strongest on this night. My offerings are ready, and so is he to accept it,' Neymat added.

'He! Who is he?' Jugal wanted to ask but he knew that his mouth shut was the wiser choice then.

Abdali, at the very next moment, asked his last living commander Malik Akhtar to provide Neymat with the necessary protection and resources. Jugal was also ordered to go with Neymat. He walked behind her unwillingly. Neymat left the battleground knowing there was no turning back now. She made her way to an isolated area far from camp the very same night. The clueless commander and his scared guards followed her. She stood barefoot under the open sky and hurriedly began to draw a circle in the dirt with a mixture of ash and blood.

'You wanted to know what I would do with the children of the traitor. I wanted to make a circle,' said Neymat cold heartedly, mocking Jugal Kishore. Jugal then realized that the ashes mixed with blood were of the children. She first extracted their blood while they were alive and then burned them for their ashes.

She then placed a soldier at each corner and ordered them to be burned. Malik Akhtar had to follow her orders to stay alive, and so he ordered to burn his own men. The burning soldiers screamed as their skin melted off. Neymat continued to chant in a language long forgotten. The words she spoke were a call to Ifrit.

'Ifrit! What's that?' asked Madhav curiously. The nameless Naga told Madhav about Ifrit, 'In Islamic texts, Ifrit is a powerful, supernatural and malevolent demon-like being. The word "*ifrit*" comes from the Quran, but it's used as an epithet to describe a spirit with an undefined nature, rather than to designate a specific type of demon. Arab philologists believe the word comes from "*afara*", which means "to rub with dust or mud".'

Ifrits are often depicted as winged creatures made of smoke and are associated with the underworld and the spirits of the dead. They are also often associated with djinns, which are similar evil and magical figures. In the Quran, Ifrits are said to live in the hidden realm, or al-Ghaib, and are described as sinister, cunning, seductive and interfering. They are believed to loiter in ruined environments, possess limbs, and take over hosts to grant people supernatural strength and bravery. In one story, an Ifrit appears in the Quran to hinder the prophet Muhammad during his pilgrimage and is defeated by the angel Gabriel.

The warzone was engulfed in darkness, and the approaching night was a moonless one. The shadow catchers were of no use anymore and many from both sides had perished. The war had halted. The giants had fallen, and the cannons were destroyed. Mahakaay was still alive but severely injured to participate any further. Many Nagas and warriors of Shakti Sena lost their lives, but casualties were heavy on the Afghan sides. By the end of the day, the number of Afghan survivors had decreased below that of the combined allied forces still standing alive. For the first time, the Naga sadhus and their allied forces were more than the remaining Afghan army. The victory seemed assured for the protectors of dharma the next day and Gokul seemed saved.

The Naga sadhus, princess Chandrika and their allies gathered around Krishna, filled with relief and anticipation. Krishna said, 'We've won the day, but we must prepare for what's next.'

'With the numbers Abdali is left with, I expect him to sneak out in the dark tonight to be alive. He is in no position or stand to attack tomorrow, because he knows that death is certain for him if he continues this war,' said Vedant with a lot of confidence.

While the soldiers and the Naga warriors were resting to heal themselves and discussing what the next morning would bring for them, Neymat completed her calling for Ifrit at 1 a.m.

With the sudden drop of the temperature, wind began to howl through the trees and the ground trembled. It was Ifrit waking up. The fall in temperature and increasing negativity could be felt in the camps of the Nagas, too, but nobody could understand what was happening other than one who was not a part of the camp, keeping an eye on everything. It was Kaaldhwaj who opened his eyes in the mountain close by. With a burst of biting chill, Ifrit appeared, freezing the burning bodies and as cold as a dead body. A being of uncontaminated supremacy and annihilation, it was a towering figure made of everything dead around him, including melting skin, dripping blood, burning tree branches and horns of dead reindeer. Its eyes were hollow yet containing a malevolent light, dark smoke coming off his ears and nose. Screams of the recently sacrificed men were heard from within its unnatural body as if they were all trapped inside him. Jugal Kishore and Malik Akhtar saw him emerging out of nowhere with all the negative forces and darkness around.

'What is this? What are you going to do with it?' asked Malik Akhtar, frightened by the appearance of Ifrit.

Neymat looked at him and replied, 'There is a reason why the dead from our troops are either left in the open or buried, but never burned. All thanks to Jugal Kishore.' She cunningly smiled while looking at Jugal Kishore after the statement and got back to holding herself strongly in front of Ifrit. But the powerful being took every ounce of Neymat's strength to stand his ground while questioning her in a hellish voice.

'Why have you called me?'

Neymat replied, 'To awaken the dead! Bring them back to fight for us.'

Ifrit's laughter crackled, 'You ask more than you can offer. What will you offer in return if I do so?' Neymat knew the cost of what she was asking. To control Ifrit, it would require a sacrifice. This was her destiny.

'I offer you a part of my soul in exchange for the power to control the dead,' replied Neymat.

'Very well,' said Ifrit. With that, a malicious spirit extended its hand that reached out to Neymat. She closed her eyes and felt a shooting pain in her chest, as if a part of her body was being eradicated from her. It was a part of her soul, the fees of her demand and fuel to follow her orders. When she opened her eyes again, Ifrit's eyes were upon her because she knew it was over. The price was paid. The offer in exchange was accepted. Ifrit was done with the ritual and was ready to execute Neymat's orders.

'Command me!'

Malik Akhtar reached Abdali at the very hour to inform him that Neymat was ready.

Abdali then called his commanders and said, 'Prepare for war. We attack now! Because the shadow catchers need shadows, we will fight at night and finish all the defenders and this war before sunrise.'

Meanwhile, Neymat also returned to Abdali, followed by Jugal Kishore, who was still trying to absorb and comprehend the series of events happening around him.

Hearing Abdali's order, Malik Akhtar, the only commander left alive, looked at his weary remaining soldiers—fewer than the defending army of Gokul—and asked, 'How?'

Abdali glanced at Neymat, who then spoke on his behalf to Malik Akhtar, 'By reawakening our final reinforcement.' Neymat smiled and walked back to Ifrit.

'What does she mean? Who was the final reinforcement?' asked Madhav, trying to recall if he had missed anything in the narration.

'His final reinforcement was the reawakening of Sardar Khan and his dead army,' replied the nameless Naga while looking at Madhav.

15

The Darkest Night

At 2 a.m. on the darkest night of Pitrapaksha Amavasya, the order was given to Ifrit. Neymat, worry etched into the lines on her forehead, finally held her breath and raised her hand, pointing toward the battlefield where the bodies of the fallen were waiting . . . some scattered and others buried. 'Order them to wake up and fight for us,' she commanded.

She experienced the jerk and throttle with which Ifrit disappeared in the very next stance. The ground shook and the sky darkened as Ifrit's presence grew stronger. Gajraaj once again realized it first and blew the shankh. It was alarming enough to wake every Naga and be warned. They started gathering, sensing that something unprecedented was coming. With a roar, Ifrit started pronouncing spells and charged the dead to rise. One by one, the abandoned, lifeless Afghan soldiers scattered across the battlefield—cold, dead, and rotting, rose to their feet. Their eyes, now empty of darkness, moved like puppets on invisible strings.

Among them, a dead man who walked was Zoravar, once the decorated commander of Abdali, killed by another commander, Sarfaraz.

His flesh hung loosely from his bones, while the other fallen Afghan soldiers, their rotting flesh crawling with worms across their faces and bodies, stood beside them. The mud clinging to their decayed bodies produced an unbearable stink in the air. Their skin, all bruised and discolored, was the evidence of the recent bloody battle. Another fragment of the recent past resurfaced in the distorted headless body of Sarfaraz Khan, brother of Sardar khan and the murderer of Zoravar. Sarafraz Khan and Zoravar were no more humans, but creatures controlled by Ifrit's orders along with thousands of other dead Afghan creatures ready to march forward to attack the Nagas. Ifrit continued pronouncing chants, which were impossible to understand for those who were still sleeping beneath the earth. As the earth opened, thousands of hands began emerging from underneath the surface. Finally, a single hand of authority broke through the dirt.

Slowly, the hand helped an imposing figure with empty eye sockets and a bruised, darkened face rose fully from his grave, his half-eaten head with maggots crawling in it. Looking at that face, Jugal Kishore's face was drained of colour with terror while Neymat smiled; the living Afghans cheered in celebration of their victory. Bearing the badge of command, he stepped over the fallen bodies lying on the graveyard of trenches, ready to receive orders and roar again. This was none other than the one killed by Ajaa himself.

This was Sardar Khan, reawakened to finish the task of destroying Gokul and the Nagas. The Naga warriors stood at a distance, watching the dead emerge from the ground like a flood ready to break the dam and sweep everything on its way. Though they remained rooted to their spots, as their orders so far were merely to wake up, the echo of their impending move resonated through every corner of Gokul.

'What's happening? What kind of sounds are they? Neither humans nor animals?' thought Krishna, looking at me.

'It's still dark! Why did Gajraaj blow the shankh of war?' I wondered, returning Krishna's glance. In less than a minute, all the Nagas and other defenders, including the leftover army of Shakti Sena and Durga Sena, along with the villagers, gathered. Before anyone could speak anything, the anxious flutter of Neelkanth caught everyone's attention. Neelkanth was clearly in discomfort while telling something to the Mayuran. 'What is it saying?' asked Dhruv and Mayuran translated Neelkanth's words: 'Dead men rising in thousands from the ground.' Neelkanth seemed terribly disturbed.

'Dead men rising! What does that mean?' asked Krishna. Neelkanth started saying something to Mayuran after which Mayuran looked at Krishna and asked, 'Who is Sardar Khan? Neelkanth says he is coming.'

The shared glance between the warriors who participated in the battle of Gokul against Sardar Khan brought terrified expressions on everyone's faces, including Krishna's and Vedant's. I too was taken aback. There was collective fear that seized the moment.

'Why is this bird so anxious with this name?' asked the princess.

'She saw her loved ones, Vanraaj and Dulari, dying because of Sardar Khan,' I replied. Neelkanth flew to me to be consoled and covered while I pampered it.

'It was Sardar Khan because of whom Ajaa, Shambhu ji and one hundred more Nagas are not among us anymore.' This enraged many, including the princess who asked, 'How is he alive till now?'

'He is not! We saw your brother Ajaa killing him. In fact, Ajaa died in the fight with Sardar Khan. We saw him dead and Jugal Kishore's soldiers buried him.' The princess and almost everyone else had blank faces as the statements did not make sense.

'If he is dead, shouldn't we be discussing our living enemies? Why and how are you people talking about his return then? Explain to me.' The princess was clearly agitated trying to understand.

'Our enemy has some dark world power, and I can feel it growing,' came a not so familiar voice that everybody turned to see. It was Kaaldhwaj standing to extend his support, but his approach to help was unacceptable.

'You need me!' said Kaaldhwaj, with a sense of pride in his voice.

'What are you doing here? I told you in the mountains that you are not one of us unless you set all the spirits free,' said the chief, questioning Kaaldhwaj's unpermitted presence.

'I followed you to Gokul,' replied Kaaldhwaj.

'You are not my follower, and you are not welcome here, and we cannot allow your participation and spoil the pious mission of sacrifice of all the Nagas,' the chief replied, breaking Kaaldhwaj's pride and elevating his rage.

'You are putting everyone in the jaws of death with your stubbornness,' replied Kaaldhwaj while raising his voice in anger and frustration. At this point, many Nagas lifted their eyebrows and some even their weapons. The chief signalled everybody to calm down and said, 'Your practices are unethical and . . .'

Kaaldhwaj contradicted the chief even before he could finish by saying, 'Why did Lord Vishnu reincarnate as Kanha and not repeat his return as Rama again? Because he knew that one can fight ethically only with an ethical enemy. These Afghan asuras are not following any rules of war. Life can win over life; life can never defeat death. Look at the sky. It's still dark, and the fight has begun. This is against the rules of war. Can't you see it? A fair fight can only be done between the men alive, and the army with souls. You can't win a war against soulless bodies that can neither feel pain nor fear. They are the dead men possessed of life. You can cut them down or stab them, you can burn them or drown them, but you cannot kill them because there is no soul in them to be extracted.'

The chief replied, 'See around you. Every defender you see here is standing on his own will. These are all free souls defending and protecting their beliefs and their land. The souls that you have under your command are your slaves. They are bound to follow your orders without their will.

Free men fight wars, slaves only follow orders. We will do whatever best we can as the protectors of the dharma. Your practices are prohibited and as the chief Mathadhish, I cannot endorse or support your war tactics. You may go now.'

Anger was the only visible emotion on Kaaldhwaj's face as he looked at all our faces, including the chief, and then turned back to leave.

'Kaaldhwaj!' called the chief again, and he turned with a glimmer of hope amidst the sea of hopelessness in his eyes.

'Do not ever come back. You are welcomed only when you set all your slave souls free,' said the chief, this time turning back to order us.

'I am the last Naga in the world who possesses this knowledge and power to capture souls, and I will never let my army and knowledge go waste,' replied Kaaldhwaj before leaving. Everybody turned towards the growling sound coming from the battleground.

Dhruv climbed a tree close to him and saw hundreds of corpses slowly rising from the ground and aligning in rows behind Zoravar, Sarfaraz and Sardar Khan. Their chests brutally caved and insects crawling out from the open wounds. Their hands clutched weapons.

Meanwhile, the princess got on her horse and rode forward to check and evaluate the danger. As she covered a little distance, she saw a group of soldiers standing at a distance, not far from the fire, giving them a ghostly glow. Few faces were eaten away entirely, fingers twitching and eyes sunken deep into the skull that looked at the princess for a moment before they vanished in the thick smoke.

'I may not be able to see them for some time, but they are ready to move towards us, and they will move quickly,' thought the princess while preparing to fight the dead lost in smoke.

The princess was right. The orders were given, and the march of the dead began.

Mahakaay, the last giant, severely injured and barely breathing, felt the disturbance before he witnessed a crawling soldier coming towards the Nagas, his both legs missing. His head appeared bald, but some hair was still clinging to his scalp. His teeth were tightened. The giant stood silently watching the horrifying creature struggle forward.

At the end, I stood on the back of my beloved Gajraaj and saw some figures moving through the darkness. To my surprise, these dead walking creatures' faces were rotten, torn, and muddy uniforms hung from their shoulders. While some had squinted eyes and sickly green flesh, others were pale white with bloodless bodies. Then I saw a massive figure in silhouette, his head wide open, his jaws broken and hanging, with a trident stabbed on his forehead and in both his eyes sockets, he was limping with one leg and another dragging behind it. It did not take much time for me to recognize the soulless body as I saw him dying recently. Now I could feel why Neelkanth was so anxious and terrified. He saw Sardar Khan walking towards us once again. I tightened my grip on both my weapon and my resolve, readying myself. The unease of Gajraaj, too, was prominently noticeable.

These undead soldiers continued marching forward, scattered across the land in unnatural form.

The tables had turned again. What seemed like an assured victory was now a war impossible to win. And once again, the number of attacking Afghan asuras, both alive and dead, had multiplied to vastly outnumber the Nagas and defending forces.

The Afghans led by their sole surviving commander, Malik Akhtar, on one side and Abdali himself on the other, attacked Gokul. From the third side, all the reawakened Afghans under Sardar Khan charged against the fourth side, the only side where our allied forces stood outnumbered by less than half still alive, defending Gokul.

'How can a dead person be alive again?' asked Vedant, fear dripped from his eyes and his voice trembled after he saw Sardar Khan's dead army moving towards them.

'And now when we see them moving, how can the dead be killed?' asked princess Chandrika, tension prominently heard in her voice.

It was all the more tough and challenging to face the dead Sardar Khan than the one who was alive as this time he had nothing to lose. We had already lost Ajaa to stand and face him.

Vedant and the princess were the young voices, but the seasoned chief knew the defenders needed a clear-cut strategy to win this battle and that this was the make-or-break war with no scope of mistakes. And so, for this, Mathadhish planned to divide everyone into specific groups.

Krishna was chosen to lead the first group which consisted of some villagers, exhausted allied forces, including

Vedant and his men. These were the men chosen to fight against Abdali's living forces.

The second group consisted of Princess Chandrika commanding the Durga and Shakti Sena, fighting the opponent Commander Malik Akhtar and his troops of live soldiers.

Third and the final group was under Dhruv, who stood with the Nagas, including me and the chief Mathadhish was directly taking on the dead Afghans that had dead men like Zoravar and Sarfaraz Khan, all under the command of Sardar Khan.

While everyone was thinking how to face the new challenge that is scary and more powerful than all the others they faced, Chandrika came forward and spoke for all: 'We faced cannons that were placed to blow us apart and men who wanted to cut us to death and horses that wanted to run through us to enter Gokul and commanders who were adamant to annihilate us from the face of the earth. But here we are . . . still standing and chanting Har Har Mahadev.'

'Har Har Mahadev!' everybody chanted as they listened to him.

I felt as if it were not Princess Chandrika but Ajaa himself standing there, motivating everyone as he had during the battle of Gokul against Sardar Khan.

'They wanted to finish us, but we reduced them to almost nothing. We have successfully done this to them once and we will do it to them again,' the chief added.

Everybody chanted 'Har Har Mahadev' again as if agreeing to the statement and motivating each other. Encouraging all the defenders of Gokul, talking about the heads and hearts, knowing that they were about to face the brainless men with no heartbeats, Dhruv spoke, 'We overpowered their numbers and strength with our unity and belief. In our heads and hearts, we are stronger and more determined than they could ever be. Together, we will rise and conquer all odds.'

Sensing some of the villagers still at unease after the words of encouragement from the princess and others, Krishna raised his hand and said, 'They are not the same men that they once were but are mere bodies without souls trapped between life and death. Strike them down, cut their heads. Let's move forward and end this.'

Vedant looked at the princess and her combined warriors of Shakti Sena and Durga Defence Forces, their swords ready, side by side, as always.

The Afghans charged upon them, but Krishna and other Nagas didn't cringe, 'Let's make this quick.' Krishna murmured before moving forward to fight.

Thinking of Ajaa and his words of inspiration, Krishna said, 'We are not humans living spiritual experiences, we are spiritual beings experiencing human lives. We are ashes of the freshly cremated bodies and whoever sees us should never forget ever that ultimately, we will be this only. The ashes . . . ashes that will be put on else's body after we are burned, inspiring more to protect the dharma unless they too turn into ashes after their death and is spread on others.'

'The situation reminds me of the Shloka from Bhagavad Geeta,' the nameless Naga said to Madhav.

नैनं छिन्दन्ति शस्त्राणि नैनं दहति पावकः ।
न चैनं क्लेदयन्त्यापो न शोषयति मारुतः ।।

'It means: While the physical body is perishable and momentary the soul is eternal and indestructible, it cannot be harmed by the elements of nature, just as the ashes symbolize the end of the physical body, but the soul continues beyond this, carrying both its purpose, including the protection of dharma.'

Dhruv also recollected Shambhu ji's thoughts that the spirit of self-sacrifice and dedication to protect dharma reflects the idea that life is temporary. It's a sacred circle.

What they meant was that they were preparing for the ultimate sacrifice to be martyred either by destroying the enemies or by dying for their sacred land and dharma. It is simple to understand: if anyone can defeat the soulless power that threatens us, it is *us*, the Nagas, the followers of Lord Shiva.

Dhruv decided to stand and fight against Sardar Khan. It was not only Dhruv that Ajaa and Shambhu ji were echoing in. Their powerful and captivating words echoed in everybody's hearts and cleared their path in the battle of dharma as every Naga was trained and preached in the same way.

'Either we finish what Shambhu ji, Ajaa and other Nagas couldn't, or we die and meet them. If anybody here could actually end the soulless monsters, it is us,' Dhruv said to all the Nagas.

While the defenders were planning their strategies, the offenders also had their plans to follow orders by Abdali himself.

'Kill the shadow catchers before the sun empowers them again with our shadows. They must be finished before dawn,' Abdali commanded.

The war with the dark forces began in the darkest night, the final day of shraddh. The shadow catchers were compelled to fight without their supernatural powers, relying on just their physical strength like other Naga warriors as it was night.

Afghan soldiers, not forgetting their faces from the previous face off, identified and attacked the shadow catchers, slashing them all as if they were only trained in the art of night warfare. Their swords swiftly hunting to find the flesh without thinking for a moment. The shadow catchers were bleeding; they were thrashed and slashed, falling apart mercilessly, and yet praying to get light and searching for the horizon as their faintest hope. But the night, like a cruel predator, did not have anything to offer them. Dhruv yelled at me, wiping his tears, seeing the shadow catchers slaughtered, 'We have to help them. They cannot fight like this, not without shadows.' But everybody else and I had their own set of enemies to handle, and we knew that it was a futile and helpless situation.

The blood was all over which triggered the cruel joy in the opponent's sensing as if they had knocked down the once-feared warriors.

This was an absolute tragedy of destiny. The chief Mathadhish, Dhruv and Krishna witnessed the other Nagas fighting their own battles and perishing. Amidst all the fallen shadow catchers, one, with his shallow breaths, was still looking up to the dark sky helplessly for a ray of hope until he too was beheaded, waiting for the blessings of the sunshine upon us all. Unfortunately, there was no hope, no light. The first light of the sun was hours away from the land of Gokul, and darkness of the night was overpowering the Nagas and empowering the asuras. Dhruv wiped away his tears as it was over for the shadow catchers. They were gone from the mortal world, brutally mutilated and then killed in the absence of their own shadows.

Everybody could feel the seriousness of the situation since the dead that walked out of their graves were now unevenly scattered. The gravity of what the defenders were facing and would face in the coming hours was devastating as they could see the dead charging madly upon the Nagas. And ironically, the dead could not be killed again. The defenders, who were bravely facing Abdali's living army under Krishna, Chandrika and Vedant, were also falling rapidly. On the other hand, the dead were moving at some unnatural speed, with their stinking and decayed limbs, defying logic as they launched themselves at the Nagas, who found themselves overwhelmed. A stench of death and decay filled the air as the battleground was covered and plagued by the bodies that were walking in unimaginable conditions. Dhruv, who was holding his sword, glanced all over and saw that panic was all around the grim battleground. The dead were killing the living, and the living were falling dead under the dark sky, hopelessly.

They were thousands in number, and more were still rising. Every defender was up against a dozen and more asuras and every Naga were going down by the lynch of the mob. The living felt like prey being caught by many predators. The number of enemies was rising exponentially upon every Naga. The dead were winning, and the night still was stretched on endlessly.

Krishna, who was watching all the chaos while fighting some Afghans, rushed to Mathadhish and Dhruv and said, 'These are no ordinary enemies. The dead cannot die again but their bodies can be burned.'

With absolute calm, calculating and focusing on his plan, he continued, 'We cannot take any more chances, we are losing our men. We need fire to burn them. We need more soldiers to set them ablaze. If we don't act now, the dead will slaughter every last one of us.'

Agreeing with Krishna, the chief said, 'Light everything! We burn them to ash.' Dhruv barked orders at the remaining firefighters. 'We will circle them in flames and set fire to the corpses.' The able Nagas lit their torches and flung fire from their mouths on to the lifeless bodies of the enemies. The advantage the firefighters had was the dry grass of the land that caught fire conveniently. The result was that the very corpses began to catch fire and were burnt. The dead made a scary and spine-chilling sound while their bodies were crackled and melted under the roaring fire. Krishna's trick was working, and the walking dead were falling, but the number of firefighters was too less than the dead targeting them.

Vidyut, impatiently looking at all that was happening, urgently appealed to the chief, 'I can help. I should be there between them, fighting with them shoulder to shoulder. Please allow me to join them, chief. The dead are too many in numbers. I can't just stand and see them fall.'

The chief Mathadhish heard Vidyut's request with a poker face and said, 'Stay down!' It was heartbreaking for Vidyut to be turned down, but orders were orders.

The firefighters burning them were losing both fuel as the dead Afghans had no sense of fear or pain. The flames only seemed to slow the army for a moment despite many perishing. It was just a matter of time; they realized when the burning dead men started attacking and eating the firefighters alive. The remaining firefighters continued throwing flames and burning as many dead as they could.

The distant Abdali soldiers were watching this with hesitation and their brutal attack paused for a moment. They could see their dead burning.

'Royal archers! Target the flame-throwing firefighters,' ordered Abdali, and around a hundred best archers of his royal fleet got into action once again. However, every flamethrower was clearly identified in the darkness of the night, serving as the source of fire from their mouth that illuminated their surroundings. Their power was now about to become their disadvantage, summoning the curse of death. The firefighters was pierced with uncountable arrows all over their bodies. With them falling, the flames first flickered and then extinguished.

Another major strength of the protectors had fallen after the shadow catchers, but Sardar Khan and his troops from the trenches still stood in thousands. Vidyut stood frozen and broke in the pain of loss of all his brothers. The firefighters were all dead and so was the idea of burning all the dead walking towards Gokul.

Around them, Krishna's army fought valiantly. But even his most skilled warriors found themselves facing an enemy that wouldn't fall. Spears were piercing hearts, swords were cutting limbs, all unstoppably. Dhruv slashed another dead, but in an instant, two more were upon him. And he could barely manage to withstand their blows.

Dhruv put his sword through the chest of one of the undead, but it did nothing. The thing continued to move.

'Chief, we need to change our strategy. They won't die like this,' Dhruv spoke with concern, slicing through another dead soldier's limb. But the chief was focusing on something else. He was totally engrossed.

'The dead army is targeting the Nagas, and I have to keep the bird whisperers safe,' the chief Mathadhish stressed. He knew that the dark and threatening battle for Gokul was still standing ahead on their faces.

'Fall back all!' Mathadhish commanded in a hurry, but it was too late for some to follow the command as the dead Afghans moved like a plague through Nagas in ridiculous fury.

Each Naga fell under the weight of numerous dead walking Afghan soldiers, fighting till their last breaths before the soulless dead men butchered them with their animalistic hunger. The shadow catchers and firefighters that seemed the biggest threat were all killed. The giants and tree controllers were also all dead. It was merely a handful of harmless bird whisperers, a few Naga sadhus relying solely on their fighting skills without any supernatural abilities, and the women warriors—none of whom stood a chance against the combined might of thousands of Afghan soldiers, both living and undead.

'Congratulations, Shehenshah! Your victory is certain now. They are finally falling back, and your dead force will march through their dead bodies inside Gokul,' said Neymat, who, by this time, was standing by Abdali's side.

Abdali turned and looked at her, smiling. The victory that Neymat was congratulating him for was clearly visible to him too.

Many Naga, other sadhus and bird whisperers lost their lives in this unprecedented night attack. But some bird whisperers were still saved. Among the few remaining bird whisperers, one of them was Mayuran, who had conversed with Neelkanth. He approached on the call of chief Mathadhish. 'Chief, we will lose Gokul this way,' he said, wiping away tears from his face, but Mathadhish replied with a grave face: 'Listen to what Dhruv has to say.'

Dhruv walked a step forward and said, 'Before Abdali's army reached here, they burned the jungle while fighting the tree whispers. We saw thousands of birds hovering over their homes—the burning jungles. They were helpless . . . just like us. The grief was not only for their burnt habitat and nests but for the earth, nature itself, the trees, the animals, the very soul of motherland that was being burnt away by the cruelty of war brought to them along with us by Abdali. They have seen what these inhuman Afghans can do and must have anticipated what they will do if we fail to stop them here. The rivers will be dried and polluted, and mountains will be melted then broken. Lives will be misused before death, the skies will cry looking at the heart of Mother Earth torn apart, scratched and molested. Call Neelkanth. We need his help.'

This resonated like the call of unity, a cry for humanity against the destruction of nature by Abdali's greed. Mayuran, to his understanding, decoded the weight of what was being asked. 'But how will we do it?' he asked. Instead of answering the question, Dhruv pointed towards Vidyut the only Naga among them who had the understanding of fire and the expertise to create bombs through the five elements and natural compounds. Vidyut looked at the chief in surprise. He now knew why he was not allowed to die with his Naga brothers.

Seeing the urgency, Neelkanth was called as he was the only one who could gather the birds.

Mayuran joined his hands in a pleading gesture in front of Neelkanth and said, 'What I am about to ask is not fair, but we have no choice. I am going to ask you to die for the residents and land of Gokul. You can deny our request and we will respect it as we are bound by our oath, but you are not. We want you to summon all the birds of Gokul and those who lost their homes in the jungle fire.' Neelkanth had a heart bigger than the army of Abdali, and it gracefully not only understood but also accepted the unfair request that ought to kill Neelkanth and all the others flying under his command. Neelkanth flew back, and with the wind, carried the message into the skies. Hope took flight, gathering birds with the sole purpose of saving dharma, securely rooted in Gokul.

Meanwhile, Vidyut, the explosive expert and Mayuran, the last bird whisperer, walked to the village women who had gathered within the strong stone walls of the temple.

'The present and future of this land need the blessings and help of your goddesses. This is our only chance. I need you, all of you, to help me prepare these pouches,' said Vidyut, humbly showing his hand that had a tiny pouch tightly packed in a piece of cloth hanging through a thread and two earthen pots that Mayuran was cautiously placing.

'What was in the earthen pots?' asked Madhav

The nameless Naga replied, 'A simple metal powder that could become a dangerous weapon, in warfare. A tool of tragedy and ruckus called sodium in today's world. This metal has the characteristics of igniting and creating explosive reactions when encountering water. It is light enough in weight to float and reacts quickly, generating sodium hydroxide while releasing hydrogen gas. This is an exothermic reaction where excessive heat is produced which ignites hydrogen resulting in flames. This powerful reaction was used strategically in historical battles.'

In the temple, there was a moment of silence, broken only by the distant cries of children clinging to their mothers and the bangles the village women were wearing. One woman stepped forward and said, 'You all are dying for us and to protect our land, our beliefs and we are ready to die for you all, for Gokul. We will do whatever it takes and there is no question of requesting us. This is our duty to stand shoulder to shoulder with the protectors of our dharma. Tell us the process of preparing it and consider it done. We are ready to do whatever is needed.'

Vidyut prepared one in front of all of them and showed how it's done. One by one, the women gathered around the pots of explosives and began to prepare small pouches with the explosive powder. Those hands and fingers skilled in household chores were now working for a purpose far greater than any task before. In no time, over a thousand pouches, with a thread hanging, were ready.

'What is this thread here for, Maa,' asked a child looking at the thread hanging with every pouch.

'I don't know my son, but everything has a purpose, whether we know and understand it or not. The maker knows it all, we are mere instruments,' replied the mother. Right then, an injured Naga warrior returned to the temple, limping in pain and looking around.

'We still have cloth and threads, but no more powder left. We've used everything we had,' said a woman. Her child ran to him and asked, 'What are you going to do with these pouches?'

Before the Naga could have answered, a shadow crossed the sky suddenly. It began with a single crow, then another, and another, until the place was overwhelmed with the sound of flapping wings. Crows, sparrows, peacocks, pigeons, hawks, majestic eagles and birds of every kind— big and small—who had lost their homes in the jungle fire, gathered in flocks, all led by Neelkanth. It was a huge mass. Mayuran said, 'My friends, it's a difficult time, but today, we do not fight for land but for the future of those yet to be born in the centuries to come.' A grand peacock, with its rainbow-like feathers shimmering, stepped forward. The whisperer said, 'We need you . . . all of you.'

Showing the explosive pouches, he continued, 'They are light, just enough for you to carry their weight while flying too. None of you will return alive if you agree to take up this task. But without your wings, we have no chance to stop them. You are our last hope and maybe after that too we lose this war, but at least the hope to revive will stand if we reduce these asuras to their minimal numbers so that they cannot continue their raid and rampage to more jungles and villages after this. You are our last weapon. I know that I cannot force you. I can only plead.'

The next moment, a single tiny sparrow, the tiniest of all the birds, flew and perched on the whisperer's hand. 'We are ready! All of us are!' All the birds nodded, affirming the task and followed by Mayuran and Vidyut, all the women started tying the threads of the pouches to every bird. It seemed like the women were tying rakhi, the bond between sisters and brothers, where the brother promises to safeguard his sister's life, honour and dignity. Birds were ready to play the roles of brothers and save the honour and lives of the women of Gokul.

Vidyut explained and Mayuran translated for them what needed to be done: 'These pouches will catch fire with the saliva in your beaks. Whenever you are ready with your target, prick the pouch and just a drop will ignite it. Then you must fly down quickly to hit your target and collide with it. The collision will create an explosion, and the body of the target will catch fire.'

Everybody, including the birds, knew that they would fall on the targets, and the women imagining their fate started crying.

One by one, like a convoy—crows, peacocks, hawks— were all ready to fly and die. These birds were live bombs in no time. They stood as a unit, looking at the women and all the Naga warriors and other allies, as if bidding goodbye with the blessing of long life to the humans fighting for Gokul. One of the women, with mother-like emotions towards the warrior birds, walked with tears in her eyes and said with a trembling voice, 'Fly safe.'

The speaker and the listeners both knew that it was a one-way flight to death. Every human eye witnessing it was numb.

'Thank you,' Mayuran muttered to the flock, barely audible. 'You are our hope.'

The Neelkanth took the lead and the birds took flight, each focusing on a single moving target approaching

Gokul. For a moment, time stopped. As the birds took off, everything turned otherworldly.

The theory and concept of war were redefining itself again, as they once changed in the battle of Gokul under Ajaa and Shambhu ji, when bulls and elephants took charge and snakes contributed too. This time, the Afghans were about to encounter the force of the skies.

As they ascended higher, they gleamed with fire, carrying small explosive pouches primed to explode on impact. This was no ordinary flight, it was a vision of defiance, a spectacle to behold, rewriting the very definition of sacrifice. However, the tragically beautiful aspect was that this air force knew this flight would be their last, with no hope of return. Their flight was for their death. These winged bombers—crows, eagles, sparrows, peacocks and hawks—gathered for a singular purpose.

It began with a scream, but it was anything but human. There was something unnatural in the air—a total silence, like a deep inhale before a scream, a haunting hum. What appeared in the sky was not normal. The birds did as they were instructed. They chose their targets and pricked their pouches while flying to hit their targets from the sky at full speed. For a moment, there was total silence, total calm.

Hearing thousands of birds hovering in a circle above the battleground like a mysterious cloud of death, the remaining Afghans, including Abdali and Neymat, raised their heads to the sky. Their hearts nearly skipped a beat as they saw the battalion of birds, appearing like stars across the sky.

'What madness is it?' Neymat whispered in disbelief upon seeing the birds circling above the battlefield. The dead were still moving, unaware of the threat that was flying above them. Both the living and the undead Afghans didn't understand what was going on in the sky, but the Nagas knew that the air force was poised for its first strike.

But before anyone could think of something, the first tiny sparrow struck down at the speed of light, producing an unusual sound as it sliced through the air with its wings, hitting its first target at full speed. The sky was filled with thousands of birds, their bodies ablaze with the desire to serve Mother Nature, resembling thousands of stars shining brightly.

That scream, echoing as it flew downward, resembled a demon set free from its cage. It collided with the nearest target. This ascent was just not a fall. It was like thunder crashing on to earth. And it was a relay then. One after another, and then another. They came with a storm of wings, fire and haste. They came not as birds but as flying harbingers of death, descending upon the enemies of nature and humanity. In no time, the defenders and the offenders witnessed the birds falling on their targets as if stars were raining down on the earth. Sparrows, tiny yet bold, peacocks, magnificent and lovely, eagles, daring and focused, all dived from the heavens on the dead, finding the right mark to hit and explode. There was a blinding flash, small but very impactful explosions, the very moment it hit the dead. The scene resembled a meteor shower cascading from the sky. It felt as if these shooting stars were turning the battlefield into a landscape of glowing destruction. It was heartbreaking, breathtaking, horrific and beautiful at the same time. The burning pouches were ripped and scattered on the bodies of the dead. After the bird and the target collided, every particle caught fire, burning the whole of a dead Afghan walking. The dead, decayed and soulless creatures erupted in the blaze and were instantly consumed and reduced to ashes before anybody could understand anything.

Neelkanth, leading the birds flying high, with his blue feathers, plunged into the heart of the enemy camp with a flock of birds following him to glory. Tents, supplies and soldiers all got caught up in the blast.

Each collision ended in a burst of flames. But as Neelkanth's body disintegrated in the fire, the camp was still standing. It was a magnificent sky show that ended with fire on one side and tears on another.

The birds gave their lives not out of hope for return, but because they understood the necessity of striving for success in this endeavour. It is perhaps the greatest tragedy of war; not the loss of life, but the hope that compels us to fight, knowing that the odds are against us. The air force perished and many dead men were burned to ashes. But the ground army of the dead Afghans still numbered in hundreds—the number was much more than the birds flying in the dark sky. Adding to the soulless soldiers were the living Afghans under the command of Abdali. Together, there stood a thousand men more than the defenders, who were not more than a hundred remaining, including Mayuran, Vidyut, the chief, Krishna, Dhruv, the princess and me.

With their wings, the birds tried their best to turn the wind of our certain defeat to an impossible victory. But unfortunately, despite all sacrifices in the pyre of their pure intentions, we were destined to be killed first and defeated thereafter.

Neymat ordered Ifrit to awaken more Afghan soldiers, and Ifrit continued his spell. With each round of Afghan soldiers we killed, more and more dead Afghans rose, swelling the ranks of Sardar Khan's invincible army.

The chief Mathadhish accepted in his heart that he had failed to save what he had sworn to protect. While we all looked up to our chief, he looked up in the dark sky with guilt in his eyes as he could not protect Gokul and his fellow Nagas. Without any prior intimation and with a sword and a trident in his hands, he suddenly ran towards the front wave of soulless soldiers.

'Har Har Mahadev' were his last words before he was consumed after cutting many enemies. Several dead soldiers tore him apart in front of our eyes, and we stood as helpless spectators with no one to lead us further. We were sleepless and tired, hungry and broken, disheartened and defeated in our hearts.

16

The Dead Against the Dead

Looking at us all lost and numb, the princess yelled while riding her horse, making sure that her voice reached each and every defender. 'We are still alive. Gather yourself back and fight for all those who died fighting so that we could be alive one more day, one more hour, one more minute or even one more moment. We know what we are fighting for, and the chief had underlined our purpose with his own death. Prepare a formation. We will fight united, and we will face them from the front. Let's not differentiate between the females that fight among us and the villagers who stand shoulder to shoulder and the Nagas warriors who travelled to defend us because the purpose is the same and so is fate. The dharma is the same and so is death.'

'Krishna! Ride with me. Vedant, handle Abdali's Commander. Charge!' she shouted like Goddess Durga herself before speeding up her horse towards Neymat, followed by Krishna, who had his eyes fixed on Ahmed Shah Abdali.

This was the final war, and we were all ready to meet our destiny, as defeating the dead was impossible, and surrendering was not an option. We all ran towards the first line of dead Afghans walking towards us. But before we could reach them, a piece of cloud suddenly rumbled, capturing everybody's attention. It was an unusually dark light. Certainly not natural as the rest of the sky was clear. As it glowed upon again and again at the very same point, some of us noticed that it was Kaaldhwaj in some kind of supernatural but unbearable pain right below. His eyes were closed and skin glowed red. Looking at the view—mesmerizing from a distance but terrifying up close—nobody could tell who the giver was, and who was the receiver.

Something was happening, something beyond the comprehension of any of us. The dead Afghans were on our faces and Princess Chandrika was escorted by a line of four terribly strong female horse riders, slicing everybody on the way.

'Secure Neymat! And somebody target the princess,' screamed Abdali. The orders were immediately followed and some of the men started making a circle of strong defence around Neymat. The other soldiers rushed on horsebacks to ensure the princess's fall and death. Before the riders reached here and the rest of us collided with the dead, the rumbling and glowing cloud suddenly exploded, and the night became darker. Every piece of lamp lost its light, and all the burning corpses were extinguished. The fire torches on both sides were put off and the darkness on the battleground spread so drastically that every soldier, living or dead, from both sides felt blind. We were unable to see our own hands. The horses, charging at each other's enemies, came to a halt, and the soldiers targeting their opponents ceased their actions. The living stopped thinking about life and death. It felt as time itself had stopped on the moonless night, the final night of shraadh. We saw many alien figures glowing dimly at a distance right below the cloud that glowed before bursting. They had radiating skin, and their faces were so bright that they could hardly be seen. All of them stood still on their spots, and in the centre stood Kaaldhwaj. We could see him moving his lips. He was talking to them.

A few moments later, all the dim glowing figures turned towards the battleground, and we heard Kaaldhwaj yelling 'Har Har Mahadev'. With the call, he ran towards us along with hundreds of alien figures, shaped like humans. As they moved closer and closer, we could see ourselves. And then, the whole battleground was alive as the shining figures scattered among the ranks of the enemies, still glowing. The directionless dead men, who could not see where we were, spotted us again and the horse riders moved again to kill the princess. The security layers around Neymat started strengthening, and Abdali himself got into the war for the first time. All of that happened so quickly that despite wanting to understand what those figures were and why Kaaldhwaj jumped into the fight even when he was expelled from the clan by the chief, nobody had a moment to find the answers.

The number of horse riders that attacked the princess was ten times more than her horse-riding female warriors. A cavalry of around fifty horse riders was sent to attack and kill the five female riders, including the princess. Krishna took charge and rode his horse past the princess before they clashed with fifty Afghan riders. Everybody who saw it was already heartbroken as the murder of the princess and Krishna along with the other four female riders was inevitable. The female fighters fought valiantly, but in some time, three female riders guarding the princess fell to the ground with multiple wounds. One of the three was beheaded.

The warzone was a mess and the formation was scattered and broken from all sides. No one knew who was fighting on which corner of the field. Right then, Kaaldhwaj rushed to me and asked, 'Where is the princess of Surajgarh?'

Disheartened, I pointed my fingers towards her and said, 'She had so much to see in life. She was too young to die and too far from us to be saved. It's too late for us to save her Kaaldhwaj.'

'Yes! You are right. It's too late for us . . .' he affirmed my thoughts and made me all the more hopeless about her life. But I did not realize that Kaaldhwaj was not finished with his statement. I realized that the most important part of a statement is the part that starts after 'but'. The complete statement was, 'Yes! You are right. It's too late for us . . . but . . . not for them.'

My face was down in sorrow, but his statement gave me some hope. I raised my eyes to look at Kaaldhwaj and saw that he was pointing towards the princess. I looked at the princess fighting at a distance and as the finger was raised towards her, three shining figures from different directions moved at the speed of light for her rescue and vanished when they reached too close to her. I could not understand anything and couldn't believe my eyes when I saw the three fallen female soldiers standing on their feet again to guard Princess Chandrika. The sight was unimaginable—one of them was wielding her sword and guarding the princess, despite having no head atop her body. The princess and Krishna were speechless at the sight before them, but we were not alone. From the other side, Neymat was also looking at the women who had collapsed after being beheaded but somehow got back on her feet. She knew she had a challenger who was equally good as her in sorcery.

Looking at these three women guards, I realized that the moves and fighting style of two of the three looked familiar. While I was trying to comprehend what was happening and why their body language seemed familiar, Neymat and Kaaldhwaj had spotted each other, and Kaaldhwaj was about to move towards her.

'How did you do that? How did you make them alive?' I asked curiously.

Still starring at Neymat and finally stepping away from my side to confront her, Kaaldhwaj replied, 'They are not alive. They are Shambhu ji and the queen trying to save their daughter along with Ajaa, her elder brother, inside the bodies of the female fighters. She is surrounded by her family. She won't die.' Kaaldhwaj left, leaving me stunned and frozen.

I now knew why I felt the movement and body language of the two seemed familiar. I had seen Ajaa and Shambhu ji fighting, and they were back with their language of war in the bodies of the fallen females as those were the closest fallen allies near the princess. The headless female warrior's body was taken by the queen who was beheaded herself in her war. And it was Shambhu ji and Ajaa in the other two dead bodies fighting. I felt exactly how I had felt when I saw Ajaa for the first time above the waterfall.

'But how did Ajaa and Shambhu ji come back to the land of Gokul? You did all their last rituals with the complete process and order,' Madhav asked the nameless Naga.

Neymat knew that the dark forces were the most powerful and easiest to summon on moonless nights. But this moonless night turned out to be a blessing in disguise for all of us. It was Pitrapaksh Amaavas, the final day of Shraddh, on which Yamraj opens the doors of heaven, and every soul is allowed to go and see their living family members. The only family member alive to Ajaa, Shambhu ji and the queen was princess Chandrika. These thousands of souls who fought for us that night were all there, but they could not interfere in the mortal world. They could only see the happenings, but then came Kaaldhwaj, who had the dark power of possessing souls and making them do things on his orders.

'Was he so powerful that he enslaved warriors and pure souls like Ajaa and Shambhu ji?' Madhav asked.

He did not only possess Ajaa and Shambhu ji that night. I noticed that all the Naga warriors who sacrificed their lives fighting Sardar Khan, and his army were all there.

'What do you mean?' asked Madhav, and the nameless Naga answered, 'That night, I saw Vanraaj again, sitting on his permanent ride, and Gajraaj blew his shankh again.' This time, when he saw his mother, Dulari, hearing the shankh, she and Vanraaj turned and looked at Gajraaj. Narayan was there, too, and so were Namah, Bhola and Shivay, the boys of Cheetah Dasta. Kaaldhwaj could possess them all only because they all allowed him to. Unless they were not possessed and ordered, they could not finish what they started. Their last wish was to finish Sardar Khan and save Gokul, which was still in danger. With Sardar Khan back on his feet, they allowed Kaaldhwaj to take control. That night, the Nagas and Kaaldhwaj both needed each other's assistance. The princess was in danger, so her parents and brother rushed to rescue her.

The three possessed bodies proved that the bond of the family is beyond life and death. They fought non-stop and a safe passage was created for the princess. Krishna followed the princess and targeted Abdali again. As the souls of the queen, Ajaa and Shambhu ji left the bodies of the dead female fighters, the three bodies fell as a stack of wheat after killing all the horse riders who surrounded and attacked the princess. All the other souls were also doing the same. They were entering the bodies of the fallen defenders and using them as their puppets to fight the dead army of Sardar Khan. We saw the giants and other martyred sadhus standing back on their feet, fighting for us. It was now the dead against the dead, the living against the living and the sorcerer and against the sorcerer.

Now the battlefield was vibrating with the sense of something that was greater than the physical presence on the ground. It felt haunted. Ajaa, Shambhu ji, Vanraaj and Narayan were no longer bound by flesh but were forces of nature. They were wandering across the battleground with their ethereal forms, casting lights in the darkness which was divine.

'These dead Afghan soldiers are soulless, empty vessels that are following orders of some authority. We too are bound to your orders. Order us to enter these soulless bodies. Only then they can be directed to death,' Shambhu ji guided Kaaldhwaj who was accompanied by a few angry slave souls and the princess, followed by some other female warriors approaching Neymat. They were looking for each other but the looks were different in the eyes of both. On one hand, where Kaaldhwaj was fearsome, Neymat looked frightened. She knew that her dark powers were no match to the darkness that Kaaldhwaj had in him. Looking at Neymat, he ordered, 'Take control of the bodies of the dead and finish them once and for all.' The spirits of hundreds of Naga souls gushed forward, entering the decaying soulless bodies like a flood of light filling the empty dark vessels. Neymat, realizing the soldiers guarding her would perish in the blink of an eye in front of Kaaldhwaj and other warriors approaching her, ordered Ifrit to defend and rescue her. Before Kaaldhwaj could reach Neymat, Ifrit stood against him, guarding her. Now, Kaaldhwaj knew that he had to find Ifrit directly and fight it to get hold of Neymat. He told the princess, 'Ifrit can't be killed, princess, but I can be. I will keep him occupied till I am alive. You have a very limited time to finish this witch. Only then will Ifrit stop.' Along with the angry slave souls he had brought with him, Kaaldhwaj attacked Ifrit. The princess and the female warriors attacked the men guarding Neymat.

Meanwhile, the souls started entering the soulless bodies, and the villagers, along with Naga warriors, fought fiercely with the remaining Afghans. One among them was Vedant, combating with Abdali's Commander Malik Akhtar. Both of their swords clashed against each other with a swift brutal force. The fate of this fight was about to be something else. Vedant, busy fighting, got separated from the rest of his troop and got surrounded by the commander's soldiers. He looked around in search of Krishna. He wanted Krishna to see that he fought with courage and honour and took the enemy's sword on his chest. He wanted to prove that he was not a coward, and that he did not fear while facing death. Krishna was occupied with other soldiers and could not see Vedant in his final moments, but I did. I saw that he finally fought as a king, as a soldier and as a warrior before both his hands were cut and his body was stabbed.

Farther across the field, the soldiers guarding Neymat were killed and the princess finally had a face-off with Neymat who stood with a dagger. She knew that she only had to fight and be alive till Ifrit kills Kaaldhwaj, and with it she can take over the battle once again. The angry slave souls that Kaaldhwaj brought with him were all consumed by Ifrit, and now he had a direct face-off with the mortal Kaaldhwaj, whose limited energy was no match to Ifrit's endless powers. In no time, Kaaldhwaj was tightly caught by Ifrit, who began sucking and absorbing all the souls Kaaldhwaj possessed, including his own life out of his body. Ajaa, Shambhu ji, Vanraaj and Narayan rushed on Kaaldhwaj's call as they were the last leftovers of his strength. Ifrit suddenly had a sudden burst of energy while trying to swipe Ajaa and others away. But his attempt was in vain. These sacred spirits pushed forward with their glowing hands to hinder Ifrit and prevent him from causing further destruction. But Ifrit was too strong. Despite their best effort, Kaaldhwaj was losing his breath while the princess's sword was clashing with the dagger of Neymat, who was filled with rage. Each of her strikes was filled with venom of her hatred. 'You cannot stop me; you are foolish girl. Your mother, the queen, could not stop me. We dragged her head, and I will drag yours too,' said Neymat. On the other hand, the princess was all set and was waiting for the apt moment to break and end Neymat's will. With her unbreakable determination and years-long training in warfare tactics and skills, she just roared with her sword, slicing through the air with a deadly intent towards the venomous Neymat. Looking at all this, Abdali ordered the men of his royal forces to reach for Neymat's rescue. He led the troop himself, but

Krishna kept him engaged so that Neymat could not get any reinforcements.

She felt the aura of her mother, the queen, as a dimly lit soul, standing right next to her; the face hidden in the brightness of her eyes gave her confidence that she was not alone. 'I am not an ordinary girl; I am the daughter of a tigress and a lion, sister of Shree Ajaa. I am the queen of Surajgarh and for you, this ends here, Neymat!' Neymat was caught off guard when the princess cut her open from the centre. She fell to the ground and so did Kaaldhwaj, as Ifrit stopped squeezing him to death. With Neymat's death, Ifrit vanished as if he never existed. The master was dead and was no longer bound to continue the fight on behalf of Ahmed Shah Abdali.

Amidst all that, the restless spirit of Sardar Khan, devoid of humanity, continued killing the residents and defenders. With him there were a few hundred still walking. All the remaining souls entered every remaining body, one after another, and made them burn themselves to ashes. While Shambhu ji and the soul of the dead queen walked towards the princess, Ajaa entered the body of Sardar Khan, and we saw Sardar Khan walking in a big fire that we had created. Kaaldhwaj was weak and the power of a few souls inside him was keeping him alive. He knew that if he released them from his slavery, he would die. He may not have lived by the rules of us Nagas, but he died an honourable death as he already granted freedom to each soul before entering the battleground and requested them to fight with him and not for him at their own will. We then learned that Kaaldhwaj honoured the chief Mathadhish's condition and released all the souls before stepping in the ground of war.

Jugal Kishore, who was all the time right beside the king, not for loyalty but for his own life, suggested sheepishly: 'We have lost the war, my lord. If we do not leave now, we may not have another window to escape.' Abdali looked around him and realized that Jugal was right. He ordered his royal fleet to fall back and leave the battleground to the fighting soldiers so that they could keep the defenders occupied.

'Gokul is invincible. It is cursed for the invaders,' said Abdali.

'Jugal! Make sure that when history is written, the world knows that we were defeated by plague and not by these nomadic Nagas. The corpses of Sardar Khan and all the other rotten bodies awakened by Neymat must be shown as the effect of plague,' Abdali ordered.

'But the Nagas will prove us wrong, my lord. They will tell the world what happened here,' Jugal Kishore suggested.

'They will return back to wherever they have come from. What happened here is unbelievable. With time, their history will become a myth, and they will call it mythology as some among them already believe in the Ramayan and Mahabharat. The residents of this land called Hindustan believe in forgiving and forgetting. They will forgive us and forget the Nagas,' taunted Abdali while trying to hide his defeat and the valour, devotion and sacrifice of the Nagas under the blanket of a disease.

He was right! They forgave Abdali and forgot us. The world still knows that Abdali was defeated because of some plague that consumed his army. It was actually us.

History is usually written by victors, but in this land, the losers had a pen. A pen strong enough to represent the haters of Shiva as guardians of the land, the enemies of dharma as seculars, the rapists as the rulers, the butchers as badshahs and the killers as kind-hearted kings.

We eventually wiped out the remaining Afghan soldiers, left as orphans in the embrace of death by Abdali. With the first ray of sunlight, the darkness named Abdali was nowhere to be seen.

Shambhu ji walked to Krishna and said, 'I know what you did for me. I am grateful to you, my old friend.'

Ajaa walked to Dhruv and said, 'You kept your promise! You found them all. The fate of this war would have been against us without you, Dhruv.'

Vanraaj and Dulari met Gajraaj and bid them the final goodbye.

The queen joined Shambhu ji and talked to Krishna: 'Take care of our girl. Finish what I could not complete. Teach her to become and stay a good and righteous queen.'

I walked to the princess and said, 'Princess! When you reach the land of Gokul, I told you that your family is all here with you, looking at you. Before they leave again, it's time that you see them. The two souls standing with Krishna are your parents and the one with Dhruv is your brother. Go bid them goodbye. The time of shraddh has ended. They will have to return to their respective places.'

The princes looked at the three of them while they walked closer to her as a family that proved the promise to keep bestowing their love and blessings to the youngest among them. All the eyes were numb. I learned that day that even souls have tears.

'You did well, Chandrika. We are all proud of you,' said Shambhu ji, the king of Surajgarh, the father of Prince Ajaa and Princess Chandrika, and also the slave of Shiva.

'We are always around you, my girl,' assured Princess Chandrika's mother.

'I will pamper and play with you in my next birth, little sister. And before that, we will all meet again in heaven,' said Ajaa with a smile on his lips and tears in his eyes. They all hugged each other before they vanished in the ray of sun.

Dhruv and all other Nagas returned to the Himalayas to their respective Mathas after burning the bodies of all the defenders of Gokul, who died gracefully fighting for the right to their religion.

The princess went back to Surajgarh with Krishna as her chief advisor and commander-in-chief. Krishna welcomed Gajraaj with him. Gajraaj humbly returned my shankh. I hugged him and bid him goodbye.

'And you?' asked Madhav, but before the nameless Naga answered, Madhav heard the roar and flapping sound of wings above his head. Something flew from right above them, very close to their heads. They were standing under the open sky, in the snow, nowhere to hide or run. He quickly sat where he was and raised his head still sitting to be safe and found the nameless Naga standing straight, smiling in a direction. He too followed the nameless Naga's gaze, and his eyes broadened with the view. As he looked around for the source of the unexpected growls and sniffs, he saw an enormous figure, fiercer than a lion and mightier than an elephant in sheer strength and size. The flying beast landed right in front of the nameless Naga, rose before him, and roared, shaking Madhav's very soul. It was an enormous eight-legged being, half-bird, half-lion, more powerful than any beast Madhav had ever imagined. With eyes burning like coals, the creature accepted the nameless Naga's greetings and then fixed its gaze on Madhav. His jaw dropped in awe. Following the gestures of the Naga he had been trailing, he realized that the massive beast before him was the Sharabh avatar of Shiva.

'We are standing exactly where Dhruv encountered the Sharabh avatar. He is the guardian and protector of the chief matha,' said the nameless Naga, walking close to Sharabh. He bowed in front of Sharabh in gratitude and said, 'Please allow me in, Lord Sharabh, that kid is one of us now.' Sharabh flapped his wings, and suddenly from nowhere emerged the gate and behind it was the math that started to be visible.

'To the chief matha,' the nameless Naga said to Madhav, answering the question that he often asked. The question was, 'Where are we going?'

The matha was huge but couldn't be seen by any man alive until Sharabh avatar permitted. Madhav followed the nameless Naga inside the matha and saw many old Nagas; some meditating, some practicing with weapons, some perfecting their superpowers, some talking to birds, some roaming around without their shadows following them under the sun and some playing with snow leopards and Tibetan Mastiffs, but all greeting the nameless Naga with utmost respect.

They continued walking and entered the grand courtyard that had a high platform. It seemed like the place of the chief Mathadhish.

'Are you the chief Mathadhish?' Madhav asked, his voice awestruck and murmuring, as the other senior Nagas of the math looked on, watching the nameless Naga, followed by Madhav, walk toward the vacant seat.

'Shhhhhhh!' said the nameless Naga and continued approaching the high platform.

Right then, another old Naga entered from the side closest to the high platform.

'What's the ground report, my old friend?' asked the old Naga sitting on the high platform.

The nameless Naga replied, 'We have got Ayodhya back. At the start of this year, 2 January, according to the Gregorian calendar, *pran prathishtha* is done and Ram Lalla is established back to his right place.'

'What about Gyanvapi in Prayagraj?' asked the chief Mathadhish.

'Prayagraj's High Court had dismissed an appeal by the Gyanvapi mosque committee against a Varanasi district court order, allowing Hindus to offer prayers in the restricted area called Vyas ka Tehkhana,' replied the nameless Naga.

It has been argued for many years that the mosque, which was built in the seventeenth century by Aurangzeb, sits on what was once the Kashi Vishwanath temple. At the heart of this dispute is a thirty-three-year-old law called Places of Worship Act, 1991, which was passed around the time of the Babri Masjid dispute. It prevents legal cases of this nature. The act states that the religious character of a place of worship will continue as it existed on 15 August 1947.

A local Varanasi court has granted permission to Hindus to conduct prayers inside the Gyanvapi mosque. The Hindu had filed a plea in the Supreme Court to unseal the *wazukhana* area within the Gyanvapi complex, based on the Archaeological Survey of India's reports. The survey has confirmed the existence of a pre-existing Hindu temple at the Gyanvapi mosque in Varanasi.

The Gyanvapi mosque has been at the centre of debates with some believing it was built on the remains of the Kashi Vishwanath temple. The claim was that the mosque was constructed under the orders of Aurangzeb, who allegedly tore down a part of the temple.

But the focus is no longer solely on Gyanvapi, said to have been destroyed by Aurangzeb. Now, attention has also turned to the Harihar temple, dedicated to Kalki, the tenth and final avatar of Vishnu, in Sambhal, reportedly destroyed by Babur.

According to the Babur-nama, Babur came to Sambhal in 1529, partially destroyed the Harihar temple, captured it and ordered that it be used as a mosque from then on. There are more such temples waiting to be explored, and their ancient pasts must be brought to light for Bharat and the world.

Madhav, listening to all that, understood why the nameless Naga told Thomas that the fight that started then continues to this day.

While the nameless Naga and Madhav reached the chief matha, Thomas lost his consciousness due to his weakness and the journey that was refusing to end. He was weak and fragile, unable to move even one step more. He knew he was very close to the plains, but every ounce of his strength was exhausted, and his will too had given up; yet he was meant to survive. His instincts were right, and he was close to civilization. Suddenly, a tired and poor man gave him a hand and served him water and covered him with an old dirty stole. He supported Thomas to stand back and took him along to the plains. The journey of the mountains finally came to an end for Thomas, as he stepped on plains with the help of this local stranger.

While he was been taken away from the mountains to the village, he turned back and saw the mountain again, as if trying to search for something. The local man helping Thomas to walk asked him, 'What are you looking at?'

'All through my journey in the mountains, I felt as if something was crawling behind me, keeping an eye all through my return, but I did not see anything,' replied Thomas.

'These mountains have their own hidden history and mysteries that we can never discover,' said the rescuer.

Never knowing that he was right, someone continued dragging his body, keeping an eye on Thomas to ensure his safety, just as it ensured the safety of Dhruv two hundred and fifty years back.

In an hour, Thomas was standing outside a village.

'The locals will immediately start to aid you with warm medical clothes. They have phones too. They will inform the authorities about you and soon you will be united with your family. You will manage from here on,' said the poor stranger who helped Thomas to the gates of the village.

'Where are you going?' Thomas asked, hardly able to stand.

'Back to where I belong,' replied the rescuer, turning to walk away.

'Thank you for your stole,' said Thomas trying to return it back to him.

'That's not mine. Keep it and give it to its rightful owner if you ever get to meet him,' replied the stranger.

Confused, Thomas kept looking at him as he walked away. And when he had gone far but still visible, Thomas realized that he did not ask the rescuer's name. Thomas was just about to shout out loud asking for his name when the rescuer shouted from the other side, 'They call me Varya, Thomas.'

Varya, who helped Dhruv at the start of his ascent, also helped Thomas at the end of his descent. He left and left two things for Thomas. 'How did he know my name and whose stole is that? Looks centuries old?'

Thomas would never know the true owner of the stole, but Madhav was about to discover where its owner was. Back in the hidden matha, the chief walked down the platform and walked close to the nameless Naga. While Madhav stood silently, the chief and nameless Naga came face to face and the silence broke with a friendly act of brotherhood. Both hugged each other for longer than usual, and the chief asked, 'Who is he?'

Madhav knelt in respect.

The nameless Naga said, 'Madhav, meet Dhruv, my old friend and our chief Mathadhish.' Madhav looked up at the old face and felt as if he were transported to the times he had heard about throughout his journey, with two of the Naga warriors standing right before him.

Before he could absorb all that was happening, a young Naga came running to the chief Mathadhish and said, 'There is something very bizarre happening in the sky above Ichhra.'

The chief Mathadhish and the nameless Naga looked at each other and the chief Mathadhish said, 'Maybe the time has come! What month is it in their Gregorian calendar?'

'Mid months of the year 2025. What's Ichhra?' asked Madhav trying to locate the place in Bharat.

'It was the old name of Lahore,' replied the nameless Naga.

'Pakistan?' said Madhav, amazed.

'Once a part of undivided Bharat,' replied Dhruv, the chief.

'Another major mysterious event on earth is about to begin with the arrival of "The Other Indian",' said the nameless Naga.

'The Other Indian! Who's that?' enquired Madhav

'He is not from this planet, but he is not an alien,' replied nameless Naga.

'This does not make any sense. If he is not from this planet then he is an alien,' countered Madhav.

'He is a mortal human who was not born on this planet,' replied Dhruv, the chief Mathadhish.

'It's time we part ways, Madhav,' said the nameless Naga.

'But what about the mysterious major event that is about to occur. How will I know about it without you?' asked Madhav

'We will all meet again in the next Mahakumbh that will happen in the year 2031. You will know it then,' answered the nameless Naga.

'You were called Adhiraj more than 250 years ago, during the battle of Gokul. I'm sure you've had other names since then. Many perished over time, and many like Dhruv found their rightful places, but you're still here, spanning the past and the present. What is your future? Who are you?' Madhav asked, desperate to know the real identity of the nameless Naga.

'You are right, Madhav. I am the Hindu, hidden in the pages of the past, who will reveal himself only when the future demands. But I can't tell you my name,' replied the Naga with a smirk, remaining nameless as he walked away from Madhav.

'Is this the end of our journey?' Madhav asked sadly. The nameless Naga stopped, turned, looked at Madhav and replied, 'It is the end of your journey with me, but for me, it's not over yet.'

Acknowledgements

Ananta Rao (Anu), my family would be incomplete without you. Everything you do silently, without the appreciation and acknowledgment from others, is not your weakness—it is our strength. What you do is not easy, and trust me, all of us know that. We all love you.

Mani Sharma, thank you for being the man I can rely on anytime, without hesitation. Your contributions to this story have truly helped make it better. I hope we continue working together. I will always be there for you.

Shweta Talwar, I coincidentally met you on 22 January 2024, the day of Lord Ram's Pran Pratishtha, and here we are, working together. You have somehow become a family member. Thank you for being there and helping me finish this. I look forward to continuing to work with you.

Sahil Sharma, we laugh, we fight, we disagree, and we challenge each other. We will keep doing this—that's what makes us . . . us.

Megha Poojari, you started working for me a year ago, and we have successfully completed one year, only because you were determined to win the challenge. If that's the case, I challenge you to always stay connected with me. May you win this challenge, too, and all the others in your life. Wishing you a wind-chiming 2025 and many more years to come. Your final read before the release of this book was a great help. Thank you for that, and for overcoming the challenges I throw at you.

Ankit Sahu, keep saving money and keep proving that you are the best at your work. Thanks for taking care of everything related to Lakshmi ji.

Avadhi Joshi, my documents-in-law called me a few days ago and assured me that they feel safe in your hands. I have asked them to give it to me in writing. They asked, 'Why?' I said, 'Because my lawyer said so.' Keep them safe for me.

Muskaan, you have a bright future. All the best and thank you for always being there.

Praveen Chilhate, thank you for paying me my salary on time every month. Welcome to our family.

Scan QR code to access the
Penguin Random House India website